CITY LIGHTS

Sizzling hot chemistry and surprises await this overzealous city girl and small-town, grumpy doctor.

Evicted!

Newly graduated, Evie finds herself broke and jobless with zero options.

That is until her friend from college convinces the older brother to hire her.

The problem?

The job is in Sugar Creek Falls, a small town in the middle of farm country—the complete opposite setting for this born-and-raised city girl.

But when she arrives and learns her new boss is the same gorgeous guy who got her fired, sparks ignite.

And not the good kind.

This job is just a means to get where she wants—a stepping stone to bigger things in bigger cities.

Or that's the plan.

Until their chemistry can no longer be ignored, and Liam teaches her skills beyond office management.

When life shifts in Evie's favor, her past catches up. Surprises and unveiled threats become real. And she finds herself facing choices where neither of them wins.

City Lights, Starry Nights is a fish-out-of-water, small-town romantic comedy featuring a spontaneous heroine and a grumpy, domineering doctor with a heart of gold. But grab those fans because these two heat up the pages! Guaranteed HEA.

Cover Design by Loganraestudio

Editing by Cait Marie from Functionally Fictional

Proofreading by Kaitie Reister

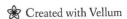 Created with Vellum

CITY LIGHTS STARRY NIGHTS

A GRUMPY SUNSHINE SMALL TOWN ROMANCE

SUGAR CREEK FALLS
BOOK 1

KIMBERLY READNOUR

CHAPTER ONE

EVIE

"You're late." Job's voice carries above the clanking of dishes and murmured conversations.

"Don't remind me." I groan and beeline to the lockers, ignoring the bitch-you're-going-to-be-fired look my friend tosses at me. Though, Job's thoughts aren't far from the truth. It's no secret that Mr. Bossman threatens to can my ass every chance he gets. His line of bullshit runs deep, but no matter how much I hate this dead-end job, I can't afford to quit. *Gah*, tonight's shift isn't starting as planned.

I shove my purse inside the designated space and spin around to the pantry that houses serving trays filled with champagne flutes. As I walk, I clip the last strands of my hair in place. Job clicks his tongue in disapproval. I can feel his eyes roam along the white oxford shirt with a missing fourth button down to my black pencil skirt. His small gasp alerts me when he spots the run in my hose above my right knee. Yes, hose, as in hosiery that Mr. Bossman makes us girls wear, as if we're stuck in a seventies time warp. It wasn't so bad wearing them during the Chicago winters, but in the summertime while riding the 'L'? No thanks.

"Girl, did you get in a fight with a beaver?"

"Beaver?" The shrill in my voice turns a few heads toward us. I give them a quick wave in greeting, which they return with a shake of their head.

"Eh, it was the only thing I could think of that's low to the ground with claws. Rawr." He pretends to swipe at me with a clawed hand. When his gaze drops, he gasps, "Where is your apron?"

I scoop the filled tray into my hands and shrug. "My interview ran late. In my rush to get here, I stumbled on the steps and fell." *Note to self: never look at your phone as you race up the stairs. That rule doubles when the caller happens to be Mom.* "When I caught the red line, I realized I didn't have my apron. There wasn't time to go home and grab it." *If there was still a home for me to go back to.* It's best I don't mention the not-so-friendly letter I received that's lining my trash with the word eviction scrolled across the top in bright red font. Nope, there's no unseeing that or changing my status. Job already thinks I don't have my shit together.

The swing door opens as a waiter breezes by us, creating enough draft to remind me of my ripped stockings. I suppose Job's assessment of me isn't too far off. It feels like life keeps chipping away at my dignity.

"Good news?" He raises an eyebrow, all hopeful-like. I hate how his face falls when he takes in my sullen expression.

"Hardly. The interviewer got stuck in traffic, which caused a ripple effect." I lift my arms as Job pulls an extra apron out of his ass. Not literally, but I have no idea where he conjured an extra one. He slaps it on my midriff and spins me around to tie it. I continue to explain, "So, after waiting over an hour, he politely told me I didn't have the qualifications he was looking for." *Things that should've been decided before I wasted my time.*

"Oh, sweetie. Maybe you'll have better luck with the next one." Job pats my butt as he secures the apron ties.

Thoroughly impressed with his ninja skills, I ignore his sympathy and force a smile. "Do you always keep spares lying around?"

"Only for you, love."

"How pissed is he?" He being my boss.

"On a scale of one to ten, he's lava bubbling over and scorching the village below."

"Great." *I'm so getting fired.* I want to scream. I need a job—one utilizing my degree. Who knew securing employment would be this difficult? I thought this economy was a buyer's market. Everyone but me found work after graduation, including my best friend, Ansley Seymour. Sure, she had to move to Indianapolis, but she still found one. It hardly seems fair. I have a shiny new bachelor's degree from a prestigious school, and I'm basically unemployable.

"Don't sweat it. Bossman will calm down. You know he secretly loves you."

I scoff. "Loves to hate me, you mean."

Job throws his hands on his hips and huffs. "I don't get it. Everyone loves you."

"I know, right?" Although, it never used to be that way. My bubbly personality drove my mother insane. Finishing school was a constant threat. Back home, women talk about charity events and gossip. Words aren't meant to uplift or cheer anyone up. Only deflate.

"Just get out there and serve all those medical professionals." Job makes a humming sound. "So much deliciousness in one room. Wait until you see the keynote speaker. Yum."

"Hope you're right."

"Trust me. He's divine perfection. Dr. Perfect, schedule me an appointment because I'm feeling—"

"Don't finish that cheesy line," I interrupt. "I meant I hope you're right about Bossman calming down."

"Oh, yeah, that was a stretch, but carry on." Job flutters his hands, as if to scoot me out the door.

I can't help but laugh—because what else can I do? It's either laugh or cry, and I refuse to shed tears over this job. I push through the swinging doors that lead to the banquet room. I don't get too far when my boss's words stop my progression.

"Give me one reason not to fire you on the spot."

I toss the middle-aged man a sweet saccharine smile that doesn't match the presto beat the marching band is performing against my chest. "Because you need me."

His lips flatten to a thin line, but he knows the advantage point goes to me. He's too short-staffed to send me home. At least, that's what I'm banking on.

"I'm watching you. One tiny slip and you're gone."

"Understandably so." I give a curt nod and hold the tray up. "Throats are drying as we speak."

His cheeks flare red, and that tiny vein on the side of his head that pops when I've done something upsetting pulses. Perhaps I should dial back my snark, but I can't seem to help myself. Asking for extra shifts is clearly off the table, so I may as well partake in what little amusement I can.

Without a word, he leaves me to attend to the guests milling around the large banquet room. It doesn't take long for the tray to empty, and after a quick exchange for a full one, I'm back serving. I work toward the far corner and stop short. Holy cow. I live in Chicago. I just graduated from Northwestern University. There isn't a shortage of good-looking men. But—and this is a huge but—I don't think I've ever seen anyone this freaking gorgeous.

The man dreams are made of runs a hand through his tousled, light brown hair as he scours over notecards. I stand in awe and watch the strands fall perfectly into place when his hand returns to his hip. I can't tell if his shoulders are normally that broad or if it's the effect of the tailored-fit, dark navy jacket. His suit isn't designer. I'm well versed in those brands, but he definitely wears this off-brand fine. He had to have gone out of his way to have it fitted.

By the way he keeps reviewing the notecards, I'm guessing this must be the keynote speaker Job had prattled on about. The man certainly checks the gorgeous box. I see why Job wanted to play doctor. And from how my insides heat, that's a game I certainly wouldn't mind joining. I stare transfixed as he works his jaw and continues to read through the notes. *My, my, what a strong jawline it is.* A short-trimmed beard splays across the hardened edges that look cut from stone. The jawline is as perfect as Rob Patterson's—*The Batman* kind of good, not the sparkling one.

Why are strong jawlines my kryptonite?

My feet unlock and pad across the floor directly toward Dr. Perfect. Because, face it, if anyone needs a drink, it's this guy. Or that's my reasoning for singling him out anyway.

A few people smile and take a glass as I close in. Nervous I'll run out when I reach him, I sidestep around a large gathering and move forward, my eyes trained on the doctor the entire time. He keeps fidgeting while studying the notecards, as if preparing for some qualifying entrance exam. The dude needs to calm down. These people are his colleagues, for Christ's sake. It shouldn't be this intimidating speaking in front of them, especially with his looks. Seriously, who cares what comes out of his mouth when he looks that pretty?

I'm within a foot from him when he tears his gaze away from his notes. Mossy green eyes settle on mine, causing my breath to hitch. There's a familiarity about his features I can't quite pinpoint. Confidence spills over me when those beautiful eyes sweep along my body with what I assume is appreciation. That is until his eyes widen in horror and cause me to misstep. Sure, my stockings may have a hole in them, but I don't look horrendous. Do I? No. Job would never let me come out here otherwise.

I close the distance between us when a jarring sensation hits my back, causing me to trip forward. The tray slips from my hand as champagne flutes bounce off the doctor's chest and crash to the floor. Champagne droplets spray across our faces and soak our entire front sides. Or maybe I'm soaked from leaning against him. My gaze rakes along his firmness before rising to meet his. There's a momentary pause where it just seems to be us.

The intensity in his stare burns into mine, leaving me captivated. Desire licks and swirls my insides. We're so close I can see the flecks of brown peppering his green irises. Those unique eyes dilate with heat, and I swear the air surrounding us is hot enough to combust.

Or maybe I'm imagining it because the moment ends as he drops his hands from my shoulders and steps back. We both glance down at the floor. I cringe at seeing his notecards soaking in a sea of champagne.

"Son of a bitch!"

Panicked from his outburst, I drop to my knees at the same time as him, crashing the top of my head into his chin.

"Jesus, woman, are you trying to take me down single-handedly?"

"I'm so sorry. He bumped into me, and I—"

"Leave it." Dr. Perfect bats my arms away. "You've done enough damage."

I stop helping and rise to my feet. "I'm sorry, but this wasn't my fault. That guy bumped into my back." I look around for the instigator to back up my claim, but all I find are widened stares and people murmuring. There is no guilty or remorseful-looking guy anywhere in the mix. *Coward.*

"You clearly aren't qualified to be serving anyone. They should fire you."

My head whips back to Dr. Perfect. Or should I say Dr. Grump? I open my mouth to tell him what I think of his entire existence, but my boss interrupts before I unload my wrath.

"What have you done this time?" The angry tone says it all—I'm fired. Turning to Dr. Grump, Bossman switches to the suck-up voice he has perfected over the years. "My sincerest apologies, sir."

The overhead speakers crackle as another guy dressed in a suit rushes around the corner. He stops short in front of us and chuckles. "Whoa."

Dr. Grump is not amused. He shakes his notecards. "Is this the type of employees you hire? Incompetent ones?" The guy scoffs as he tries wiping off the excess champagne, which only smudges the pencil marks further. It serves him right for using something erasable. *Who even uses lead anymore? Isn't it bad for your health?*

"Miss Thornhill, grab your belongings and leave the premises. We'll mail your last check to you." My boss offers another apology to the asshole, who just stands there speechless and nodding, as if he agrees.

"But this was an accident. Didn't you see the guy who bumped into me?" I'm pretty sure Dr. Grump tried warning me before it happened. Why punish me?

"I'm tired of your excuses. Leave before I call security."

Oh, this is rich. I scowl at my boss and slice my icy glare toward the asshole. "Word of advice, asshole: permanent ink." With those parting words, I spin toward the prep kitchen and march out with my head held high. I refuse to let them see the desperation brewing inside me.

CHAPTER TWO

EVIE

"No. No, no, no, no, this can't be happening." *Can it?* I stare at the blockbuster bomb taped to my apartment door as the phone slips from my grasp and crashes to the floor. Muffled sounds scream in the background as I fumble with the keys, but I'm barely able to breathe—too shocked to register where the voices are coming from.

Please, please, please let the keys still work.

Panic grips my chest as my shaky fingers slide the correct key in place. The rush of air leaving my lungs when the door clicks open is so loud I'm surprised nosey neighbor Ms. Hines didn't stick her head out to see the commotion. But I don't care about her. All I can think is, *thank God I can still get inside.* Seriously though, what would I have done?

I move to go inside, but faint screams pull my attention back to the phone lying on the ground. I swoop it off the dingy tile and snatch the notice from the door.

"I'm here. I'm here," I say to my best friend.

"Are you okay?" Ansley's frantic voice causes a strangulated laugh to escape. Or more like a choke, stemming from the imaginary vice grip around my throat. There certainly isn't anything laughable in my life right now.

"Yes, sorry. I dropped the phone." I step into my apartment, crinkle the offending paper, and toss it in the trash with the one I received in the mail the other day. I bite back a sigh as my world implodes around me.

I'm so screwed.

"What happened before that?"

"It's more like what hasn't happened." I close my eyes and shake my head, trying to regain control of my life. I toss my Chanel purse on the stand and kick out of my heels. I slip on my bunny slippers and head to the kitchen.

"You're not making sense."

"That's because I don't want to tell you." Who wants to admit that they can't take care of themselves? Not me. All I wanted to do was break free from the stranglehold my parents placed on me at birth and help people. So far, I can't even help myself.

"Evie, what's going on? You're starting to worry me."

She isn't going to let this go. I cringe as I open the freezer door, preparing for the onslaught of judgment.

"I got served an eviction notice."

"No! How'd this happen? I thought you had enough money from selling your car."

Oh, my precious baby.

"Just dig the knife deeper." *And twist it while you're at it.* Because that blade hurts. When my parents cut my funding six months ago, I sold my beloved Audi to cover rent. Otherwise, I would've been homeless until graduation. Chicago's real estate market isn't cheap.

But I only have myself to blame for this predicament. I would still have my nice car instead of the crappy one I replaced it with and my credit line if I had gone home after graduation. My home being Philadelphia, and the credit line that came with the stipulation of being under my parents' thumb.

I grab the chocolate fudge brownie non-dairy ice cream and a spoon, not bothering with a bowl. It's a straight-out-of-the-carton type of night. I totally deserve this.

"I'm serious. You had your budget figured out. I wouldn't have sublet my apartment had I known you'd come up short."

"I thought everything was under control, but you know how it goes. Those unexpected graduation fees sucked up the rest of my cash. It was either graduate or pay rent."

On my way to the couch, my gaze wanders to the closet housing my Louboutin heels. I mentally whimper. Okay, in retrospect, paying more than a month's rent for the latest pair wasn't the brightest decision. But I needed them like I needed the air to breathe. The mixed black velour sculpted my feet, as if they were specifically made for me. I caved. Closing my eyes, I shake my head from yet another rash decision that went awry. Will I ever learn? Perhaps being homeless will drive the point home that I'm no longer wealthy. Honestly, I thought I'd be working a permanent job by now and using that degree I worked so hard to obtain.

Maybe I can sell them. I've heard there's a big resell market for shoes. If those hideous Yeezy Slides can catch an exorbitant price, surely my Louboutins could buy me another month. Half a month? *Ugh*, why was I so careless?

"I, uh, came up a little short, and the landlord must be tired of my excuses." I dig into the chocolatey goodness and relish in the flavor.

"What about the grace period? That was one of the selling points when you moved in." Ansley's voice rises in pitch.

"I suppose I dipped into their generosity too many times." *Like the last two months.*

"Flirting?"

I flinch. I can't believe my best friend is suggesting

succumbing to that level. She's all about women's equality and fairness and how sexism has no place in the world. "Really? This coming from you?"

"Hey, desperate times and all."

"Lessening the whole feminist movement wouldn't matter in this case. I lack the proper working equipment if you catch my drift."

"Well, crap." Her frustrated breath fills my ear.

"Exactly." I eye my apartment that cost me my car. The chipped stucco wall with peeling paint in the corner isn't much. In fact, the five-hundred-square-foot studio would classify as a dump, but it's been my sense of freedom for the past few years. The nicest part of the entire space is my wardrobe, including a bitchin' pair of black heels residing on the closet floor.

Totally worth it.

I rocked the stage during graduation with those. No regrets.

"Sorry the interview didn't go well. Any other prospects?"

"Just the one in a couple of weeks. I have so many applications filled out, but most places want someone with years of experience. It's the same song and dance."

"Gets old, doesn't it?"

The crumbled piece of paper resting on top of the trash mocks me. It's a constant reminder of yet another failure. I close my eyes to stave off the tears. "Let's hope I can hold off my landlord until the next interview. In the meantime, I'll look for another waitressing job."

"Have you given any more thought about working for my brother?"

The moan rests at the base of my throat. I swallow it back because the last thing I want to do is offend my best friend. Well, that and leave the city. "You mean move to a town you don't want anything to do with?"

A beat of silence passes before she speaks. "Sugar Creek Falls isn't so bad. Or it won't be for you."

"I can see the headlines now: Evie Thornhill moves to southern Indiana and dies from total boredom."

Ansley laughs. "You're exaggerating. I lived there for seventeen years and survived just fine."

"Yeah, but you left and never went back."

"True, but..."

Her voice trails off, so I steer the subject back to my current situation. I met Ansley four years ago when we shared a dorm. Not once, in all that time, has she mentioned the reason for not visiting home. The fact that she even mentioned her brother needing help, much less suggesting I help him, surprises me. "I can't see myself living in a small town."

"Don't worry. I'll call him just in case. You'll be perfect for the job, and he'll finally have the position filled."

"Wait, why is it taking so long to fill the position? Should I be worried?"

"Uh, no. It's just... he hasn't been in a good place lately."

I don't like the sounds of that. "What do you mean?"

"It's complicated. But don't worry. He'd treat you fine. The only thing I'd worry about is you falling for him. Not that you would, considering he's my brother and all, but still, ew."

I'm unsure how to take that, but I shake it off. The point is moot. He's thirty-seven, and there's no way I'm moving to the middle of nowhere. I wouldn't know how to act in a small town. Give me glamour and lights. I like the hustle and bustle of the city. Here, I blend. The constant noise keeps the attention off me. And dating is so low on my radar it doesn't even register. I need to focus on myself and prove I can make it on my own. Prove that I'm not like my parents. That I'm not another self-centered aristocrat.

"Believe me, I won't fall for anyone, let alone your brother.

Even if I did move there, and that's a big if, the stay would be temporary. I'd be gone with the first job offer that drags me back to the city."

The truth is, her family has always been a big mystery. Ansley never talks about them or her hometown. Since Liam's a doctor, I assume he wouldn't be a serial killer—a person who takes the Hippocratic Oath doesn't usually slash people—but the fact that he can't fill the position is concerning.

"Which is why I'm warning you. Look, all I'm saying is, he's coming off a bad breakup. His fiancée broke it off five months ago, and he hasn't gotten over her. I don't think you'd fall for him, but heed the warning."

"You don't have to worry about me." Dating ranks at the low end of the priority list—a constant for the past four years. I did the whole boyfriend thing back in Philadelphia before leaving. I close my eyes and let the shudder race down my spine. Nope, quick hookups are all I do. The guy back at the banquet pops into my mind. He stirred something inside that I haven't felt in a long time. But like the rest of the assholes, he revealed his true colors. I shake off the thought and double down on my rebuff. "The last thing I'm looking to do is fall in love. But I think we're getting ahead of ourselves since, you know, I'm not moving."

"We'll see about that."

"I can't believe that asshole fired me," I say around a mouthful of ice cream.

"Bossman's a douche. He only hates you because you wouldn't kiss his ass. You darn well know you're his best employee."

"Thanks, but I think you're biased."

"I am not." There's a pause, and I know she's biting her lower lip. She always does that when contemplating what to say. "Don't worry about your apartment. Everything will work out. This is only temporary."

A smile tugs at my lips. "You sound like my old nanny."

"See, you throw me off when you talk like that. Who grows up with nannies?"

"What? You didn't?" I feign shock and laugh, but it's more for her benefit. If it weren't for my nanny, life growing up would've been horrible and lonely. Miss Carmichael was my lifesaver.

"Oh, yeah, sure. Right there along with the butler."

"Now, that would be Jeffries, and he was more of a house manager."

"Jesus, I was kidding. You sure you want to leave that lifestyle?"

More than you could ever know.

A pounding at the door saves me from responding.

"Who's that?" Ansley asks.

"I don't know." *But I have an idea.* The sound wasn't friendly.

"Do you want me to stay on the phone?"

"No, I'll be okay. I'll talk to you soon."

"Okay, but remember, my brother is still an option. You know, just in case."

"Do not make that call. There's no way I'm moving to Sugar Creek Falls." The small town would eat me alive and spit me back out.

We hang up, but another round of rapping has me clutching the tub of ice cream like a security blanket. The soles of my bunny slippers pad across the floor, and I peer through the peep-hole. When the balding man comes into view, I groan.

He's here to kick me out.

This day has been nothing but a nightmare. I'm already jobless, penniless, evicted, and broke. Wait. Broke and penniless mean the same thing. Whatever. That's me—flat busted and embarrassed. It can't get any worse than this. Maybe I can pretend to be gone. Technically, I should be at work.

"I know you're behind the door, Miss Thornhill. Open up."

But I don't want to.

I straighten my shoulders and tug open the door, the container of ice cream in hand. I force a smile as I muster my cheerfullest voice. "Hello, Mr. Burge. I'm surprised to see you this late."

"It's only eight o'clock." He doesn't look amused.

Glancing at my bunny wall clock, I cringe. It seems later. I guess one loses track of time when getting fired and eating half a pint of Ben & Jerry's. This whole feeling sorry for yourself takes a toll. I'm freaking exhausted.

"Oh, I guess you're right," I manage to say.

"I'm assuming you got the notice?" My landlord gives me a once over and curls his lip when he notices my tub of non-dairy ice cream. Don't hate on my life choice. Or maybe I'm wrong, and he doesn't appreciate my bunny slippers. They look worse for wear with one of the right eyeballs missing from a tragic accident with a sweeper.

"Yes, sir, I sure did." I keep smiling and don't add anything else. Mr. Burge stares open-mouthed. He really is a nice guy, but I can tell he's at his wit's end with me. I don't blame him.

"If that's the case, then why aren't you packing?"

"I have a plan on how to get you paid." *Another lie.*

"It's too late. I have this unit rented. I was being nice by not changing the locks on you. If you can be gone by Sunday, I'd appreciate it."

My stomach dips as I scramble with what to say. I thought I'd have at least another month to make arrangements. It's Friday. If he wants me gone by the end of the weekend, that means I have one full day to find somewhere to live. "That can't be legal. My rent is paid up for the entire month."

"You haven't paid rent in the last two months."

Slight technicality.

"I have heels. Good ones," I blurt, working the secondhand shoe angle.

"Why would I care?"

"They're Louboutin."

His eyebrow perks, as if he's considering it. "Color?"

"Black crushed velvet."

"Size?"

"Six."

His eyes seem to gleam, and for a moment, I think he'll cave, but then he waves his hand and shakes his head, tossing me a pitying look. "Look, if you don't fight me on this and leave by the weekend, I'll use your deposit for what you owe. Call it a clean break. That way, it won't go against your credit. But I need you gone."

My stomach does a weird flip-flop. He acts as if I should thank him, and maybe I should—he is, after all, doing me a solid—but where will I go? And now that I have zero income due to an incredible jerk with beautiful green eyes, I'm totally screwed.

"Fine, I'll be out of here," I concede, even though what he's doing is illegal, *I think*. But let's face it, it's a little late to be filing a complaint. And who in their right mind will take my side? He's been more than patient with me.

"Okay." He claps his hands together, as if he isn't singlehandedly crushing my dreams. He stands there expectantly.

Uh...

His eyebrow rises at my continued silence. "The shoes."

"You want my Louboutins?" I may have whimpered.

"I believe that was part of the deal."

My shoulders slump. I was half-joking, but okay. "I'll be right back."

I grab my latest pair and hold them up to my chest. It's not as if I don't own more, but these were special. Why couldn't I have offered a pair from last season?

"Here." I shove them at him.

"Gorgeous," he says as his greedy paws grab hold.

Yes, they are, I think sadly.

He turns to leave. "I wish you well."

I close the door and sink to the floor. All I wanted to do was escape my parents' hold over me and prove I could make it on my own—not to depend on their money and the rules attached to it. Living shouldn't be this hard. I put in the hard work and dedication. I was supposed to be rewarded at the end of a rainbow. *Where the heck is my pot of gold?*

I take a bite of icy goodness and smile around the spoon. I can practically hear Miss Carmichael telling me not to worry. She would always tell me everything was temporary. What seemed like a major problem now would be a blip along your life journey. She was extremely optimistic given her circumstances. But she was my godsend. Whenever prep school was too much, she would sneak me a bowl of ice cream—the real kind. The strict diet Mom had me on banned the dreaded cream, but that didn't deter Miss Carmichael.

"To find a decent man, you have to maintain your figure," Mom would say whenever sugar carbs came within five feet of me. By decent, she meant someone whose inherited wealth would enhance our net worth. As if I would want to be in a relationship based solely on my looks and his bank statement. Talk about a match made in gold-digging superficialness.

There's no way I want that lifestyle. I witnessed first-hand the lack of empathy toward others while they were in need. I was part of the culture. Part of the problem. But no more. I won't return to it, no matter the circumstances.

My self-pity gets cut short by my ringing cell phone. I instantly groan. *The Imperial March* ringtone is never good. I slip the phone from my pocket and reluctantly answer, "Mom."

CHAPTER THREE

EVIE

"You've graduated. It's time for you to come home," Mom says in lieu of a greeting.

My gaze shifts toward the heavens. Her timing is impeccable. But one can argue it's my own fault since I've ignored her calls and texts all day. Trying hard to keep the frustration out of my tone, I say, "We've talked about this."

"No. We agreed that you'd attend college, not actually work. It's been two weeks since you graduated. It's time to come home while a few suitable men are left."

You mean suitable to your standards. And I'm surprised she even remembers I graduated, considering neither parent attended the ceremony. My dad refused to come. He said, and I quote, "It's not as if Northwestern is an Ivy League school." And Mom, well, she wouldn't stray from the cage Daddy built for her. I do what I do best whenever I talk to her; I lie. "I have a long-term lease."

"I'll pay it off. Daddy doesn't need to know. Just come home."

Of course, she would pay it off. Mother has turned wasting money into an art form. "I can't. I have a job starting soon."

Silence greets me as my lies pile up.

"Other than waitressing?"

"How did you know—"

"I know everything." Her frustration seeps through the phone. She huffs and continues, "It's bad enough you've embarrassed the family, but no one needs to learn about your shenanigans while you were away. Just come home, and we'll smooth it all out."

My jaw clenches shut. Graduating college and working as a waitress are not shenanigans, but screaming this to her is pointless. Her mind is like cement. Once it sets, it's permanent. My thoughts race for a way to get out of this. I can't go back there. I just can't. If I do, I'll be stuck in that world with no escape.

"As I said, I have a job. I've accepted an office manager's position. I won't quit before I start." For a crazy moment, I thought the faux management title would impress her, but I should've known better. The only thing to impress her will be my future husband's portfolio.

"That work is beneath you, dear."

"Let me guess. I'm better suited to planning charity events and sipping tea while degrading the people serving me. You're too much. I have to go."

"You're better suited to have someone pamper you, yes. Thornhill women aren't bred to work. I'll give you a month, and then I'm coming to get you. It's time for you to take your place in this family."

She hangs up, and I'm left staring at the now blank screen and wondering how I ever grew up in that toxic environment. I drop the phone on my lap and look at my apartment. Sirens sound in the distance, along with the squeal of brakes. I blink away the threatening tears. This place may not be much, but these four walls are my freedom. Something I fought very hard for. I won't crawl back to Philly and conform to my parent's wishes. I won't. But what am I going to do? I have to live somewhere.

You have an out, the small voice in my head reminds me.

Ansley's offer to contact her brother comes to mind. Can I really leave the city and move to a small town in southern Indiana? The only time I've been to small towns was when Ansley and I stopped for bathroom breaks on our California-or-bust road trip. We busted. Knowing my car was being tracked, we took her old Hyundai. The passenger tire blew. She made the mortal sin of slamming the brakes, which is the opposite of what you're supposed to do. The car jerked to the right and rammed us straight into a farmer's fence pole.

Another rush of panic works through me. Will my current car even make the trip? I glance at my now melted container of chocolatey goodness and sigh. *I can't even do misery right.* I sit the container aside and dial my friend. Before I bring up her number, a text message appears.

> I'm here waiting. I won't wait forever.

I close my eyes and try to will my heartbeat to slow. *The words mean nothing. Just as before.* With shaking fingers, I delete the message and call my friend. I'm so screwed if this doesn't work.

"What's up? I didn't expect to hear from you again so soon." Her cheery voice conjures a smile. I can always count on my friend to make me feel better.

Biting back tears, I say, "I need you to call your brother."

CHAPTER FOUR

EVIE

Two days later, the "Welcome to Sugar Creek Falls" sign comes into view. I give the car's dashboard an appreciative pat. *I arrived.* It was iffy for a while. The car's engine light kicked on about ninety miles back. I didn't know whether to pull over or not. I'm fluent in one language—English. I don't speak *car*. My knowledge of vehicles consists of filling up the gas tank and pressing the pedal to drive. And drove I did. *To the middle of nowhere, apparently.*

"At the next stoplight, turn left." The deep Australian voice says, as if other stoplights exist. I'm not so sure they do.

How small is this place?

I heed the advice and take the left turn, veering to the right shoulder due to the orange and white striped barricades lining the inside of the street. *Are they removing the turn lane?* The construction spans the entire town, but it looks like they're widening the road or making multiple lanes. *Strange.* I wouldn't think the traffic would be that heavy through town to constitute four lanes.

My gaze takes in the downtown area, or what I think is their downtown. A sinking feeling that I somehow stepped back in time settles in the pit of my stomach. I take in the row of storefronts to my left. The two-story brick buildings appear to be original to the town, which, according to the welcoming sign, was founded in eighteen hundred and twenty-four. Large display windows cover most storefronts, with black awnings covering the entrances. A rather sizable, grassy, squared-off section sits to my right, and the road wrapping around it houses another row of storefronts. I frown. The town is small but quaint. I can do quaint, right? I'll have to. It's not like I have many choices.

Pressing the gas pedal, my car jerks and makes a grunting noise. "Come on, Lyle. We just have a few minutes before we're there." I give my dashboard another pat, showing more love. I named the beast Lyle as a play on the word reliable. The irony isn't lost on me that lie would be the more realistic take. I'm sure the seller stretched the truth about the engine's "tip-top" performance. But being desperate and all, I took him at his word.

It's another rash decision that hasn't panned out. I'm racking them up. *Go me.*

Heading straight, I make it past the construction and drive through the residential section. Single and two-story homes line both sides of the road before tapering into a heavily wooded area. My destination is beyond the S-curve on the road. Once I round the last bend, I pull into the parking lot at what is supposed to be my temporary home. *This can't be right.* I check the GPS and glance back at the motel with a look of horror. I've time-traveled to the nineteen sixties. An uncontrollable shudder sweeps through my body as the realization sinks in that Ansley's brother booked me at the Bates Motel. Okay, it may not be the same motel from the horror flick, but the single-row units and god-awful faded beige walls with weathered brown trim look eerily familiar. The only thing missing is the creepy mansion in the background.

I sit inside the running car, debating whether to flee. The problem is, I wouldn't know where to go. I take a deep breath to calm down. It seems to work until a strange gurgling sound erupts followed by complete silence. And steam. Lots and lots of steam billow out from under the hood. *Great. Even my getaway car came here to die.* I guess I should've taken the check engine light more seriously.

Clenching the wheel, I will myself not to cry. I can do this. This is temporary. This town serves as a way station until I land a job that will lead me back to the mass population. Back to where the odds are more favorable for helping people. But it's not as if I have a choice to leave. I spent the last of my cash at the gas station thirty miles back. I have a whopping fifty bucks to my name. No, living here is my only option until I grow my bank account or land a real job.

I let out a breath and grab the door handle. *I've got this.*

Maple trees provide a canopy of green as my heels click against the broken concrete. I take care to watch where I step. A gal could lose her heels in these craters.

A bell chimes through the air as I open the rickety door.

"You must be Evie," a grey-haired lady says from behind a mahogany countertop. She straightens a stack of flyers.

"I am." I grab the straps of my purse and squeeze them closer to me, a little perplexed by her recognition.

"Welcome to Sugar Creek Falls, dear. I'm Amabel, but folks around here call me Mabel." She wears a friendly smile. No creepy son, and she's alive. That's a plus.

"It's nice to meet you, Mabel. I guess I'll be staying here for the week." I step to the counter.

"Yes, dear." The older lady hands me a block of wood with a

key dangling from the end. "You're in room 1A. This isn't anything fancy, but your room is clean. Breakfast is served from five to eleven."

"I didn't realize this included a complimentary breakfast."

"I don't like folks to go away hungry." She points to a red barn across the street. "That's the restaurant where you'll eat. Order whatever you like. They'll know you're a guest."

"Oh, that's unexpected." Sit-down breakfasts served hot don't happen in other hotels. When she mentioned breakfast, my mind went straight to fake scrambled eggs or self-made waffles. At least I'll have one daily meal taken care of.

"You're all set. Little Liam took care of everything."

I pop an eyebrow. "Little Liam?"

She blushes. "I suppose it's Dr. Seymour now, but he'll always be Little Liam to me. He's like a second son."

I let out a chuckle. "Now, that's a story I may have to revisit."

"Anytime, dear. Anytime. Oh, here, take a flyer. You don't want to miss the festival. It's held at the square. People from all around come here. I just hope the construction will be done as promised."

"Thanks. It sounds fun," I lie, folding the flyer and placing it in my purse. The date isn't until Labor Day. That's practically three months away. No way will I be here, but I keep that information to myself. Mabel practically beams with pride, so I don't want to burst that bubble, but I just came from Chicago. We have street fests and outdoor concerts all the time. Not that I went out much, but that's beside the point.

Once I'm standing in front of room 1A, I creep inside, expecting the worst, but much to my surprise, it's clean and smells of cleaning supplies. The look isn't modern, but the crisp white duvets have a fresh appeal. The walls are stucco and painted white. Two sets of different-sized black and white covered bridge photos are positioned on the wall above the bed frame. The matted, black metal frames hang in an alternating symmetrical fashion to complete the gallery wall. The display is eye-catching, but the photographs are remarkable. I scan the photos for an artist's name but come up short.

Shrugging it off, I place my luggage on the dresser and step over a grease mark marring the otherwise clean but dated green carpet. My phone buzzes with a call.

"Yes, I've arrived at Slasher Motel," I say to my best friend, plopping my ass on the bed.

"Did you say hi to Mabel for me?" Ansley asks through a laugh.

"No, you didn't ask me to. Otherwise, I would've. Say, she doesn't happen to have a creepy son lurking around the property, does she?"

Silence.

Why is she silent?

"Ansley?" I prompt, peering out the window in search of anything odd. The only movement is a squirrel digging around a flower garden.

"Well, not creepy, no, but she does have a son."

Of course she does.

"Will I be able to take my shower in peace?"

She laughs. "Oh, yeah, you're good. Matthew may be a jerk, but he's not a psychotic killer."

"That makes me feel so much better." I lie back on the bed, which admittedly feels nice.

"You'll be fine. Have you met my brother yet?"

"No. I literally just pulled into town. I haven't even unpacked." I close my eyes and stave off the tears welling in my eyes. "I have no idea where I'm going to live. Maybe coming here was a bad idea."

"It's not a bad idea. I'll text you a number to call. It's an old friend of mine. She'll be able to help you get settled into a place."

"How many people quit this job before me?" I question my decision-making altogether. Even if I had no choice in coming here, I still made a hasty decision. And my record hasn't been good.

Ansley hesitates. "Those people don't matter. They don't have your spunky personality."

"I'm not feeling too spunky at the moment." I feel somewhat deflated. If I sunk any lower, I'd lie next to that grease spot on the floor.

"That's not true. Once you get a few steady paychecks under-foot, you'll be back on your game."

"I suppose."

"And you did it on your own. No help from your parents. That means you have a backbone. Quit selling yourself short."

"Okay. You're right. I'm just... feeling sorry for myself."

"I know you're down, but things will improve. I promise."

"It'd be better if you came and visited me."

"Yeah, I don't see that happening anytime soon."

One of these days, she's going to spill and tell me her story. I don't press. She'll deal with her demons on her own time. "Oh, I almost forgot. Do you know a good mechanic around here?"

I chew on my nail as she takes her sweet time to respond.

"Matthew."

"The psycho son?"

This earns a laugh, breaking the sudden tension. "He's not that bad. But, yeah, the same one. What happened to your car?"

"I don't know yet. But the steam coming from under the hood can't be good. I'll get his number from Mabel and call him in the morning. For now, I'm going to take a hot shower and chill for the rest of the evening. I miss you."

"I miss you, too."

"I'll let you know how day one goes."

She laughs. "Sounds good."

We hang up, and I stare around the room that will serve as home for the week. It's not as bad as I thought it would be. As much as I look forward to starting work, I also dread it.

I hope you're ready for me, Little Liam. I need this to work out.

CHAPTER FIVE

LIAM

"This town has less than four thousand people. Why the hell are we always double-booked?" I slam the schedule on my desk and turn my sharp gaze to my nurse. Rachael levels me with a stare, not intimidated by my height towering over her.

"I take it the conference didn't go over well?"

The low grumble escaping my mouth causes her eyebrow to lift. "You have no idea."

"I'm sure it went better than you think."

"It was a clusterfuck." *One I'd rather forget.* "Back to my original question. Why is the schedule always in utter chaos?"

"No one can figure out the archaic system. I've shown them countless times, but I can only lead a horse to water—"

"But you can't make them drink it. Yeah, yeah, I get it." I cut her off because I've heard this a thousand times. I realize the office needs some serious updates, but that shouldn't negate people's competence. Hopefully, this new hire will live up to the expectations set by my sister. Ansley promised she was worth the trouble.

You better be right, sis.

And speaking of, I glance at the black-rimmed, Grand-Central-Station-styled clock hanging on the wall above my office door. My jaw tics. Miss Highly Recommended is five minutes late.

"Where's our new office manager?" I cock an eyebrow, letting the question hang, but an unsettling feeling sinks in my stomach as confidence slips from Rachael's expression.

"She isn't here yet."

"Jesus," I mutter under my breath. So much for doing my sister a favor. I need to call her out for having horrible taste in friends. I wave my hand dismissively. "Let's keep the walk-ins to a minimum, shall we?"

"Yeah, okay. I'll be sure to do that right after you attend to the ankle injury that just arrived. You know, the one you told to come in before opening hours," she quips, tossing the chart on my desk. She about-faces and exits without another word.

I glance at the chart and curse. The last thing I need is a pissed-off Rachael. She's the only constant in my life since returning to town. I need to apologize. It's not her fault the walk-ins are never ending. We're the only medical provider within a forty-five-mile radius. Our reach stretches farther to the west if you include the Amish lands.

As my cell phone rings, I make a mental note to apologize later and grab my phone.

"Why are you calling me so early?" I round my desk and flop into the chair, waiting for my childhood friend Matthew to reply. My sleep deprivation from rolling into town late last night caught up with me, and I just want to get through this day without difficulty. The faster I get home and forget about this shitty weekend, the better.

"Good morning to you, too, sunshine. I take it you didn't enjoy your weekend."

I grunt. "What do you think?"

His answering chuckle serves to sour my mood further. "I know you hate making speeches, but I don't know what you have against big cities. They're fun to visit."

They are, until every turn reminds me of my ex-fiancée. Chicago may not be New York City, but it's pretty damn close. Even the whiff of fresh goose feces in Grant Park reminded me of the picnics we took in Central Park. The hustle of people, the never-ending skyline, and the constant noise remind me too much of my time in the Big Apple.

My time living with *her.*

"Then, I suggest you go and visit," I say, my tone laced with irritation. "And you haven't answered my question. Why the early call? You're not hurt, are you?"

"No, nothing like that. I wanted to warn you that your new hire is running late."

"How would you know about my new hire's work ethic?" No doubt his mom told him about Evie coming to stay since I put her up in his family's motel, but how would he know her schedule?

"Because I'm staring at her sorry excuse of a car while she Ubers to work."

"*Uber?* We don't have any Uber drivers."

He chuckles again. "I know, but Miss Thornhill didn't quite trust me to give her a lift. I have a feeling she'll be hoofing to work in those fancy heels girls like so much."

My eyes narrow in concern. It's only a couple of miles from the motel to the office, so the walk won't be bad, but the cost she'll incur to fix the car won't help her situation. The impression from my sister was Evie spent her last dime to get here. "What's the damage going to be?"

"The estimate comes in around twelve hundred dollars. I'm trying to get some parts from the junkyard. That should lower the cost."

I give a low whistle and scrub a hand over my face. "Don't get used parts; order the factory ones. I'll cover the cost."

"Hmm, I knew this girl would get you out of this funk."

"What are you talking about? I haven't even met her."

Another low and irritating chuckle slips past his lips. "You'll see. She's your type."

"I have no idea what you're talking about. I'm just doing this as a favor to my sister." Although, I know exactly what he's insinuating. Evie is another highfalutin, city girl like my ex, Ciera. But I don't have a specific type of woman I'm drawn to. I met Ciera during my last year of residency in New York City. Of course, Evie would be "citified," as the locals call it, but that doesn't make her my type. I mean, sure, I have a specific type sexually, but he doesn't know anything about my sexual preferences. No one in this town does.

"Okay," he says, drawing out the word. "We'll see what you say after you meet her. I wanted to warn you about her car so you wouldn't fire her on day one."

"I haven't fired anyone." *They quit.* It's not my fault I can't find a competent person within a hundred-mile radius to run the office.

"Uh-huh. Sure. I'll see what I can do with these parts and let you know."

"Fine. I'll talk to you later." I no more than hang up when Rachael knocks before letting herself in.

"Our new hire called and said she's running late. She had car trouble."

"Hope this won't be a trend," I can't help but bark out.

Rachael's face softens. "I think the excuse is legit this time."

"Yeah, Matthew called and told me."

"Timmy's ready in exam room one. My guess is a sprain rather than a break."

"Great. I'll be there in a minute."

As Rachael retreats to the hallway, I replay Matthew's words. *She's exactly your type.* I love living in a small town—that's why my future consisted of moving back—but there are drawbacks, like everyone knowing your business and making assumptions. After introducing Ciera to Sugar Creek Falls, the townsfolk labeled me a snob, claiming none of the girls around here were good enough. That's pure bullshit. *Somewhat.* I may not be attracted to anyone local, but that doesn't mean I prefer high-maintenance women. I don't. I'd rather stay away from them. They're nothing but trouble. My ex didn't fit in here, and it will be a cold day in hell before I make that mistake again. You can't take a fish out of the water, and that's what I tried doing by bringing Ciera here. Everyone saw that but me. I thought she was happy. I thought we were on the same page. Turns out, not only were we reading different books, but we weren't in the same library. Our goals couldn't be any more opposite, and I'm not as bright as I initially thought. I missed the signs that she wasn't happy.

I missed a lot.

Regardless, Matthew's wrong. There isn't any way I'll fall for my new office manager. I've crossed high-maintenance women off my list. Besides, she is too young for me. She's my baby sister's age, for fuck's sake.

But the age difference didn't stop me from lusting after that waitress who couldn't have been much over twenty.

Christ. When the woman walked toward me, carrying a tray of champagne flutes, all I could focus on were her mesmerizing eyes. Sure, she had the body to match—slightly thicker legs and enough curves to satisfy my wettest dreams—but those smokey gray eyes drew me in. They were unique. And her confidence. When she walked toward me with a mission, I paused, visualizing my hands running along those curves. Every objectified thought ran through my head. I'd say I wasn't proud, but that would be a lie. Give me some credit for not vocalizing them. But I was so transfixed I forgot why I was at the conference in the first place. That was until that asshole bumped into her and caused her to trip forward.

My hands curl into fists on top of the desk as I remember the chain reaction that mishap caused. My notecards flew from my hands and landed in a sea of champagne. But that's not the worst part. Oh no. I had to go and make a complete ass of myself by not handling the situation like a grown adult. I succumbed to my anxieties and just lost it. But there was a moment before realization hit. The surrounding crowd disappeared with her in my arms while my stare held hers. With my hands wrapped around those curves and her body pressed against me, the wet shirts left little to the imagination of how she would feel if the clothes were off. And yes, my mind totally went there. Her shorter frame against my taller one couldn't stop those wicked thoughts. Hell, neither could our age difference. Something about her sparked a feeling I didn't think would ever ignite again since Ciera left. My hand twitched as I visualized my handprint across her ass cheek, and that thought, coupled with thoughts of my ex and ruined notecards, fueled my anger.

I'm pretty sure my tirade caused the girl to be fired. I wasn't proud of how I handled the situation, which wasn't the woman's fault. I searched for her after the speech to apologize, but she was nowhere to be found. The woman plagued my thoughts the entire weekend. I let out a humorless laugh. Hell, she's still haunting them.

I shake off my guilt and go examine my patient's ankle. Twenty minutes later, I access the films from the portable X-ray machine.

"The X-ray doesn't show any fractures. Luckily, it's just a sprain. Apply a combination of ice and heat, alternating for twenty minutes. Do this four times a day, and your ankle will be good as new. Rachael will give you further instructions."

"Thanks, Dr. Seymour."

I nod while stepping out into the hallway and placing the clipboard on the wall mount. I turn to head to my office and come to a dead stop at the sight of the woman standing in the hallway.

"You!" we say simultaneously.

CHAPTER SIX

EVIE

Tone conveys everything.

Tone deciphers actual meaning.

And the tone behind our simultaneous "you" couldn't be any more opposite. Where his was in shocked surprise, mine was accusatory.

Because what the actual living hell?

Why is the guy who got me fired in front of me right now?

At my new job.

Then, it sinks in as I take in the white lab coat and the stethoscope hanging around Dr. Perfect's neck.

Doctor.

As in medical doctor.

The very one who is my new boss.

Sweat breaks across my forehead. I want to melt into the dark, dingy brown and beige asphalt tile. You know, the kind that looks like it belongs on a chessboard, which it may as well be since I feel as isolated and exposed as a chess piece left hanging.

Holy shit.

Why am I focused on flooring and figurative chess games when I should be directing my attention to the guy who uprooted my life? Focus Evie. This guy is Ansley's brother. My new boss. The same guy I wanted to hit on back in Chicago. Oh my God, I tried to hit on Ansley's brother.

That was until he went from Dr. Perfect to Dr. Grump.

Guilt flashes in those devilish green eyes a moment before they harden into steel.

"Why are *you* here?" He fires the question at me, as if my presence isn't welcomed. As if I'm the source of his sudden stress.

"Seriously?" I scoff. I see it didn't take long for Dr. Grump to surface. I mean, the audacity of this man. Just when I feel terrible for lusting after my best friend's brother, he has to remind me why I labeled him. Liam folds his arms across his chest and glares at me. Me! The one who did nothing wrong. I look behind him in search of a hidden camera. This has to be a joke, right? Some sort of twisted prank gone wrong. My luck cannot be this bad. "Why do you *think* I'm here? *You* hired *me*."

That perfectly defined jaw clenches and has me so mesmerized that I forget why I'm standing here in the first place. That is, until he speaks.

"You're Evie?" He clears his throat, as if that would help wipe away the disdain in his voice. "Sorry, Miss Geneva."

Geneva. So, he wants to play with formalities, does he? That is not going to work for me. "Yes, but please call me Evie."

Liam drags his gaze along the length of my body, lingering a moment too long on the small amount of cleavage my silk blouse exposes before pushing past my pencil skirt and settling on my legs. His small intake of breath stokes flames of desire as the air around us electrifies.

Shut those thoughts down now!

There is no good that can come from them.

This tension would be easier to ignore if the heat in his

eyes wasn't so prevalent during his slow perusal. Then, maybe my body wouldn't buzz with this unwarranted need. But it's hard not to react when I can practically feel his touch from his stare alone. I may not like it, but I can't deny what he does to me.

He's Ansley's older brother, I remind myself.

"I think we should keep this professional," he says, snapping me out of the lust-induced trance he put me in and straight to reality—the one where Dr. Grump hates me for no apparent reason.

"It's a little late for that, don't you think?" I snap.

"What do you mean?"

"I mean, you're the one who made it personal when you got me fired."

He steps closer, and my resolve wavers. I'm transported back to Chicago when his hard chest pressed against mine. Back to the moment where it was just us and his fingers tightened their hold around my hips. Back before the moment was shattered by him being a dick. An older woman dressed in pale blue scrubs steps from the exam room, breaking that memory. Her eyes widen as her gaze ping-pongs between us.

"You fired her already? Her car broke down. You knew this."

"No," Dr. Grump says while I say, "Yes."

Our gazes connect, and my body betrays me again. But I can't help it. He stands so close I can smell him—a woodsy scent and something else I can't quite distinguish. It smells good, whatever it is.

This time, he has the decency to grimace before resting a hand on the back of his neck and letting out a sigh. "I didn't mean for that to happen."

"Really?" I place my hands on my hips, not believing his string of bullshit, and glower at him. Good scent or not, he still acted like an ass that night. "Please, by all means, explain how asking my boss why he hires incompetent help works in my favor."

As soon as the words leave my mouth, I cringe, wishing I could take them back. I shouldn't poke the bear—the bear being my boss. What if he fires me? What would I do then? I spent every dime I had getting here. I'm stuck. I'm too broke to leave. Even my car is broken. Not to mention, it's his dime paying for my motel. God, if he cans my ass, I'll be forced to live in the woods surrounding this town.

I see why the previous employees left. The guy is grouch-o numero uno, which is a shame. He seemed nice on the phone. Well, nice might be a stretch, but he was decent enough. He offered to put me in a motel for a week. Huh, perhaps he's the slasher I need to watch out for. What did Mabel call him? Her second son? *Well, this story just took a major spin.*

"Look, I think we got off on the wrong foot," Slasher says.

My eyebrows shift up of their own accord, unable to hide my unspoken sarcasm as his words snap me back to the current situation. But give me a break. There is no *we* in this scenario, only *he*. He is the one who got off on the wrong foot. All I did was lose said footing. But to save my job, I keep my mouth shut.

"I seem to have missed something in translation," his nurse says, interrupting the tension between us. "But we need to get back on schedule before the day gets away from us. Why don't I show you the office? I'm Rachael, by the way." She pats my arm and side-steps around me. I hold Liam's gaze for a beat longer before conceding and following behind her.

"I'm sure you guessed by now, but I'm Evie." As I make the unnecessary introduction, I can't shake the weight of his stare as she guides me to the front. I don't dare turn to look, though. I'm not sure if his expression would be hostile or intrigued. Both, maybe? And I'm not sure which one I want at this point.

Ten minutes later, I find myself having another mini freak out.

"Sorry, I don't have time to show you how the office works properly. You're going to have to wing the scheduling today. But don't worry. I'll cover everything tomorrow when we have a lull in our schedule. Just do the best you can for now and *try* not to double-book. You'll be fine once you get the schedule down."

My quick nod of assurance is more to satisfy myself than Rachael. But the reprieve is short-lived when my gaze sweeps across the waiting room. Multiple sets of eyes stare back, leaving no doubt that this is what an overbooked day looks like. Hopefully, the blame won't land on me. I glance back at the computer and ignore the sweat pooling under my arms.

What have I gotten myself into?

This program looks as dated as the CRT monitor taking up half the counter space. I'm exaggerating. Kind of. The counter is relatively large, but this setting will take some getting used to. No wonder he has such trouble keeping help. If it's not his grumpy demeanor, it'd be these antiqued working conditions making people leave.

I force a smile at the aging woman. "I'll do the best I can."

"That's all I ask, dear. Okay, let's show you how to check in a patient." Rachael pulls up a chair, her face growing almost whimsical. "I don't know the history between Dr. Seymour and you, but don't let him fool you. He means well."

"Noted." I sink into my seat as she nods. Why does everyone speak so well about this guy? I've found him nothing but irritating. Perhaps I shouldn't judge him too harshly, but Dr. Grump needs to undergo a complete personality transformation to change my opinion. And that reminds me, I need a different name for him. I doubt I last long if I call him a grump to his face.

Rachael gives me a quick rundown of how to check in a patient when the door bursts open.

"I don't need a doctor." A loud voice booms into the waiting room.

Our heads snap to the outburst and land on a grey-haired, elderly gentleman being wheeled through the door by a guy who looks around Liam's age.

Rachael groans. "Great, you get to meet the lovely Mr. Cusack today. Talk about tossing you into the fire on day one. Hope your will to work outweighs the need for unemployment because you're about to be tested."

She bypasses the clipboards made for the scheduled patients and pulls one from a nearby stack. Attached are a few blank forms. These must be the forms for the walk-ins she mentioned. "Looks like Melvin fell and split his head. Give this to his grandson—he'll know what to do with it—and bring Melvin back to examination room three. I'll go get it ready." She hands me the clipboard and disappears to the back.

"I don't need to be here." The gruff voice says as he bats his grandson's hand away. "And I don't need this contraption." The contraption being a wheelchair, and by the dripping blood and grandson's eye roll, I'd wholeheartedly disagree. He's exactly where he needs to be.

"He fell again. I think he may need stitches this time," the guy says. He's good-looking. The tips of dark curls spring from under the faded blue baseball cap, giving him a boyish appearance. He's hunched over, pushing his grandfather, but I can tell he leans toward the taller side. Maybe not as tall as Liam, but above average height.

"Don't listen to him. All I need is a grandson who isn't a yellow-bellied canary and let me be."

My gaze shoots up to meet his grandson's. Amusement dances in those big, shining eyes instead of the anger that I expected to see. *Hmm.* The old man can't be too awful if his flesh and blood can still smile after that insult. I spring into action.

These moments are where I shine. I love winning over cantankerous people. For the first time in a long while, I feel useful.

"Well, Melvin—" I hand the clipboard to the grandson and take over the wheelchair—"If you don't mind, I'll get you back to the exam room. I can't have you bleeding all over my floor."

CHAPTER SEVEN

LIAM

Sitting at my desk, I scrub my hand over my face while the other flicks a pen repeatedly. I stare mindlessly out the tiny window in my office as a hummingbird flutters around the evergreen bush. Other than an occasional passing car, it's quiet and calm—the state of being I usually crave and the opposite of the storm cloud I just hired.

When my sister asked me to hire her friend, I had no idea it would be the same waitress I got fired. The same attractive woman I spent all evening feeling guilty about because of my behavior. And felt even guiltier later during my shower when I visualized her on her knees and those unique gray eyes staring up at me, waiting for my command.

Jesus.

My new office manager is the star of my late-night fantasies.

I want to hate her on principle. I want to hate every high-maintenance bone in her pampered, posh body, from her silky blouse to her expensive perfume that smells like a damn orange grove. My grasp on the pen snaps the plastic. I don't know why

I'm obsessing over this. *Over her.* There's no way she's cut out for this town. She won't last two weeks.

Rachael knocks before popping her head through the door. "Mr. Cusack fell again. I'll set up room three. It looks as if he'll need stitches this time."

I stifle a groan. I should have known the day wouldn't go smoothly. We're already double-booked thanks to our last office manager's incompetence. I squeezed Timmy's twisted ankle in this morning with the hopes of keeping on schedule. I should've anticipated the recipient of the worst-patient-of-the-year award to thwart the morning. Melvin's timing is impeccable.

"Laceration to the head?" I guess.

"Yes. Right temporal region. Should be cut and dry."

I shoot her a look, but it falls on her backside. Rachael is already on her way to prep the room. This should be fun. Getting Melvin to cooperate isn't easy. He's stubborn, belligerent, and refuses help. He's the typical eighty year old, who has nothing nice to say. Ever. No one, and I do mean no one, is safe from the wrath of the old geezer. I should know. The stubborn ass happens to be one of my best friend's grandfathers. I've had the pleasure of dealing with him my entire life. I stand but pause when Evie's voice echoes down the hall.

"Mr. Cusack, this visit won't take too long. The doctor will have you fixed up in no time, and you'll be on your way."

"I don't need a doctor. They're all quacks, wanting to send me to the old people's home."

"Now, you know Dr. Seymour isn't that way."

"What do you know? It's your first day. You'll be gone by the end of the week."

My stomach tightens from the truth in his statement, even though his thoughts echo mine. But the last thing I need is Melvin running off another manager—not yet anyway. I place my hand on the door to intervene when her laughter echoes down the hallway and stops me. The genuineness in her tone makes my stomach flip, but the sensation hits differently this time. Which only serves to irritate me further.

"That may be so. Not all of us are lucky enough to have a designated suite like you. Rumor has it you're a regular."

My lips twitch at Mr. Cusack's answering grunt. He knows he has been bested. Putting up with Melvin was the common complaint from the revolving door of office managers. The other common denominator was my demeanor. I don't know what problem they had with me—I'm rather lovely. I just want people to do their job. *Correctly.* I didn't think holding them accountable was too much to ask.

"And speaking of your suite, here you go."

"Thank you, Evie. I'll get him prepped if you could get Dr. Seymour," Rachael says.

Before being trapped in my office with her, I step out into the hallway. Evie takes the paperwork from Ethan and turns toward me.

"Oh, great, you're here."

My gaze drops to her silk blouse, which has a small spot of blood seeping into the expensive fabric. I wave my finger toward it. "You may want to put some hydrogen peroxide on that. Perhaps in the future, you shouldn't wear expensive clothes. This isn't the city. People aren't impressed by your fancy outfits. It puts people off more than anything."

She flips her long, blond hair back as she straightens her shoulders, eyes narrowing. "I don't dress to impress others. I dress for myself." She points a perfectly manicured finger toward the exam room. "You have a bleeding patient. You may want to attend to him rather than give me fashion lessons, *Doctor.*"

Her emphasis on the word doctor makes it sound like a nasty virus. Our gazes lock in a battle of wills neither of us wants to back down from. I refuse to let this woman get under my skin. We stay this way until a chuckle breaks our staring contest.

"This one may just stick around." Ethan looks from me to Evie, the corners of his mouth curving into that cocky grin that has worked in his favor since high school. "At least, I hope so."

Evie raises an eyebrow in amusement as she shoots Ethan a look. Was that a look of interest? My jaw clenches. Ethan and that damn grin of his.

"This is a doctor's office, not a pick-up station," I say hastily.

Her gaze cuts back to mine, and if looks could kill, I wouldn't be standing upright.

Ethan's smile widens. "This is going to be fun." He slaps me on the back and dips inside the exam room.

"Hydrogen peroxide," I repeat. And why my conscience picks this moment to stab me in the back, I'll never know, but I cave. "After we're done working, I'll take you to the Wagon Wheel. We can discuss your living arrangements over supper."

The amusement she had for Ethan disappears. "That's okay. I've contacted a realtor."

She has? I study her for a long moment. When Ansley called yesterday, she insisted I take care of Evie. She said her friend was flat broke and spent all her money to get here. Why would she turn down a free meal if that's the case? I take in her designer clothes and red-soled shoes. I know those had to cost a pretty penny. I know this because my ex-fiancée wanted a pair. It's not that I didn't want to buy them for her, but I didn't have an endless amount of cash. And it wasn't just one pair she wanted. She wanted a pair to go with every designer outfit she owned. So, how the heck did a privileged rich girl become so broke?

"I know the Wagon Wheel sounds hick-*ish* and beneath your standards, but they serve a tender filet mignon. Rated best steak in the county." Why am I pushing this? My gaze dips to those heels, and I have my answer. She isn't walking far in those. How she walked here in the first place is beyond me.

"I'm vegan."

Of course she is. She's more like Ciera by the second. I grit my teeth. "They make good salads."

"I'm good." She nudges her chin toward the door. "Your patient is bleeding."

I don't say a word and duck inside the room.

Mr. Cusack isn't the only one with problems around here.

CHAPTER EIGHT

EVIE

"You did a good job today, despite how crazy the day went. As I said, don't worry about scheduling. I'll show you how the system works tomorrow."

I give Rachael a warm smile. "Thanks. I know I messed up a few times." And by a few times, I mean a lot. I can see why today's appointments were overbooked. The system is horrible.

"We'll work through it. I have a good feeling about you." She glances down at her watch. "I need to go. I'm on the planning board for the Sugar Festival. Too bad you won't be staying for that long. I hate for you to miss it."

"It does sound like a good time." *If I was twelve.*

"Biggest festival in southern Indiana." She laughs. "Anyway, do you need a ride? It looks like the clouds may cut loose."

"No, I'll be all right. I wanted to do a few more things before heading out. Oh, I have one question. Why is this day blocked? It looks like patients are listed but not assigned times."

"The day is blocked for rural checks. We list the names but don't assign times as a way of overriding the system."

"Rural checks?"

"Yeah, it's like a home visit. Liam's dad started the program years ago. One day a month, we check on the individuals who can't come to town. I'm glad to see Liam continuing the service."

"Oh, that's nice."

"Yeah, once you get past the gruffness, you'll find a good guy." She rechecks her watch. "Okay, I'll see you tomorrow."

I let out a long exhale at her departure and delve into the program. Rachael said she would teach me, but what if other emergencies occur? I can't go another day of double-booking patients. I need this job. I also need to figure out where to live. I have approximately four days left at the Bates Motel and fifty dollars to my name. Not exactly a good starting point. I lied about getting ahold of a realtor. It's embarrassing enough to be flat-broke. Why contact someone if I can't afford their services? I don't see the point.

Pushing aside that worry, I settle into figuring out this scheduling program. There is no way I'm letting some outdated system be my demise. Navigating through the program, I jot down notes in my spiral notebook every time I figure a function out. I'm in the middle of writing another one down when the sound of loafers pads up behind me.

"I don't remember approving any overtime."

"I'm off the clock." I point to the computer screen and turn to face Liam. My breath catches in my throat when I take in the sight of him. He shed the lab coat he wore earlier and rolled up the sleeves of his dark green oxford shirt, exposing corded fore-arms. His tie sits loosely under the collar, where he unbuttoned the top button. A scant amount of chest hair peeks out from the gap. I'm not going to lie; he wears casual dress clothes well. Drawn to him, I lean in closer as my gaze roams along the cotton fabric stretching across those shoulders that are indeed broad. His suit jacket from the convention didn't lie. When I finally force my gaze back to his face, my cheeks heat from the smirk planted

across his lips. Yeah, he totally knows I checked him out. I clear
my throat. "I, uh, wanted to learn the antique scheduling system."

"Updating the system is on my to-do list." His lips flatten as
he shifts his focus to the paneled walls and yellowed medical
room chairs, although I think their original color was white. The
only impressive piece in the room is the art. They're the same
style as the black-and-white photos from the motel. I wonder if
the photographer is local.

"It's a rather extensive list." He turns those mysterious eyes
back to me and holds our stare. "I appreciate your enthusiasm for
learning the system."

He says that with so much convection I believe him. I open
my mouth to say thanks, but a bear burst through the front doors,
growling. Okay, it wasn't a bear, but the sound coming from my
stomach may have well been one.

"My offer for dinner still stands. I've heard they serve a good
vegetable stir fry."

Tempting. So tempting.

My breakfast wore off about ten patients ago, but I don't want
him paying for my food as if I'm some charity case. He has
already paid for my housing. I may not have much left to my
name, but I still have my pride. Another deep growl escapes,
louder than before.

However, my pride won't keep me fed.

"I'm fine," I say, too stubborn for my own good.

His lips twitch. "It's no problem."

"And I said I'm good."

He cocks his head and studies me, my denial irritating him.
He leans against the counter, stretching his long legs out. His
woodsy cologne makes another appearance, and I will my face to
be passive.

"I *am* sorry for what happened at the convention."

"I hated that I ruined your notecards. How'd the speech go?"

"Terrible," he says through a humorless laugh. "I talk to patients all day, but public speaking is the one thing that terrifies me. I may have unleashed that anxiety onto you."

"May have?" I slap my hand over my mouth from my retort, which elicits a chuckle from him. But one that sounds genuine this time and throws me off. I never expected laughter to escape from those lips.

"I deserve that. And yes"—he leans over, placing his hand over mine and peeling my hand away—"I projected my anxiety onto you. For that, I apologize. There's no excuse for my behavior."

With his fingers still wrapped around mine, tingles shoot everywhere his flesh touches. My heart thrums in my chest. The desire to erase the distance between us becomes overbearing. It wouldn't take much. We're already a breath's distance away from each other. As if realizing what he is doing or what reaction he elicits from me, he drops my hand and backs away.

"Has Matthew called about your car?" He stands to his full height.

"Yeah, he has to order some parts and said it will take a while." That news sounded painfully expensive. I didn't even ask for a quote. I figured ignorance was bliss.

"If you're not going to have dinner with me, at least let me drive you to the motel."

I hesitate. I don't think being confined in a tight space with this guy is a good idea. Not after I almost made a fool of myself.

"I enjoy walking."

He glances down at my heels. I press my lips together and raise my chin in defiance. No way am I going to admit how treacherous the walk was. I probably damaged my soles.

My thirteen-hundred-dollar soles, thank you very much.

A thunderclap breaks above. Our gazes break from each other

and shift to the picture window. To my horror, rain falls in sheets. It looks as if I won't be walking anywhere.

He eyes me expectantly. I swear I can read this man without him saying a word.

Feeling cagey, I try getting out of dinner one more time. I don't think I can last an entire meal with this man. "Honestly, you can just take me to the nearest Starbucks and I'll be fine. We can talk over a latte."

"That would be a forty-five-minute drive." He says it so matter of fact that I start to panic. What if this town doesn't have any espresso? I wouldn't know how to survive.

"Is there any cafe in town?"

"Yes, the Java Hut."

"Great! Take me there," I say with too much enthusiasm. Cafe snacks may not be solid food, but they're substances. And I really need a caramel latte. I deserve it, especially after the horrible breakfast experience I had. The Red Barn wasn't overly friendly or accommodating. I frown, thinking about how my morning went.

"I'd like a caramel latte with almond milk, oatmeal with blueberries, and a glass of your best freshly squeezed orange juice," I said as the waitress rolled her eyes.

"We have regular half-and-half for the coffee. No caramel. I can substitute grits for the oatmeal, but a muffin is the only thing with blueberries, and the orange juice... I'm afraid that's straight out of the carton."

"Oh, um... On second thought, I'll stick with the orange juice and try the grits, but no milk in them."

"You want a side order of bacon or sausage?"

"Neither, thanks. I'm vegan."

The woman looked at me as if I claimed rights to her firstborn.

"Where'd you go there?" Liam asks.

I force a smile. "Nowhere. I was picturing that caramel latte."

"Sorry. They closed at three."

My face falls along with the last of my energy.

"Let me grab the umbrella and we'll head to the Wagon Wheel. I know you're starving." He stalks to the back, leaving no room for arguments.

I try not to stare at how those black dress pants wrap around his backside but fail epically. Whether I want to or not, it looks as if I'll be spending my evening with Dr. Grump.

CHAPTER NINE

LIAM

Never before has the desire to burn every orange tree—domestic and wild—been so strong, but here I am. Orange blossoms should remain on trees, not in women's perfume. And certainly not inside the cabin of my truck.

It's going to take a week to get rid of her scent.

I take a deep breath. And then another. It's not because her scent is pleasant, but more like I'm trying to increase my lung capacity. Ethan and Matthew talked about resurrecting our high school basketball team for some recreational games. I'll have to be in top shape if they pull it off. I'm only looking out for my best interest, not her or her intoxicating scent.

Pulling the truck into the gravel parking spot outside the restaurant, I grumble out a sigh. Rain sheets off the windshield, prolonging this torment longer. We're not escaping this truck anytime soon.

I pull out my phone and open the weather app. "I'll check the radar to see how long this downpour lasts. We can't have City Girl getting soaked."

Evie bristles. "I'm not afraid of rain."

My gaze roams over her silk blouse. "No, but your blouse is." I ignore her huff and show her the radar. "It should be easing soon enough. That other cell there will hit once we're inside."

Her gaze flicks back to the restaurant. "The Wagon Wheel, huh?"

"Uh-huh." I kill the engine and study Evie's expression. The trepidation in the way she bites her lower lip and the slight crease between her brows as she eyes the two-story brick building gives me some severe déjà vu vibes. My ex hated everything about this town, including this restaurant. That's the thing about high-society women—they can only slum it for so long. I take a calming breath. Why I insisted on taking her out to eat is beyond me. I could've driven through Burger King's drive-thru and ordered something to go. That would've been the most practical solution. Am I practical? No. Instead, I torture myself by taking her to the nicest restaurant in town.

The gossip hounds will be clucking their tongues before sunrise.

New plan.

We'll sit down, order, and eat so we can leave, and then I'll get as far away as possible from this woman. I can endure another hour or so to make sure she's well-nourished.

"The building looks like an old hotel." She turns those dark gray eyes toward me, but there isn't a trace of judgment in them. Had I imagined it earlier?

"You're close. It was a typical Midwestern saloon with rooms for rent."

"Interesting." She turns back to eye the building right as a loud thunderclap roars overhead. She flinches, as if the noise intimidates her.

"You may not mind the rain, but you don't seem to like thunderstorms."

She gives me a tight smile and stares out the windshield. "I'm not a huge fan."

I remain quiet. It's not my business to know the reason behind her fear. She's nothing more than my temporary office manager. I'm nothing more than her boss. She's here because she's my sister's best friend. She means nothing to me.

But if that's true, why am I consumed with the sudden need to comfort her?

"I assume you've lived here all of your life?" she asks, still watching the rain beat against the glass.

"Yes, apart from medical school."

"Ansley never mentions home."

That's because Ansley left and never had the desire to move back. Unlike me. "I wish she'd come to visit more. Mom misses her."

"Where did you do your residency?"

"New York City."

She gasps but tries hiding it with a cough. "You lived in New York City and moved back here?"

My shoulders tense. I'd have my student loans paid off if I had a dollar every time people are shocked by my life choices. "City life isn't always bright lights and glamour."

"No." She tilts her head, as if in thought, her hair falling behind her shoulders, exposing beautiful, pale skin at the swell of her neck.

My fingers clench into fists. *Do not look at my baby sister's best friend's flesh.* And don't think about brushing my lips along any part of said creaminess that looks as delectable as taffy. Jesus, I can't be thinking about licking and tasting my office manager. I shift in my seat and focus on what she's saying.

"There's a certain amount of struggles you deal with daily, but so many exciting things happen. People all around."

"Strangers who never talk to you," I counter.

"That's not true." A small smile that looks more troubled than good forms on her lips. "There's plenty of grumbling and mumbling under their breaths. I'd think you'd fit right in."

I chuckle at that. "I like the slower-paced lifestyle. I like walking down the street, where everyone knows your name." *It just makes my sex life more difficult.* "I'm smart enough to realize this way of life isn't for everyone."

"Is that why your ex called off the wedding? She didn't like living here?"

I quirk an eyebrow, shocked she went there. Not too many things surprise me, but her question sure has. Evie gnaws on her thumbnail and hangs her head, a flush creeping along that creamy skin.

"Sorry, that was out of line. I have a bad habit of cutting to the chase."

"That's okay. You pretty much guessed it." *For the most part.* I let out a breath and stare into the darkened sky. The rain pellets fall like acid rain against my soul, uncovering truths I wish to be buried. "We had a plan. We would live in the city until Dad retired. Then, we would move here, take over his practice, and start a family." At least, that was what I assumed she wanted.

"But then, your dad passed away unexpectedly," she guesses.

Grief washes over me, along with guilt. Mainly, I miss my dad. I miss his wisdom immensely. But a tiny fraction—the one I'm not proud of—resents him. If we had more time in the city, maybe, just maybe, Ciera would have gotten her fill. Instead, our time was cut short, and she resented the move. Resented me.

"Then, Dad passed away. I moved into his practice, and Ciera... was full of ideas. I thought maybe she'd learn how to adjust." *I thought that maybe our love was strong enough.* "But this town couldn't hold her down." I shift my focus to the woman currently occupying my truck cabin.

"Sorry things didn't quite go as planned. I'm also sorry about your dad." She gives me a weary smile, and I think she means her apology.

"Thanks." We hold our gazes for a beat. Everything about this woman is magnified—her scent, fancy clothes, and expensive shoes. They all become too much. Luckily the rain lessens to a soft drizzle before I lose complete control and do something stupid, like grabbing a fistful of her blond hair and bending her to my will.

"Looks like we're getting that short reprieve. Hang tight. I'll come around and get you." I grab the umbrella and hop out of the truck, letting the fresh air clear my head. I open her door, holding the umbrella for her. She steps one heeled leg out, followed by another. I try not to think about what those luscious legs would feel like wrapped around me. I concentrate on the dirt smudge along the floorboard instead. That seems to work until her skirt bunches up, and I catch a glimpse of her thighs. I straighten, jaw hardening. I will not let this woman affect me.

She's off-limits.

The equivalent of a no-fly zone.

Not only is she my office manager, but she's my baby sister's friend. What kind of brother would I be if I hit on her best friend? I wouldn't want my sister hitting on one of mine if the roles were reversed. I offer my hand to help her down, and she accepts. Sparks ignite and set a fire rushing through my veins the moment we touch. The same rush hit me back in the office when I peeled her hand from her face. This ends now.

As soon as she's steady, I let go.

"Come on. Their food's good, I promise," I say harsher than intended.

We step into the restaurant, and her legs draw short. She takes in the rough, saw-cut plank flooring and knotty pine panel-ing. When her mouth falls open at the wild game heads mounted on the wall, I can't help but chuckle. I don't know what it is about this girl. She has a way of pulling me out of my anger.

"Not classy enough?" This earns me a glare.

"I've been to Houston."

"Is that supposed to mean something?"

"It means, I know how to do country."

My chuckle deepens. If I know anything about this girl, it's that she most definitely cannot *do* country. "Come on, City Girl."

"I am not prissy. I'm just—"

"Out of your element?" I guess, giving her a side-eye.

"A little. I didn't sign up for small-town life."

This is why I don't want to get to know this woman better. She'll be gone the first opportunity she gets.

Just like the rest.

CHAPTER TEN

EVIE

I've known several highly influential men in my life, and most are straight-up assholes. But I've yet to see someone turn from hot to cold in a split second like Liam. We were talking and getting along, but then he went from being a decent human being to Dr. Grump so fast my head spun. Perhaps these tiny glimpses of decency are what everyone else latches onto since the entire town seems to think he's this nice guy.

"Liam, it's so good to see you," the waitress Brenda says, setting glasses of water down in front of us as we seat ourselves. Her eyes land on me for a moment and back to Liam. "And it's good to see you moving on so soon."

I prickle at the snark in her tone. Ansley told me his ex-fiancée called off the engagement and left town five months ago. I suppose people consider a few months too soon, but his ex is the one who did the leaving. How long is he supposed to pine over her? I'm not sure why her suggestion bothers me. We're not on a date, but she doesn't know that. Her statement is still rude either way.

"Brenda, this is Geneva, my new office manager. Geneva, this is Brenda. We went to high school together."

I go to shake Brenda's hand, but she doesn't notice. She's too busy eyeing Liam.

"We were more than that. You make us sound like long-forgotten acquaintances." Brenda shakes her head while playfully swatting Liam's biceps. She turns to me, her smile as fake as her bleach-bottled hair. Her gaze flashes to my shoes and then back to my face. "Ah, I see. I guess there's no point in getting to know you. You'll be gone in no time."

My eyes narrow. So far, the servers in this town are zero for two in my book. I clear my throat. "Perhaps you're right. But it's still good to know who to stay away from in the meantime."

Liam's lips twitch as Brenda's fake smile falls.

"Perhaps you can get Geneva a menu," Liam suggests.

Her smile transforms into a genuine one when she looks at him. "Sure thing, sweetie."

When she's out of earshot, I can't help but say, "Wow. That's not obvious or anything."

"Her rudeness?"

I study Liam for a beat. He genuinely looks like he's asking. Surely, he isn't that clueless. "No, her attraction to you."

He rears his head back, as if I've slapped him. "Brenda? No, she's rude to everyone. And a town gossip. You weren't wrong in your assessment. You'd do best to keep your distance."

"Are you sure about that?"

"Yes, her nickname is Blowhard Brenda." He cocks his head and looks thoughtfully. "I suppose that could have a different meaning."

"Oh my God, I meant about her not liking you. Although, it sounds like you may have experience." A pang of jealousy hits me in the chest from out of nowhere. It's no secret I find Liam attractive, but not enough to warrant jealous vibes. The man frustrates the heck out of me.

He laughs. "No, I wouldn't know anything about that. I took her to a homecoming dance back in high school, but that's the extent of our story. Trust me, there's no chemistry between us."

"If you say so." I guess he is that clueless, but at least he's no longer grumbling. Trying to lighten the air, I can't help but tease, "How many old flames am I going to run into?"

"None."

"None? Why do I find that hard to believe?" Considering the size of the town, I can't imagine the dating pool is vast. I'm sure to run into ex-lovers.

"Because I didn't date anyone from here."

"If you wanted to start, I'm sure Brenda would help you out." I scoff, wondering why I even care. I'm acting like a jealous girl-friend. I clear my throat, preparing to apologize, but pause. His once relaxed handsome face darkens and holds a maddening hint of arrogance.

"Let me rephrase. I *can't* date anyone from here."

"What? Why not?"

"My tastes are unique. I wouldn't want to scandalize the townsfolk with my preferences."

An unwelcome surge of excitement ripples through me. I don't know if it's his commanding tone or my wild imagination, but his words draw my body to attention. Mouth suddenly dry, I grab the water and take a sip. Looking over the glass rim, I dare ask, "What do you like?"

"To be in charge."

My breath stills as his gaze boars into me with an intensity that has me picturing myself on my knees, looking up into those mossy green eyes, waiting for his command. I blink, trying to dispel that image because what the fuck? I can't lust after my boss.

Before I can respond properly, Brenda arrives and shoves a sticky, plastic menu in my hand. I internally cringe, trying hard not to show my disgust.

"Are there any tofu options?" I ask, hoping the Wagon Wheel is as accommodating as my boss led me to believe.

Brenda cocks her head and shoots Liam a look. Placing a hand on her hip, she asks, "Again? You can't seem to stay away from these fancy snobs, huh?"

All traces of a relaxed Liam disappear with that comment, and I've decided I don't care for Blowhard Brenda. I don't particularly appreciate being classified as a type, and I'm guessing she boxed me in the same category as his ex. She doesn't know me. She doesn't know anything about me. I may not fit in this small town, but someone calling me a snob for preferring a healthy life choice is new.

"I don't see where that's any of your concern, but as I said, Miss Thornhill's my new office manager. Her eating habits aren't up for discussion. I'll take the filet, medium rare."

Her gaze lingers on Liam for a moment before turning toward me. Since I never had a chance to review the menu, I play it safe and order a vegetable salad. The tension leaves with her.

"I'm sorry about that. My ex never treated her well when we came here. I'm sure she's projecting."

"Uh-huh." *Doesn't like you that way, my ass.* It may have been one dance years ago, but that woman still holds hope for more. It's written on every lingering, starry-eyed glance she tosses Liam's way.

"Ansley told me you went to Northwestern with her. What degree did you obtain?"

"American studies with a minor in humanities."

"Hmm, why that particular degree?"

Because I want to help people instead of hosting fake ass charity events while pretending to be a martyr. Don't get me wrong, certain charity events raise awareness and money for particular causes, but a specific demographic of people needs help daily. I want to funnel my efforts into getting these people real life-sustaining help.

"My goal is to work as a Public Health Advisor. I wanted a degree in health communication, but Northwestern didn't offer it. So, I chose something as close to the field as possible."

"Why Northwestern?"

I needed to escape my parents while figuring things out.

And needed to escape *him.*

"I wanted to get as far away from home as possible while still being in a major city. New York City was too close to home. That left Chicago or Los Angeles. There's no way my mom would allow me to go as far as California, so Chicago it was."

"Liam, it's good to see you out and with such a lovely lady."

"Mr. Bungles." Liam smiles at the elderly gentleman. By the thinning gray hair and leathered skin, I'd place the man to be in his eighties. "Mr. Bungles, this is Geneva." He swoops his hand toward me and then back to the man. "Mr. Bungles has been a family friend forever," Liam says with a tight smile.

I'm guessing Liam doesn't want to make small talk tonight. Who can blame him? His presence in town and present company seems to be their entire focus. I'm guessing that the gossip mill Liam spoke about will be in hot use tomorrow.

"Nice to meet you." I extend a warm smile in an attempt to appear friendly. That's sort of my thing—try to put everyone at ease. If there's one thing I'm good at, it's winning over cantankerous old men. Hmm, maybe I'll convert Liam to team Evie before leaving town.

"You do have an affinity for the fancy ones." Mr. Bungles chuckles and pats Liam on the back, as if that erases the fact that he's being rather rude.

"We're just trying to get a decent meal. Geneva won't be in town for long."

My eyes meet Liam's, the muscles in my stomach tightening. For a slight moment, I wish I wasn't leaving. But that's absurd. I don't belong here. I belong in a place where tofu is on menus and people don't show pity for ordering a salad. I certainly don't belong in a town with a grumpy doctor who'd rather snarl than smile.

"That's a shame." The older man turns to me and winks. "Sugar Creek Falls could use someone to brighten this man."

"I'm sure he could. That's why I'm here to help his practice." I smile politely and lower my voice. "It seems he's been rather moody."

The man's face cracks into the biggest grin. He wags a finger at me. "I can tell you're going to fit in this town rather nicely."

"Too bad it's temporary. The town is charming." Thunder cracks overhead, causing me to jump and erasing all the smoothness I built.

"That it is." He dips his head at me. "Well, I'll let you two get back to your discussion. Good seeing you, Liam."

"Likewise." Liam watches the older man shuffle away before cutting his gaze back to my shaking hands. "You really don't like storms, do you?"

Before I have a chance to answer, Brenda approaches the table, carrying a tray.

"Here's your salad." She plops the bowl in front of me and diverts her attention to Liam. "And your filet mignon. I'll be back in a while to check on you." Without another glance at me, she takes off.

"Should I be worried about having spit in my lettuce?"

He chuckles, and I decide right then that I like the sound of him laughing. It's the only time he doesn't seem tense or stressed.

We're halfway through our meal when Liam asks, "I take it you haven't had any luck finding a job in your field."

"No. I don't know why it's been so hard. I've had multiple interviews, which seemed promising, but nothing comes of them. There is always some flimsy or cookie-cutter excuse when I follow up."

"Are you still pursuing?"

"Yes, I have an interview coming up next week."

His eyebrows narrow as he chews. I know that look. He wants to know something but doesn't quite know how to ask. I sigh. "Go ahead and ask."

He quirks an eyebrow.

"I can tell you're contemplating something, so ask away."

"All right then. You obviously come from money. What happened?"

"I, uh—"

"Sorry, that was rude. I'm just trying to piece together how you ended up here."

"No, it's fine. It's my parents. They want me back home, and to make sure I come crawling back, they cut off my credit line about six months ago."

His hand pauses in the air, halfway to his mouth. "Before you even graduated?"

"Yes. They paid for tuition but not rent. My job working for the hotel didn't pay much, and I fell behind. I got evicted on the same night I was fired."

A look of mortification crosses his face before his back straightens. "You can move into the cottage on my property. I won't charge you rent."

"Uh..."

"I'm serious. It's the perfect solution. You'll have your privacy, and I'll repay my debt to you." He says that with such conviction, but I'm not sure he's thought it through. I don't want to be a knee-jerk reaction.

"Stay on your property? I couldn't possibly."

Another loud crack makes us both jump.

"This is one heck of a storm," Liam mumbles and then looks back at me. "I'm serious. It's been years since someone used the cottage."

He looks rather pleased with himself. There is a finality to his tone, as if the discussion is closed, but I couldn't possibly live on the same property as him. The man doesn't even like me. Although, his actions make me wonder if that's true. Like right now with him looking at me as if he wants to devour me.

Yeah, staying with him is a bad idea.

I go to protest one last time when sirens wail in the distance. I swear every head turns toward the front windows. I quickly realize how immune I am to the sound. I was going to mention it when the front door swings open, and someone yells, "The motel is on fire."

CHAPTER ELEVEN

EVIE

This can't be happening.

I cover my mouth and stare out the windshield as the nightmare unfolds. Flashing lights swirl around us. People shout. I feel stuck in a horror film of my life as my temporary home burns to ashes. Not literary. I can't see too much from this vantage point—not with the firetrucks obstructing our view—but I assume the smoke billowing above is from the last of my possessions burning to ash. This is bad. This is the worst-parts-of-the-past-six-months-mixed-with-childhood-memories level of bad.

I can't catch a break.

"I think the office building caught fire. The guest units look spared from what I can make out." The confidence in Liam's voice soothes me—somewhat. He could be saying that to settle my nerves, though. I don't know his personality too well, besides his cranky side. Who knows, lying may be his superpower. It hardly matters. I'll take whatever he offers—lies and all. I may not have much left to my name, but I can't afford to lose what little I do have.

"I hope you're right," I answer barely over a whisper, staring out the windshield.

A tap on the driver's side window jolts us out of our daze.

Liam rolls the window down a few inches. Mr. Cusack's grandson comes into view.

"Ethan," Liam says in greeting. "Was it a lightning strike?"

"Yep, it struck the electrical box."

"Did Mabel make it out okay?"

"Yes, she's with Matthew."

Ethan's gaze cuts to me, the corners of his mouth dipping down. If he is surprised to see me with his friend, he downplays it, but I have a feeling he would've jumped all over the opportunity to tease Liam had the situation been different. "Sorry, ma'am. Looks like you'll need to find a different place to stay tonight."

"Is it possible to grab my belongings?"

"Not tonight. You'll be able to grab them tomorrow morning. There's a hotel about forty-five minutes—"

"She's staying with me."

Ethan's eyebrows rise. "Oh?"

"In the cottage house at the farm."

"The cottage house?"

The surprise in those three words puts me on high alert. There better be a real cottage.

"Yes, it's the perfect solution."

"Right," Ethan drags out.

"It's only temporary." I don't know why I feel the need to speak up, but they're discussing my fate as if I'm not a part of it. As if I don't have any say. I'd go home if I wanted to be treated like a china doll.

Liam's jaw tics. "I told you before it would be beneficial."

"That may be so, but I don't want to impose."

"You're not. As you said, it's *temporary.*" He emphasizes the word, as if it's some dirty curse word. As if he's mad that my stay isn't permanent, which makes zero sense. The entire day, he has done nothing but growl and order me around—*sort of*. Making sure I eat and providing shelter isn't necessarily awful. And while waiting for the rain to stop outside the restaurant, we had a decent conversation. There was a calmness about him that made it easy to talk to him. That was until he stared at me for a beat too long. Everything went downhill after that. I'd say he doesn't like my looks, but I don't think that's true—not with that hungry gaze he gets. Whatever happened between us earlier is gone. He's running cold right now. And from the way Ethan's gaze ping-pongs between us as rain sheets off his fireman's uniform, I'm pretty sure he's picking up on it too.

"Okay, I better get back. As I said, you can obtain your belongings in the morning."

"Thanks." My voice quivers. I don't want to cry, but I think the evening has caught up to me. I've been riding this whirlwind high for far too long. If you can call it a high. It's more like prolonged crashing, and I'm about to bottom out. The question is, where will I land?

THE RAIN EASES to a drizzle as the headlights illuminate a wrap-around porch, but the blanket of darkness makes it impossible to see anything other than a silhouette of the two-story farmhouse. We're a few miles east of town, surrounded by farmland and woods, and admittedly, it's a little intimidating. Or creepy. I've never spent time in the country. Let alone on a starless, moonless night. Is it always this dark? I remain quiet as he bypasses the house and turns onto a small gravel road lined by evergreen trees. I clutch the grocery sack Liam insisted on grabbing tighter and peer ahead.

"The cottage is down this path."

"It's so dark."

He gives me a side glance. "It's the country."

"No kidding." I punch his arm playfully but withdraw my hand just as quickly. I'm no better than Brenda from the restaurant.

Do. Not. Touch. My. Boss.

He chuckles, and I hope he doesn't realize my thoughts. "I was kidding. It's brighter on a cloudless night. You'll see."

"The property looks large. Has it been in the family for a long time?" I shuffle the bag of groceries to the other leg to keep my hands from fidgeting. Liam insisted we go to the store and grab some essentials.

"This was our grandparent's farm. Grandpa worked in the fields until he passed away five years ago. Since Mom is an only child and Dad never had any interest in the farm, they cash rent it to Mr. Bungles, the guy you met earlier."

"Oh. I sensed some tension there."

He winces. "A little. He has been after Mom to sell the farm ground to him, but she refuses. Me living in the house gives her more bite. There's no way she'll sell now."

"The house sat empty for five years?"

"Yeah, my parents had zero desire to move out here, and Ansley... she never expressed interest. Too many memories. But I love the property."

"It seems nice." *From what I can tell.* I can't wait to see the property in the daylight.

We pass a pole barn, and I sit straighter when the headlights shine on a cobblestone, one-story bungalow. It certainly isn't anything to brag about, as far as size goes, but I don't need much space. A workable kitchen, bathroom, and bedroom will suffice until I land a permanent job.

The truck comes to a halt outside the front door. My stomach sinks as I take in the vines weaving through the mortar joints, snaking their way to the roof. It's hard to tell in the darkness, but the shingles appear to be made from clay, with some busted. Wouldn't it leak?

Suddenly unsure about sleeping here, I ask, "How long has it been since the last person stayed here?"

"It's been a few years. Grandpa's hired help stayed in the cottage back in the day. Nobody has been inside for a while, so I'm sure it's musty."

I turn to look at him, expecting a smile, but he seems stone-cold serious. "Musty?"

"Just a little. But don't worry, I'll turn on the dehumidifier."

Lovely. I turn back to the weathered shack. *Years or decades?* I think to myself.

I clutch the sack of groceries tighter and step out of the truck. Liam jars the front door open, and staleness assaults our senses. He wasn't lying about the odor. I stand straighter, not wanting to appear ungrateful, but this dump is so far beneath my standards that it couldn't sink any lower.

Liam flips on the light, which surprisingly works. My eyes widen in disbelief as the room comes into focus. I thought the motel was stepping back in time, but this had that beat by ten years. Patterned wallpaper, yellowed with age, lines the walls. A brown and gold flowered afghan drapes the back of a silver vinyl couch that sports sleek lines and a metal frame. A rocking chair with many years of dust cover sits in the corner. And a circular, braided wool rug is displayed in the middle.

"A few years?" I ask, voice squeaking.

Liam runs a hand through his hair and rests it on his neck. "I guess it's been a bit longer."

Chittering sounds in the distance. My head snaps to the kitchenette area. "What was that?"

"What was what?"

The chittering grows louder.

"That!" I scream and jump when a clanging sound zips through the air. I drop the grocery bag and race behind Liam as two raccoons dart from the kitchen. Liam chuckles. *Chuckles.* Masked killers attack me, and all he does is laugh. Opening the door wider, Liam directs the beasts out. They dash past us.

My heart starts beating again. "How'd they get in here?"

"I better check the back door." He walks through the kitchen and lands at the opened back door. "This certainly doesn't help."

"Do you think there are more animals in here?"

"Maybe a snake or two."

My eyes grow wide. "You have poisonous snakes?"

He presses his lips together as if suppressing a smile. "They're rare. More in the northern region. You're fine as long as you stay away from any snake with slit-like or cat-like eyes."

I wrap my arms around myself and scope every nook and cranny.

"Relax, I was kidding about a snake being in here." He grabs the door and tries to shut it. A popping sound assaults our ears. The door shifts, falls off the hinges, and crashes to the floor. Liam jumps out of the way. "Jesus."

I stand transfixed. Could this day get any worse?

"Come on. You're staying at the main house. This was obviously a bad idea." He brushes my shoulder as he heads toward the front door.

Stay with him? At the house? Panic grips hold. There's no way I can stay with him.

"No, I'll make this work," I blurt out. Eyeing the layers of dust coating every visible surface, I shudder.

"You're not staying here. It's unsafe. And don't worry. I'll run into town and grab your belongings first thing in the morning."

I nod, suddenly feeling vulnerable. Tears prick my eyes. These past few months, I've encountered losing my allowance, graduating, selling my car, being fired, being evicted, and moving from a city I adored. If I lose my independence, I fear I'll break. "Seriously, I'll be okay here."

"Absolutely not. It's unsanitary." He points to the far corner where water streaks down the aged walls. "The roof leaks. God only knows what animal is lurking in the shadows. Not to mention the fucking door fell off its hinges. I don't know what I was thinking by bringing you here."

"I'll be fine." I stand my ground, unsure why I'm choosing this hill to die on. I would never voluntarily stay in a place like this. Never. It's beyond creepy and stinks. But we couldn't possibly stay together.

Could we?

No, no, no. That's a horrible idea.

"I just need a blanket and pillow. Really, I hate to impose."

Liam huffs a frustrated breath and steps closer to me. His furrowed brows and the hard set of his jaw show every ounce of frustration. I'm being unreasonable. I know this. But I can't stay in the same house as my boss. That's too overwhelming.

Too *everything.*

"You're *not* staying here." The sternness in his voice and the determination in his stare kill the rebuttal on my tongue, but it sparks something else inside me as warmth races up my spine. I have never considered myself a submissive—I don't like losing control—but from the way his command lit my body, I foresee an extensive internet search on how to be a good sub.

Holy cow, I just want to melt into him.

Before I can say something regretful, screeching howls cut through the silence. I let out a yelp and jump into his body, wrapping my arms around his torso. His arms catch me, but his momentum pushes him backward. His heel kicks the almond milk container and sends it crashing into the wall. The container slits in the corner, spilling the content over the dirty floor. My gaze raises to meet his, and I swear his body relaxes against mine. A sense of security washes over me, and for the first time, I feel I'm right where I belong—inside his embrace—even when attacked.

"What is that? *Silver Bullet's* call sign?" Apparently, right before my death, I become a comedian. And not a very good one at that, considering that's the name of the wheelchair not the werewolf.

"It's a pack of coyotes," he says, voice barely over a whisper. His woodsy scent wafts over me, and I snuggle closer to him. His gaze holds mine for a beat before dipping to my lips. Those mossy green eyes darken as flecks of brown become more abundant. That look right there—the one that screams desire and want—confuses me. He gets this way right before turning grumpy. I instinctively lick my bottom lip and watch the slide of his Adam's apple. His hands grip my sides tighter, and I wonder if he can feel the thrum of my heart against his chest. It's beating a mile a minute.

"Is that common?" I ask, trying to diffuse his grouchiness but killing any chance of him kissing me. Wait? Do I want him to kiss me?

I look at those hooded eyes and full lips, and I decide, yes, I very much want that kiss. And that's precisely the reason why I shouldn't move into the main house.

His mouth forms a complete smile and breaks the spell he had me under. "Yeah, City Girl. We're in the country."

"We're on a farm, not the Wild West."

"We're also surrounded by woods."

"Oh." Embarrassed, I back away, hating how much I miss his touch. "So, no werewolves?"

"No werewolves." He picks up the bag of groceries scattered on the ground, grabs my hand, and pulls me out of the cobblestone cottage. "You're staying with me, Geneva, whether you want to or not."

"But what about the milk?"

"Leave it. It'll give the animals something to drink."

I'm unsure whether he's joking, but I don't protest and follow behind him.

What the hell did I get myself into?

CHAPTER TWELVE

LIAM

I heard you moved the new girl in with you.

As I drive the truck down the gravel road, I grind my teeth, replaying the barista's words. It hasn't even been twenty-four hours, and the news of a girl moving in with me is hot gossip. Damn that Ethan. He can't keep his mouth shut to save his life.

They don't understand Evie's living arrangement isn't permanent. I only volunteered the cottage to help her out. It was a temporary solution to an unexpected complication—a means to help a displaced and distressed woman. I didn't ask her to stay with me because I like her. I asked her out of obligation and guilt. For God's sake, these people live in a distorted reality. She clearly needs a place to stay and doesn't have the funds to cover anything. Since my meltdown got her fired, providing temporary shelter is the least I can do. It's not my fault the place was covered with years of dust and infested with animals.

Getting her belongings from the motel before she woke was just another way of me being nice. I wanted to bring them to her before my morning jog in case she was an early riser and wanted to get a shower. When I returned from my run, I realized I was out of coffee.

Out of obligation is the only reason I drove back to town and picked up her caramel latte. It's not because I want to make a good impression. Or because I *like* her. I couldn't care less what she thinks of me. I feel sorry for her, that's all.

But still.

If all that is true, why did I almost kiss her when she jumped into my arms?

Fuck. That can't happen again. No matter how good she feels pressed up against me.

No matter how much I want it to happen.

I pull into the driveway, kill the engine, and grab the coffee out of the cupholder. My guest should be up by now.

As I push through the back door, I stop short at seeing Evie standing on a chair, bent over the kitchen countertop, and studying the circuit breaker set underneath the cabinet. Her satin robe rides high, showcasing those silky legs. The hem stops short of revealing her ass cheeks.

Sweet Jesus, what's not to like about this girl? She's a goddamn wet dream.

"What are you doing?" I ask, perplexed.

She startles and bumps the back of her head on the cabinet's underside. She whips around, and I almost crush the coffee cup in my hand. Her robe slips open, leaving nothing to the imagination. Another half inch and her nipples that stand erect through the satin fabric would be on full display. I drag my gaze away from her breasts and force myself to look at her feet. Are those bunny slippers? Correction: mutilated bunny slippers?

"You scared me."

"Are you okay?" I ask, voice cracking as I place the coffee on the kitchen island.

"Yes, I'm fine, whoa..." The stool teeters beneath her weight, causing her to wobble, her hands flailing in the air. I dash to her and don't think about anything else but steadying her. That is until my hands wrap around her waist, and those sweet curves are under my touch. My dick, which has been silent for five months, jolts to life as those perfect breasts crash into my face. She may as well not be wearing anything as thin as her robe is. A hint of orange consumes the air around us, and it takes all my restraint not to devour her. I'd give anything to trace my tongue along her soft flesh right now. She's so fucking close. Once she steadies herself, I drop my hands and step back, the need to adjust my pants weighing heavily.

"Shit." Pink coats her cheeks as she wraps her robe tightly around her. "Sorry. This was supposed to be a quick fix. I thought all I had to do was flip the flippy thing and then finish getting ready."

"Flippy thing?"

"Yeah, you know. The thing you flip when a fuse blows."

"I know what you mean. I just haven't heard it be called a flippy thing before."

"Whatever. I'm not an electrician." She laughs, and the sweet sound makes me smile. She points at the breaker box. "But that ancient relic baffles me. I'd Google it, but the internet on my phone doesn't work."

"Yeah, the cell service can be spotty out here." *Which is another reason my ex hated living in the country.* She was a social media influencer and lived on her phone. I can't blame her for not liking the location, but there were options we could've explored. All she had to do was be patient enough and wait for the satellite installation. "I forgot to tell you about the low amperage in this old house. And those are fuses. They unscrew, and you have to replace them."

"Oh." She huffs out a breath. Damn, she's cute when she's flustered.

I pick the coffee up and shove the medium-sized to-go cup in her hands. "Here, I brought you a caramel latte."

She hesitates, staring at it longingly.

"Don't worry. They made it with almond milk."

Her mouth falls open. "How'd you know my favorite coffee?"

"You mentioned you could use a caramel latte yesterday, and I guessed you make it with almond milk since that was the milk you chose last night."

"Oh, that's incredibly observant of you." She bats away the mist collecting in her eyes and doesn't hesitate this time before bringing it to her mouth. "Thanks so much."

"You're welcome."

Her eyelids close as she sips the coffee. The moan escaping her mouth makes my half-hard cock twitch. Needing to purge the feel of her tits from my mind, I walk over to the circuit board. "What were you trying to do before the fuse blew?"

"Blow dry my hair."

"That shouldn't have done it." I unscrew the fuse for the upstairs bedrooms. Sure enough, it's singed. "What else was plugged in?"

"My flat iron and make-up mirror."

"All in the upstairs hallway bathroom?"

"Yep."

"Yeah, that's a bit too much for this house. I need to get it rewired." *Another task on my to-do list that my ex complained about constantly.* All these reminders of Ciera are starting to put me on edge, erasing all the good my morning run brought. "I should have spare fuses in here." I rifle through a drawer but come up empty. "Well, this isn't good. It looks like I'll have to pick up some from the hardware store."

"What does that mean?"

"It means you'll have to finish getting ready downstairs, but only plug one item in at a time."

"This entire trip has been a nightmare," she whispers.

My back goes rim-rod straight. With her words sounding too similar to Ciera's, I snap. "Sorry, this old house isn't the Hilton. You'll have to slum it for a while."

"I didn't mean—"

"And I suggest putting on clothes." Needing to get away from her and old memories, I push past her and head to my room. Moving her here is the worst mistake I've made.

Even as the words are uttered, I have a hard time believing them.

CHAPTER THIRTEEN

EVIE

There is no end to Dr. Grump's endless hot and cold streak. He does something nice, like surprising me with my luggage and a latte made to my specifications, but then he turns around and treats me like a bug infestation he wants to fumigate. The drive to the office is silent. I don't know what I did to warrant the cold shoulder—other than parading around him half-naked. The silent treatment continues as he opens the door to his building and motions for me to walk through, proving my point. Even in his grumpy state, the man remembers his manners.

Rachael emerges from the hallway. She manages a small grunt out of Dr. Grump as he breezes past and heads to his office.

"Did something happen?" she murmurs.

Do you mean besides me taking out half of the electricity and flashing him my tits? Nope, nothing at all. In my defense, I thought it'd be a quick flip of a switch, and everything would be back to normal before he returned. He was gone, so I just grabbed my robe. I had no idea fuses like that existed and got caught up trying to figure them out.

"It has been a long night."

"Oh, I heard about the motel. It's a shame. I'm glad Mabel's safe. I'm guessing they'll get the damage repaired in no time. Sorry you're displaced. Where are you staying in the meantime?"

I lick my lips. "Um, I'm staying with Liam."

A smirk slides into place. "Ah, that explains his attitude."

"What does that mean?" Is his distaste for me that obvious? Or is she picking up on the times he tolerates me?

"Nothing, sweetie. Nothing at all." But the low chuckle following that statement leads me to believe there is definitely something.

"I need to make a few personal phone calls before we open." I grab my cell out of my pocket for show.

"If you need me, I'll be getting the rooms prepared."

I pull up the local mechanic's number when she exits down the hallway. First, I need to find out if my car will be ready for my interview next week. I'll worry about the payment later.

"Tillman's," the profound, baritone voice answers.

"Hi, this is Evie Thornhill. My 2013 Honda Accord is in for repair."

Matthew chuckles. "Yes, ma'am. I know who you are."

"Yes, well, I was wondering about the status."

"It's scheduled to be done at the end of next week."

"I don't understand. Why is it taking so long?" Panic grips my throat. I need transportation before then.

"Not sure if you heard about the fire that destroyed a factory. Anyway, it caused a parts shortage which affects your vehicle. The part we need won't be in until next Thursday."

I close my eyes, shaking my head. I swear I'm in the middle of a *Doc Hollywood* set. "Is there a rental agency?"

"Yeah, but it's—"

"Let me guess, forty-five minutes away?" I ask, cutting him off.

"You've got it."

Holding back a sigh, I say, "Okay, just keep me informed."

My mind reaches for possible solutions. I could see if Liam would take me to this elusive town under an hour away, but I hate to put him out more than I have. Besides, I would have to ask for an advance on my paycheck, and I think they prefer credit cards. All of which my parents made sure didn't work. This leaves me no other choice than to reschedule my interview.

Biting back tears, I pull up the email chain and find the number to call. After I introduce myself, the human resource lady throws me for a loop.

"Miss Thornhill, I was going to call you."

Dread sinks in. I don't want to ask, but I may as well rip the Band-Aid off. "I guess I saved you the trouble. What did you need to know?"

"We regret to inform you that the position has been filled."

"You filled it without waiting until after my interview?" Tears prick my eyes. How many interviews does this make where I didn't even have a chance?

"The last candidate came highly recommended and was a perfect fit for the job. I'm sorry if you were looking forward to it, but at least I've saved you the trouble of traveling here."

Her chipper voice doesn't sound sorry. She sounds almost giddy. This doesn't make sense. I feel as if I'm being blackballed. But how would that be possible?

"Thanks for your interest in me. If things change or don't work out, please keep me in mind for the future."

"We certainly will. It was very lucrative meeting you."

She hangs up, and I contemplate what she meant by lucrative. We never officially met. How lucrative could it have been? I hang my head and bite back a sigh. I'll have to keep my feelers out. Maybe I need to hire a headhunter? But the jobs requiring headhunters typically come with higher salaries. My entry-level position won't pay much. Not worth a headhunter's time. *Gah*, why is this so hard?

My phone rings with my mom's ringtone. I want to send her to voicemail, but she'll just continue to call until I answer. I glance at the clock. With twenty minutes to spare, I flop into the chair and reluctantly hit answer.

"Good morning, Mother."

"It would be a good morning if you were home where you belong and not embarrassing me."

"I'm not sure how working can be considered an embarrassment. People go to work every day."

"Not Thornhill women." Her stern voice makes me flinch.

"What do you want?" Her entitlement is the last thing I need this morning.

"I made arrangements for you to be home. Your flight is Monday at nine o'clock. You'll be flying out of O'Hare."

"No, I won't. I'm committed to this job."

"That tiny medical office?"

So, they found me. I shouldn't be surprised by their type of resources. "Yes. I'm their office manager until I land a permanent job."

"I heard on good authority that you don't have any prospects."

The air gets sucked out of my lungs. Surely, my parents wouldn't stoop so low as to sabotage my interviews. They use their money as leverage and try squeezing me to comply, but I can't see them outright sabotaging me. They're entitled elitists, sure, but they're not low-life assholes. Are they?

"How would you know that?" My voice is eerily calm and even.

"I told you I know everything. Now, pack your bags and be on the plane."

"Mom, I am not coming home. I'm going to ask, and I demand an answer, have you interfered with any of my interviews?"

She gasps. "How could you accuse me of such a thing?"

"Because you keep meddling in my life. So, is that a no?" I need her to verify one way or another.

"It's most certainly a no. I may not like you slumming around, but I would never do something that caddy. I can't believe you'd accuse your own flesh and blood of betraying you."

These dramatics are coming from someone who's manipulated me at every turn.

"Fine, but stay out of my affairs. And quit trying to force me to come home."

"But you need to find a man. I know you don't want—"

"Stop! Don't say another word. I know what you and Dad want for me. It's not going to happen."

"We'll see."

"I have to get to work. We'll talk later."

"We most certainly will. Be on that plane."

I hang up and pinch the bridge of my nose.

"So, you weren't lying about your parents, huh?"

I jump and spin my chair around. Those jade green eyes bore into me, and I wonder how much he heard. "They are every bit as frustrating as I said."

"Sorry, I didn't mean to eavesdrop, but I came to grab a schedule." There's an ease to his gate that was missing before as he strides over to me. He plants his backside against the edge of the desk and peers down at me. "I take it the interview got canceled?"

"Yes." I let out a shaky breath. "I guess they filled the position."

His gaze softens, and I have to look away. I can't bear to see any empathy coming from him. Not when I'm in this state. And definitely not when he's standing so close we're almost touching. I can smell his scent. I already have some weird attraction to the man. I don't need to fall for some grumpy, small-town doctor. If I catch a glimpse of compassion in him, that'll be my undoing.

And that's something I can't endure right now.

"I'm sorry. I know you were looking forward to it." He places a hand on my shoulder, and my body zings with awareness, dissolving the thoughts that are seconds old. We're way too close. Or still too far, depending on how you look at this. I want to erase the gap and see how his hands would feel on the rest of me. Is crushing on your boss so bad? What's one little kiss?

"Two apologies in less than five minutes. What's going on?"

He withdraws his hand and grabs the schedule, his reasoning for coming out here.

"Don't get used to it." He flashes me a rare smile before letting it fall. "In all seriousness, you'll bounce back from this."

"Thanks." I huff out a small breath. "I'll scout for more opportunities."

"That a girl." He stands, his gaze lingering on me for a moment before stepping toward the hallway. "Oh, that reminds me. The passcode for the home Wi-Fi is 1Bitchbegone."

"Seriously?"

He shrugs. "It was installed two days after Ciera left. I felt it was appropriate at the time."

And number one-hundred and twenty-fourth reason presents itself as to why kissing my boss is a bad idea. He's obviously still hung up on his ex-fiancée. Despite my attempts at hiding a smile, I fail. "You may want to change that someday. Otherwise, it'll be a constant reminder."

He grunts. "You're right. I'll work on that."

"Speaking of work, I better unlock the door. We have another full day."

He steps farther into the hallway. "When you accepted this position, did you think we'd be this busy?"

"I don't even know where all these people come from."

He chuckles. "Okay, City Girl, let's get to work."

CHAPTER FOURTEEN

EVIE

"There, that should do it," Liam says as I walk into the kitchen, my laptop in hand. His gaze peruses the length of my body before settling on my face. His lips flatten to a thin line, as if he disapproves of the biker shorts and halter top I changed into after we returned to his house. What's it to him what I wear? It's hot outside. Shouldn't it be my prerogative if I want to be comfortable sitting on the porch and searching for a job?

Liam grumbles and closes the panel to the fuse box. A wave of guilt washes over me. Luckily, he picked up some fuses during lunch. For once, this town had something stocked.

"I'm so sorry you had to deal with this. I'll be more mindful from now on." *Now that I know about overloading the electrical system.* I never dreamed that could be a thing. The house on Charleston Bay would never have electrical issues. Even my apartment, which wasn't built during modern times, handled the amperage fine. No matter my ignorance, I feel bad for making him go through all this extra trouble.

He takes in my expression and lets out a defeated sigh, seemingly letting go of his foul mood. "There's a learning curve to living here. This house wasn't made for modern-day appliances."

Then, he does something I never dreamed possible. He winks.

And I about die.

My body stills, mesmerized by that wink and tiny smirk playing on his lips. It's the most casual look I've seen on him yet, and seeing it does something to me. My mouth dries. And I swear my legs go weak. I place the laptop down on the small butcher block island as a sudden need to quench my thirst hits me. Although, I have a different type of thirst fulfillment in mind. *Holy crap. Where did that thought come from?*

Needing to regroup, I walk to the cabinet where the glasses are stored. I'm not sure I can take a civilized-acting Liam. I shove to my tiptoes and reach for a glass on the middle shelf but come up short. These cabinets are freakishly high. I get that the base cabinets aren't a standard size—a fact I noticed the other day when I had to grab a chair to look at the fuse box—but their height places the upper ones out of reach. "Was your grandma an Amazon descendant? These cabinets are way too tall."

"Here, let me grab that for you." Liam chuckles and goes to grab a glass. As he leans across, his arm brushes against my breasts. My breath hitches as heat curls down my spine. He backs away quickly, but I don't miss the want in his eyes when he hands me the tumbler.

"Thanks." That word comes out more breathless than I intended. I clear my throat and continue, "Seriously though, your grandparents must've been tall." *Like you.* Liam is at least six feet tall or more. He stands a good eight inches above my five-foot-four frame.

"My grandpa was, but not Nana. She was short like you." He walks to a pantry, opens the door, and points to a step stool. "Right through here, you'll find the stool Nana used to reach the

CITY LIGHTS STARRY NIGHTS 99

upper cabinets. She always teased Grandpa, saying he built the kitchen for himself, not her. With a devious grin, she'd add, 'But he forgot who cooked the meals'."

There's a sweetness to his tone which causes me to smile. The mental picture of a loving family gathered around the butcher block island or sitting around the rustic kitchen table is easy to visualize. I glance around the farmhouse kitchen and take in the milky-smooth, green finish coating the cabinets. The white-tiled backsplash accents perfectly against the soft green and frosted glass on the wall cabinets. The kitchen has a homey vibe to it. I breathe it all in. This house has so much love seeping from the walls—a stark contrast to the sterile environment I grew up in. Other than a few modernizations, like updated wiring and freshly painted walls, I wouldn't change a thing.

"I bet you have so many good memories here," I say in a dreamlike trance.

Liam closes the pantry door and leans against it, studying me. The moment is so intense. I stand transfixed as something dark passes through his eyes. It's as if I can see the transformation from playfulness to grumpiness in real-time.

"Yeah, there's a lot of memories." He shoves off the wall and pulls his keys from his pocket. "I'm heading to town. You'll be okay here, right?"

"Uh, yeah," I answer, a little taken aback by his clipped tone. "I take it you're not staying for dinner?"

"I'll grab something in town." Without looking back, Liam walks out the back door.

I shake my head, wondering what set him off. Was what I said that bad? I would've thought mentioning his grandparents would invoke good vibes, not put him in a bad mood. Maybe he hasn't gotten past their loss? People cope differently. I grab my laptop and head to the porch. It's not as if I'd have gone with him had he asked. I need to search for job openings. But as the taillights disappear down the lane, one thought goes through my mind, *an invite would've been nice.*

Dismissing Dr. Grump's weird behavior, I settle onto a wicker chair with a floral print cushion that must be a leftover from his grandma. There's no way that grouch of a man picked out frilly cushions. Once seated, I take in my surroundings. With the evening sun casting down, the place seems peaceful and not as scary as it did during nightfall. It's a typical two-story farmhouse-style home with white siding and black shudders. Even the wrap-around porch features a white slatted railing. But my favorite feature is the widow's peak with an actual rooster weathervane. The only modernized addition to the house is the satellite dish. The sizable yard edges against farm ground, where two feet of corn stalks grow in symmetrical rows. I feel as if someone dropped me into a Hallmark movie. Birds chirp in the distance. A strong breeze comes from the east, and aside from the approaching dark clouds, the setting is peaceful. Surreal. I can see the appeal. It's perfect for raising children.

I code the 1Bitchbegone! passcode, but after it connects, I close the lid. I'm still pondering what I said to chase Liam away. One second, he seemed relaxed, and the next, he seemed unsettled. Mystified, I call my friend. I could use a friendly voice right now. Ansley answers right away.

"How's Sugar Creek Falls treating you? Isn't Mabel the best?" Ansley asks.

"I suppose the town is fine, minus the waitresses, and Mabel's doing okay, all things considered."

"Wait. I'll jump back to the waitresses in a minute, but what's happening with Mabel?"

"She's fine, but a storm came through last night. Lightning struck the motel and caught it on fire."

"Oh my God. Was anyone hurt?"

"No, but the main building was heavily damaged. They shut the motel down until it gets repaired."

"Where are you staying?"

I cringe. "At your brother's house."

Silence greets me. Then, she lets out a low whine. "You're totally going to fuck my brother."

"What? No! That's gross." *Gross?* Of all the descriptors to use, that's what I go with? Fucking Liam Seymore would be anything but gross.

"Well, yeah. To me it is, but I can see the inevitable. You're the type of girl my brother is into. Once he sets his sights on you, you'll cave. It's the Seymour effect."

"The what?"

"The Seymour effect. Never mind. Moving on now."

"Not so fast. I want to know what you meant by *type of girl.*" I keep hearing this tossed around, and I'm unsure if it's a good thing.

"You're sophisticated. Put together. I don't know. He's always had an affinity for fancy girls. His ex-fiancée was very highfalutin"

"You mean snobbish?"

"She was, but you're nowhere near that realm. You have this way of making everyone feel welcome. That's why he'll fall for you. And since every one of my friends crushed on my brother, I predict it's only a matter of time before you'll cave." She lets out a groan. "My best friend will be doing the nasty with my brother."

"Stop. We won't either." He proved that from the way he rushed away from me.

"What's big brother up to?"

"Not sure. He left to go into town."

"He left you alone... in the country?"

"Yep."

"Hmm. Interesting."

"It's not interesting. I said something to upset him. Or maybe he wanted to eat out. I have no clue. One moment we're having a nice discussion about your grandparents, and the next, I'm eating his dust as he hightails it out of here."

"It's already happening."

"What are you talking about?"

"Nothing. Nothing at all. Tell me about the waitress problem. It's Blowhard Brenda, isn't it?"

Laughing, I spill the details of how rude both waitresses were, from each eye roll to their blatant dismissal of me.

"Jealous bitches!" She huffs. "One thing you'll learn about small towns is the cattiness that occurs. I'm not sure what Marla's problem is, but Brenda has had her claws stuck in Liam for years. He's wanted nothing to do with her since sophomore year, but she won't move on. Ignore them."

"I'm trying, but they have a point. I don't belong here."

"You belong anywhere you want to be. Don't let societal norms define you."

Isn't that the crux of my entire existence? I've let my social circle rule me for years. I allowed them to choke the essence that makes me who I am. That's why I broke away. So I can live my life the way I want. If I want to be funny and laugh, I will. I refuse to sit like a puppet, waiting to be told what to say. I refuse to yield.

We talk for another half hour before we say our goodbyes. My phone buzzes with a text the moment we disconnect. I laugh, thinking she forgot something, but my smile dies as soon as I read the text.

I'm getting impatient.

I almost drop the phone. Why won't he leave me alone? I slam my eyes shut, all bravado from my inner speech forgotten.

Suddenly, I don't want to be out here by myself anymore.

CHAPTER FIFTEEN

LIAM

"How's playing house going?" Ethan flanks my side, the tease in his voice unmistakable. He motions to the bartender and settles onto the barstool to my right. I should've known escaping to The Pump House to be alone wouldn't fly in this town. Eyes are everywhere. But I couldn't stay another minute at home with her.

I slide my gaze across the shellacked wooden bar top and land on my soon-to-be ex-friend's wide-ass grin. "I won't humor you with a response to that dumbass statement."

As expected, Matthew's chuckle follows as he joins the impromptu party. Matthew and Ethan are cousins, but they may as well be brothers. Where one goes, the other shortly follows. It's just a matter of time before they seek me out. I swear they installed a tracking device on my truck. Even though they're annoying as fuck, I missed them when I went away for college. A secret I'll take to my grave.

"Oh, come on. Ethan just wants to know how it's going. Moving the city girl into your home is the hottest rumor around town. It trumps my mom's fire."

"Her name is Geneva," I bite out, swishing the bourbon in

small circles, the ice clinking against the sides of the tumbler. I don't know why Matthew's nickname for her angers me. Haven't I been calling her the same thing? Somehow, hearing "City Girl" slide off his tongue hits differently. It sounds more condescending than endearing.

"Look who's getting all defensive." Ethan laughs, slapping a twenty on the table. "I knew you wouldn't be able to resist."

"I have no idea what you're talking about. I'm just helping out someone in need." I twist and shoot Matthew a glare. "You, of all people, should know she needs a place to stay."

His toothy smile tells me he's not buying my excuse. "Yeah, and I know she goes by Evie, not Geneva. And since you refuse to call her by her nickname, I'm guessing it's to set some type of boundaries. Since, you know, you've already fallen for her."

Thoughts of her waltzing into the kitchen with her ass and tits on full display come to mind. She looked so damn innocent *and clueless* about what her top and biker shorts did to me. I had to turn away to hide the evidence. Even now, thinking about the Lycra squishing her breasts to where they practically begged to be free and those ass cheeks dipping below her biker shorts have me shifting in my seat.

"Yo, Earth to Liam," Ethan said, snapping his fingers in front of my face. "Damn, he does have it bad."

I raise my glass to my lips and mumble, "How did I end up with assholes for friends?"

"Lucky draw of the straw," Ethan answers, chuckling. "The bigger question is, why are you here and not at home with her? Her company seems better than this crowd."

It is, especially with these two bozos.

I can't admit that, though. And I certainly can't disclose why I left her to fend for herself. It was a dick-*ish* move on my part, but if I had stayed, I would've done something regretful like devour that mouth of hers. I came close. Her lips were mere inches away when I retrieved that glass for her. I didn't expect the rush of heat after my arm brushed against those perfect-sized tits. It was purely by accident, but the results were the same. My body craves her touch.

Matthew's right. I've tried to maintain a distance since she came to town. I've tried to keep things professional, and addressing her by her birth name helped establish those boundaries. There are so many reasons why I should stay away: she's my employee, her age, she's my sister's best friend, and the fact that she's leaving.

She's leaving.

That reason alone should be enough.

The woman reminds me so much of Ciera. Those similarities were all I've focused on for the past couple of days. *Except tonight.* There was a shift or a change in my perspective if you will. Evie showed a glimpse of her true personality, and that tiny peek tilted my world. Evie may dress like Ciera and come from privilege, but that's where the resemblances end. That was evident after I talked about my grandparents. Her whimsical expression when she eyed the kitchen nearly brought me to my knees. And when she spoke about the good memories, it triggered what I lost when Ciera left—a family. All my dreams of raising a family in my grandparent's house went out the door with Ciera. I never thought I'd find someone to have that with again. I hadn't banked on Ciera not wanting kids and hating country life. She had once mentioned not wanting to alter her figure, but I thought she meant for now. She was five years younger than me. I figured she'd change her mind. I figured wrong.

Watching Evie feel so at ease and comfortable leaning against the kitchen cabinets sparked memories long forgotten, like Nana standing by the island dishing out supper, laughing and teasing as Grandpa snuck up behind her. The slight pat to her ass when they thought I wasn't looking. The way he snuggled in the crook of her neck and whispered Lord only knows what in her ear. Those memories morphed into the present, and I could visualize a future with Evie. I could envision myself standing there having fun with her, and that scenario scared the living shit out of me. I had to get out of there.

I'm not stupid. I know I'm not in love with a woman after two days of getting to know her, but I can't deny our instant connection. My biggest fear is getting to know Evie on a deeper level. She's not the privileged, spoiled debutant I thought. She's someone I could fall hard for. And that would be detrimental. She'll leave as soon as an organization or agency realizes her potential and hires her.

She's leaving.

I sip my old fashioned with a passive expression and then ask, "Why would I need to stay home?"

"Because you like her," Ethan mumbles into his bottle before taking a drink.

"I don't have a thing for my new office manager," I lie.

"Sure, that's why you're here drinking on a Tuesday night instead of home entertaining your guest," Matthew says with a laugh. "I smell avoidance."

"You just worry about getting her car fixed so she can get to her interviews." I steer the conversation to a safer, more manageable topic. Enough talking about me.

Matthew tosses his hands up in surrender. "I'm trying. It's not my fault there's a parts shortage."

"She's not sticking around?" Ethan asks, frown lines creasing his forehead.

"No." That admission should shut down the gossip mill and make me feel better, but somehow, it doesn't.

"You should definitely try getting your dick played with since she's leaving. Maybe then you'd be less grumpy."

Ethan spits his drink out. "Jesus, Matt."

I glare at my lifelong friend. "I am not grouchy."

"Says the man through a growl."

"Why are we even friends?"

"Come on. You'd be lost without me."

"I can't believe you moved the new girl in." Olivia Berge, the only female our seven-year-old selves allowed in our friend group, says as she approaches the bar. She's the younger sister of our friend, Daniel, by ten minutes. A fact Daniel never let her forget when we hung out, which was a lot throughout the years.

I roll my eyes, ignoring the bite in her tone. "Is my every move talk of the town?"

"Apparently, when a shiny new toy is involved." Olivia flops in the chair beside Ethan. She never hid her disdain for Ciera, but the feeling was mutual. I can't count the number of times Ciera bitched about Olivia's presence. She bitched about all my friends and was jealous of our group dynamic. No matter how often I tried to include her in our conversations, she felt like an outsider. She especially didn't like Olivia. She mistook our friendship for more, but it isn't like that between Olivia and me. She's like a sister to us. Ciera never understood childhood pacts.

"Geneva needs a place to stay. What was I supposed to do?" I bring the tumbler to my mouth, staring at her over the glass.

"Always the martyr, huh?"

"She isn't Ciera." I don't know why I feel the need to defend Evie, but Olivia's assumption isn't fair. *Kind of like mine, in the beginning*, my self-conscience whispers.

Olivia's eyes widen momentarily before narrowing. "Since when did you become so defensive."

"Since a certain city girl showed up in town," Matthew jokes.

"Stuff it," I say into my glass. As I take a drink, I can't help but think they have a point. I never defended their barbs against Ciera. And while they were *all in good fun*, it still pissed her off. So, why am I defending Evie's honor when I hardly know her? I change the subject before I delve into what that means. "What's your brother up to tonight?"

"He's securing the barn. We're under a tornado watch."

Unease creeps up my spine. "We are?"

After all the rain we received last night, the humidity was stifling. I never dreamed another cold front would come through so quickly.

"It's starting to rain, but the wind picked up about a half-hour ago. According to the radar, the storm will hit any minute."

I stand abruptly, guilt clawing my throat. "I need to get home."

"What's the hurry?" Matthew asks, with *it's just another storm* Midwest mentality. No one around these parts takes storm warnings too seriously. We'd hunker down all the time if that were the case. That's not to say an actual tornado is something to take lightly. Olivia's family has seen up close the destruction they cause, but there's less than a one percent chance of personally experiencing a tornado per year in the Hoosier State.

"I just need to get back." No way will I explain how Evie hates storms. Or how her hands shook last night when the thunder clapped overhead. The things that frighten her aren't their business.

Their ribbing falls on deaf ears as I exit the bar into complete darkness. I look up at the ebony storm clouds blanketing the sky. I can't believe I left her with a storm coming. Why didn't I check the radar? Storms seem scarier out on the farm.

I dart to the truck, the rain pelting my face. The moment the engine roars to life, the tornado siren wails through town.

Shit.

CHAPTER SIXTEEN

LIAM

"Evie!" I burst through the front door, my heart beating wildly in my chest when silence and darkness greet me. Toeing off my shoes, I flip the light switch on, but the room remains black. *Great, no power.* It's not uncommon to lose electricity living out here, but why did it have to happen now? I shouldn't have left. What the fuck was I thinking?

"Evie," I yell again and sprint to the living room. My feet halt when I spot a silhouette occupying the far end of the couch. I let out a sigh of relief and beeline across the hardwood floors to her. Once my feet hit the rug, I kneel beside her. "Are you okay?"

"I'm fine." Her voice, low and shaky, screams she's anything but fine. She's tucked in the corner, shoulders hunched, looking anywhere but at me. I chastise myself for my stupidity.

"I'm so sorry I left you alone. Are you sure you're okay?" I search her eyes for any reassurance that my selfishness didn't cause harm, but the shadows blanketing her face make it impossible to see.

"Yes, I'm okay."

"We're through the worst part. There's one more cell pushing through, but once it passes, the storm will be over."

She nods but remains quiet, still not looking at me. Crushing pain like I've never felt squeezes my chest. I'm used to a more vibrant Evie, not this timid, lifeless girl. It's as if I snuffed her candle flame, leaving behind a cold, empty shell. *Damn it. Why was I so thoughtless?* This whole asshole routine I've fallen into isn't me. It's not who I am at my core. I've always been reserved, but my compassionate side usually showed. That's why I became a doctor. Ever since Ciera left, I've been content to condemn everyone and everything around me. I blamed the move back to town, the small-town gossip, and my friends' behavior. Hell, I even blamed my dad's death. Blaming others masked the real source for Ciera not getting what she needed—my shortcomings and failures. I realize we wouldn't have worked long term—our goals were too opposite—but I was blind for far too long. It only took five months to get here, but seeing Evie tucked in the corner of the couch curled in on herself is an eye-opener. Actions have consequences, and I'm witnessing firsthand what asshole-like actions bring.

And I feel gutted.

"I shouldn't have left you," I reiterate in a soft, apologetic voice.

"It's fine. You don't owe me anything."

That phrase hurts the most out of the few words she has said. *You don't owe me anything.* Oh, but I do. I need to tell her the truth. To come clean. She deserves to know what went through my mind before I left. She deserves so much more.

"I left because I was afraid of what I would do."

This grabs her attention. She turns toward me, her legs bumping against my hands. Part of me wishes for light so I could see her face. If I could read her expression, I would know what she was thinking. But I'm thankful for the darkness. It makes what I want to say easier.

"Earlier, in the kitchen, we were having a good time. Too good of a time. I had to leave before I did something stupid."

"Something stupid?"

"Yes." *Just be honest,* I tell myself. "Like kiss you."

"You wanted to kiss me?"

"I wanted to do much more than that," I admit.

A gust of wind beats against the windows, causing this old farmhouse to creak and whine. A shudder works through Evie, but I don't know if it's from what I said or the weather. I wrap my hands around her thighs and lean closer, her knees pressing into my chest. I ignore the stirring in my pants. This isn't the time to think about how soft and smooth her skin feels against mine. Or how I want to spread her thighs apart and bury my mouth into her pussy. But damn, the hint of her perfume permeates the air, and I want to taste her to see if she's every bit as sweet as the orange scent besieging my nostrils.

"I won't deny my attraction to you, but I've been fighting it since this hot-as-sin woman carrying a tray of champagne approached me in Chicago." Her slight gasp gives me the courage to continue my verbal vomit. "You surprised me earlier. I realized that you weren't this self-centered, privileged girl. You genuinely care about people and can see the beauty in your surroundings. That's why I left."

"Because I'm a glass-half-full person?"

I grunt. I'm messing this up. I have a Ph.D., for fuck's sake. I should be a master at communication, not some blundering idiot. I take a shuddering breath and try again. "Earlier, when you stood in the kitchen around the island, it reminded me of everything I want: a loving wife, family. It reminded me of memories—the past and the present ones I want to create. I could fall hard for a woman like you. I thought the best thing for us was to remove myself from the temptation."

"Because you shouldn't be attracted to me?"

"Because I wanted to bend you over the table and fuck this attraction out of you. *That's* why I left."

The rain beats against the side of the house, the wind howling around us, but the only sound I focus on is the uptick in her breathing.

"I thought you hated me." Her voice comes out in a husky whisper.

"No. Never."

It's so damn dark in here. I can't read her face to know what she is feeling. I'm blind, letting the sound of her breaths guide my moves. I inch my fingers up her thighs while my thumb works small circles against her flesh. The slight hitch in her breath cuts through the air, causing me to pause, but then her legs spread ever so slightly. My dick strains against my zipper, clearly not feeling the same conflicting thoughts as me.

The right thing to do would be to back off, but damn if I don't want to. What I want is to explore this attraction between us and see where it leads. The woman has driven me crazy since I first saw her. We would be good together. I know it. But I can't take her like this. Not tonight. I go to slip away, but her fingers weave into my hair, and the tips tug the nape of my neck closer. Evidently, I'm weak because that gesture is all the signal I need.

I move my hands farther up her thighs, stopping short of her hips. "Are you sure?"

"Yes."

"Thank fuck." I shift forward and press my lips against hers. My mouth absorbs the small gasp she makes when our lips join, and I take advantage of the opening by thrusting my tongue inside. An explosion of lust and heat slams into me when our tongues collide. Every earlier thought that this was a bad idea loses the battle of wills. Nothing this good could ever be wrong.

Pushing off the floor, I shift my hands under her ass and lift her, not once breaking the kiss. I'm painfully hard as I move myself to the couch, but this isn't about me. This is all about her. Placing her on top of me, I let my hands roam along her curves. I moan into her mouth because she feels like heaven. With her legs straddling my hips, I grind into her core, letting her feel what she does to me.

"You make me so hard," I say before kissing her again. Her little whimper tells me she likes dirty talk, which is good because I don't want to hold back. "Do you like that? Do you like knowing what you do to me?"

The "yes" falls from her lips, and I reclaim her mouth, exploring every crevice. Our tongues slide across each other in a give-and-take motion. I pull back for a second, running my fingers along the hem of her halter top. I lift it, my gaze matching hers. "Is this okay?"

She nods and raises her arms straight up in the air. I remove the harness, albeit not sexily, since the thing is like a chastity belt for tits. We laugh when I finally get it over her head, but two perfect globes stare back at me once it's removed. I groan, wishing the power hadn't gone out. I skim my fingertips along the swell of her breast. Her body shivers, and I take a taut nipple in my mouth as she grinds down on me. I nibble ever so slightly before moving to the other one.

"Are you wet for me?" I whisper against her skin, my fingertips drawing circles on her back.

"Yes."

"Good." I plant small kisses along the crook of her neck. When I get close to her ear, I whisper, "Because I can't wait to taste you. I bet you taste sweet. Would you like that? You want my mouth on your pussy?"

She grinds down and lets out another whimper, nodding her head. My hands roam back down, round her hips to her inner thighs, and I lightly brush my thumb across her clit. A full-body shudder ripples through her, and this time there's no question what caused it. Hint: it has nothing to do with the weather.

Wanting the feel of her skin on me, I shrug out of my shirt, not exactly sure at what point she unbuttoned it. Her palms land on my bare chest, and I press into her core as she explores my pecs down to the ridges of my abdominals. I'm not ripped, but I'm not exactly soft, either.

When I can't wait any longer, I smack her ass. "Up on your knees." She lifts, and I shove those too-short biker shorts down, along with her underwear. I wish I could see how glorious her pussy looks, but at the same time, the surrounding darkness feels liberating. It's like having an out-of-body experience. One I don't have to be in the present for, which is good. The present is where rational decisions are made, and I don't want to be rational right now. I want to be reckless. I want to let my inhibitions rule instead of my ever-present sensible side.

I pick her up and flip her on her back. I shove her clothes the rest of the way off and practically growl, "Spread those legs for me."

She complies and runs her hands across her tits, squeezing them. Fuck, she looks so sexy. I may not be able to see her completely, but my imagination fills in the blanks. Wasting no time, I run my tongue along her folds and breathe in her musky scent. The woman is intoxicating. With the slightest pressure, I swirl my tongue around her clit in a mixture of kissing and teasing strokes but never quite touching the most sensitive part. Her breaths increase, hips bucking and searching for more. I continue this onslaught of kissing and licking until I brush my tongue over her clit and blow ever so slightly.

"Oh my God."

"You want more?" I ask.

"Please."

"Tell me what you want?" I take the tip of my tongue and flick it over that precious nub once more before removing it.

This causes her to cry out, "Your tongue. Mouth. I don't care. I just want more. I *need* more."

"Okay, City Girl."

I curl my tongue and plunge inside her wet heat before circling her opening and licking my way back to her swollen clit. She writhes beneath my touch. As I plunge two fingers inside and work them in and out, I continue my delicious assault while her appreciative moans fill the dark, night air.

"Yes, just like that. Never stop."

I chuckle against her skin but keep going. I keep up this pace and don't stop until her thighs tighten around my head and she bucks beneath me with my name spilling from her lips in repetitive succession. Damn, this girl is responsive.

And I love it.

Not worried about my needs, I rise and stare down at her. My hands trace figure eights along her thighs as her breath catches up. She opens her eyes, and even though it's too dark to see their hidden expression, I sure feel her continued arousal deep-seated in my bones. It's in the tiny goosebumps beneath my fingertips, the subconscious thrust her pelvis makes as if she craves more of my touch, and her—

"Fuck me, Liam."

Her verbal command.

It doesn't get more straightforward than that, but even so, I want it to be as clear as possible. "Are you sure?"

"Yes, I need you." She sits up and grabs my waist. Unbuckling my belt, she pants, "It's all I can think about."

Okay, then. That has me sliding off my pants and grabbing a condom at record speed. The moment I sheath myself, I tell her to straddle me.

Her thighs situate on both sides of mine, giving me perfect access to everything. This lustful haze has me so drunk on her body I'm at war with wanting to slow down or speed up. I run the tip of my dick along her folds. She's so wet for me; it takes sheer willpower to keep from ramming inside her. I break the barrier when the room illuminates, exposing everything. I freeze as the concept of what we're doing crashes into me like the portfolio's best-performing stock bottoming out.

Fuck. Fuck. *Fuck.*

I tug her up and off me. She plumps onto the couch, and I have to turn away, the confusion on her face killing me.

"I'm so sorry." I stand, my dick erect, just as perplexed as her. "Shit, I should've never done that." I run my hands through my hair and squeeze. *I screwed my office manager.* No, I ate her for dinner and *almost* screwed her. What the hell was I thinking? She's my sister's best friend. I found her tucked away on the couch like a scared child. God, did I take advantage of her vulnerability?

Her exasperated breath causes me to face her. She's curled in on herself, her arms wrapped around her legs. Another pang of guilt hits my chest.

"What do you mean you shouldn't have done that?"

"I..." I let out my breath and run my fingers through my tousled hair. How could I be so stupid? Yes, I wanted her, and she acted as if she wanted it too, but this is a bad idea. She works and lives with me. *Fuck.* This is bad on too many levels. "I shouldn't have taken advantage of you like that."

"It's not as if I didn't consent." The ice in her tone tells me exactly how pissed she is.

"Still doesn't make it right."

She flinches, and I immediately regret my phrasing. But I'm

right on this. I shouldn't have taken advantage. It's okay to lust after her, but not act upon it. It's my practice on the line. My reputation. Jesus, why am I so weak?

She snatches her clothes from the ground and uses them as a shield, but the scraps of fabric barely cover anything. She marches up the stairs, leaving me standing in my living room naked with a condom covering my shrinking dick.

Yeah, buddy, that's exactly how I feel—pathetic.

CHAPTER SEVENTEEN

EVIE

"I hate to leave you like this, but I need to get to the committee meeting." Rachael looks at her watch. "It starts in fifteen minutes. I didn't expect today to run over so late. However, I should've known since it's Friday. The end of the week never goes as planned."

"That's fine. I don't have much left to do." I straighten the last of the magazines in the waiting room. The remaining charts need to be put away, but I'm stalled, waiting for Liam to get done dictating. He certainly didn't have time in between patients. Today put chaos to shame. If anything could've gone wrong, it did.

I rise to my full height, my gaze even with the black and white covered bridge photos hanging on the wall. Like the motel ones, they lack the photographer's name.

I really wish I knew who the artist was.

Rachael hands me the keys to the filing cabinets. "Thanks again for offering to file the charts. I appreciate it."

"Not a problem." I pull my gaze away from the photos and offer a smile.

Her eyes bounce from me to the photos. "Those pictures are great, aren't they?"

"Yeah, I tried looking for the photographer's name, but it's not listed. Is she local? I saw similar prints back at the motel."

"Yes. The photographer is Olivia Berge. She's one of Liam's friends."

"Please learn how to schedule if you continue to work here." Liam slams the last chart on my desk and storms back to his office.

Great. It looks as if Dr. Grump will carry his title into the weekend.

The tension has been thick between us since he gave me one hell of an orgasm. He refuses to talk to me. He barely looks at me. I can't wait to get my car back to drive myself to work. That would alleviate the awkward tension right before work—not to mention the confusion. His hot-one-minute-and-cold-the-next actions give me whiplash. He goes out of his way to bring me a latte every morning when I could wait to get one before work. When I mention it, he blows me off, saying he knows I'd prefer one when I rise.

I do. But how the hell does he know that?

Rachael's eyebrows lift, watching the tails of Liam's lab coat disappear behind his door. "He does realize this schedule is still the fallout from the last manager, right?"

I huff out an exasperated breath. "I don't know. I don't think he's in a good head space right now."

She pats me on the back.

"Sorry for cutting on you and leaving you with Groucho, but I *really* have to go."

"I'll be fine." I toss her a smile for good measure as she darts to the door.

"Have a good weekend," she says behind her.

"You, too." I let out a breath as the door closes and glance around the waiting room. *Have a good weekend,* I muse. The weekend would be better if the awkwardness between Liam and I dissipated. The only thing consistent since Tuesday night is the latte he brings me every morning. Other than the occasional work question, it's been radio silence between us. That ends tonight. I refuse to spend the entire weekend in misery. I just have to figure out a way to get past this awkwardness.

Technically, I should be upset with the way he left me hanging. And I am. I've never been cared for so thoroughly, only to be left sexually hungry. But he left himself hanging more. I understand where he's coming from. Like, I get it. His ex broke his heart, and he doesn't want to fall hard again. Blah, blah, blah. That's typical for every breakup story. But being together intimately doesn't have to turn into something complicated. We have chemistry. That's obvious. It would be a shame not to see where that leads. Yes, I'm leaving, but that doesn't mean he has to become a monk.

Hello, who is this girl wanting a fling?

This isn't me. I don't have recurrent sex with a partner. I stick to one-night stands. One hella-amazing orgasm later, and he has me breaking my casual-only rule.

I close my eyes and try to push these thoughts away. This is where I need my best friend's advice. Ansley would tell me exactly how to proceed. However, considering the mere thought of her brother and me together grosses her out, she isn't an option. I could call Job, but I already know what he'd say. He'd tell me to jump on that ride and never let go.

The swish of the door cuts through my musings. Thinking Rachael forgot something, I spin on my heels to tease her but startle at Ethan wheeling in Mr. Cusack, holding a handkerchief to the left side of his forehead.

"I'm glad you're still here. I left my phone at home when I went to check on Gramps."

"Boy, you worry too much. I don't need to be here. This is nothing more than a flesh wound," he says while holding a blood-soaked cloth.

Ethan shoots me an apologetic look, which I guess is for his grandpa's behavior. But the old man doesn't bother me. He's a relief from this constant tension.

"What's the matter, Mr. Cusack? Are you trying to match scars? Even out the damage? Or are you trying to change your name to Bruiser?"

"Ha," he grunts. "My snowflake grandson thinks every bump and bruise needs to be seen. He wouldn't know hard work if it—"

"Hey, that's enough," Ethan says. "You're bleeding every-where. Again."

My lips twitch at Mr. Cusack's scowl. I wink at the old, cranky guy before taking the reins and wheeling him down the hallway. "I guess you do have your own suite here."

"It's been a week. Why are you still here?"

"My life's mission is to annoy cranky old men."

Ethan barks a laugh while Mr. Cusack harrumphs.

"I knew I liked you." Ethan shakes his head, still chuckling.

"You're about as funny as this construction through town." Mr. Cusack's words may come out as a grumble, but there's an undertone of humor.

"It's a pain, isn't it?" I ask. Although Liam has been the driver, getting to work is still a hassle. Who would've thought it possible in a small town?

"It's the stupidest thing I ever heard. There's nothing wrong with a turn lane down the middle of town. Making four lanes is plain ignorant."

"It will only cause people to drive faster."

Mr. Cusack nods. "Huh, no wonder you've stuck around. You're actually smart."

"What is this? You're paying my office manager a compliment?" Liam comes out of his office and walks over to us. I expect to see the grumpy doctor who blessed us with his misery all week, but who stands in front of us is a man using humor to mask his concern. I can tell because his soft laughter doesn't entirely hide the wheels turning inside that mind of his. I don't understand how I know this about him already, but it's evident with one look in his eyes. This opaque green color means concern.

Liam stands beside Mr. Cusack and examines the gash. "You did it this time, Melvin. What were you doing?"

"Not a damn thing. This is nothing. You're making it a bigger deal than it should be."

Ethan sighs. "Gramps, it wouldn't hurt for you to tell us."

Melvin harrumphs again, his hands gesturing for him to go away. Before either one blows a gasket, I wheel Mr. Cusack into the exam room.

"Here you go. You know what to do." I pat the exam chair. The same one he refused to sit in last time he was here.

Then, Melvin does something I never thought I'd see. He transfers out of the wheelchair and into the seat without protest. Liam stands slack jawed. Our gazes lock and hold for what seems like an eternity. I wish his thoughts were readable because, at this moment, he doesn't appear mad. He seems stunned.

Once Melvin settles into the seat, Liam shifts to retrieve a linen-wrapped package labeled suture kit and places it on a stainless-steel stand. Ethan shuffles to a chair in the far corner. Liam explains what he's doing.

"I'm going to open this up. Usually, Rachael assists, but I don't expect you to scrub in. The sutures are kept in here." He pulls out a couple of different ones. He pulls the foil apart and flips one onto the sterile field. "If I need more or something different, grab from here and open it just as I did."

My eyes widen. Had I known there was a chance to participate, I would've paid closer attention to Rachael's job. But I find myself nodding when all I want to do is bow out.

Liam washes his hands and directs me to the sink. He leans down next to my ear, and the proximity of his body ignites tingles that shoot across my skin. "He likes you. See if you can get him to confess what happened."

My nod is subtle as I give the slightest inclination to play along.

As Liam starts injecting Mr. Cusack's forehead, my stomach growls. All eyes land on me, causing me to blush.

"Sorry, I guess I need to eat something. What did you have for supper?" I direct the question toward Melvin.

"Nothing. I was going to fix Tex Mex."

"Hmm, I don't think I've ever heard of the meal. What's all in it?" I put the question out there as Liam keeps injecting.

"Hamburger, something you city folk don't take too kindly to." There's humor in his statement that makes me smile. I adore this man.

"Oh, that's not true. Plenty of people like beef. They wouldn't have steak and burger joints otherwise." I pause, meet Liam's gaze, and then continue, "What else besides hamburger is in it?"

"Macaroni."

"Sounds interesting. I bet it's tasty," I lie. I'd agree to anything as long as it keeps Mr. Cusack occupied and gives us additional details of what led to the fall.

"It is, but the damn dish requires spice."

"That's a bad thing?" I laugh.

"Not usually, but they're stored on the shelf above the stove. I almost had the cumin until the damn chair slipped from underneath me."

Liam's head jerks up, and he looks at Ethan. They exchange a look and then stare at me in awe. And do I dare say they seem impressed?

Ethan's mouth opens, but I cut him off before he makes things worse. He means well, but the aggressive way he goes about things fuels Melvin's temper.

"Those chairs can be tricky. I bet you can devise a solution to prevent that in the future." The room stays silent. "Do you enjoy cooking?"

"I hate it."

I burst out laughing. "Maybe there's a better solution altogether."

"Like dying?"

"No!" I draw out. "I can check into it if you want. Anything has to be better than always coming in here and seeing this grump." I bite my lip. Did I just call my boss/roommate a grump? To his face?

Liam eyes me before going back to the gash.

"You're right about that. I don't need help."

"No, I'm sure you can handle it. But options are better than none, right?"

"Where'd you find this girl?" Melvin asks Liam.

"She's Ansley's friend. They went to school together."

"At Northwestern?"

"Wildcat for life," I say.

"Knew you were smart."

The room stays silent after that. A smile rests on my lips. I'll look into options for him. Once I find something, I'll worry about convincing him then.

When Liam finishes with Melvin, we wheel him into the hallway.

Ethan speaks up, "Guess I'll see you later?"

Liam stands straighter. "Oh, uh... maybe." Liam looks at me and then averts his gaze.

"Take the girl out. She's probably bored stiff at your place," Mr. Cusack says. "Don't you know how to treat a woman?"

"Yeah, I just didn't want to... What do you know, old man?"

"Apparently, more than you," he huffs and wheels his chair to the door. "Come on. I don't want to stay here all night. He's likely to have me committed."

"Twenty-four seven supervision wouldn't be such a bad idea," Liam grumbles under his breath.

"Okay, see ya later." Ethan pats Liam on the back and heads toward his grandpa.

When they exit, Liam turns to me. "You handle Melvin really well."

"Grumpy old men don't scare me." I quirk an eyebrow and smirk.

He studies me, and I bet he's wondering if I'm labeling him in that category. Spoiler alert: I am.

"Let me dictate this, and then we'll grab something to eat." He stalks off to his office. "Looks like you're about to be initiated into the gang."

"Should that scare me?"

"Oh yeah." His half-hearted shrug gives pause to worry.

CHAPTER EIGHTEEN

LIAM

"We don't have to stay long." We exit the truck, and I eye the bar for a beat before redirecting my attention back to Evie. She steps to the sidewalk, her face full of strength. I frown. How can she be so composed meeting my friends? Usually, that would be a good thing, but she doesn't know what's in store. My ex hated my friends. Ciera would bitch every time they came around and reached the point where she wouldn't go out if they were there. It didn't help that my friends treated her like an outsider, but she never gave them a chance.

"It's fine. There's no rush to get home." Evie beams as she looks up at me.

Home.

The innocent word nearly knocks the air from my lungs. Evie doesn't mean anything by it. There are no underlying implications, but referring to my house as our home causes a wave of emotions that baffle me. I should want to run for the hills, not feel elated. An email notification pings my cell phone, stopping my spiral descent into what a single word means.

"Hey, hold up. I've been waiting on an email from a

colleague. I sent him Mrs. Jones's lab results." I open the app and frown. The email isn't from my colleague but from a corporation I don't recognize. The subject line "Urgent regarding recent hire" intrigues me.

From: BSC Group
To: Dr. Seymour

Dear Dr. Seymour,

It has come to our attention that you've been working on receiving grants for a wellness clinic. Our corporation would like to donate $100,000 to the cause. I believe it would be lucrative for you to accept the offer.

In exchange for a monetary donation, we would like to hire Miss Thornhill. As you're aware, her talents far exceed that of a small-town medical office. Don't worry about her well-being; we are prepared to cover any moving expenses.
I look forward to your response and congratulations. The wellness clinic will be a significant asset to the Sugar Creek Falls community, as I'm sure you're aware, given the circumstances behind your departure from New York City.

Sincerely,
The BSC Group.

I close the email as unease niggles at my conscience. This doesn't seem right. The fact they mention my reasonings for leaving New York seems like an underlying threat. Whoever

BSC Group is has done their research. I glance up at Evie. *Who is this woman?*

"Was that the email you wanted?" Her innocent eyes widen as she asks, "Was it bad news?"

"No. It wasn't about Mrs. Jones." I resume walking, debating whether to ask if she knows who would send a threatening bribe. Is this what happened during her other interviews? Were they paid off? The bigger question is, who the hell is she that this company would shell out a significant amount of money to bring her home? Her parents are wealthy. And by the way she made them sound, they're rather shitty parents, but would they sabotage their daughter like that? As we reach the bar's entrance, I decide against telling her for now and make a mental note to check out the corporation. There's no need to get her worked up before meeting my friends. She'll be overwhelmed the way it is. I force a smile and pull the door open for her.

"Ready or not, it's time to meet the gang." I point to the table in the back, where everyone sits sans Ethan.

We reach the table, and I nod to my friends. "Geneva, this is Olivia Berge. The guy to her left is her brother, Daniel, and his wife, Jeanette. You know Matthew already. Everyone, this is Geneva."

Evie shakes her head. "Evie. Please call me Evie."

Olivia's eyes dart to mine with an unreadable expression. I force my hands into my pockets to avoid reaching out to my office manager. I need to shake loose this overwhelming need to protect her, but I admit it's getting harder each passing day. Olivia's sharp eyes don't miss a thing. She smirks before turning her attention to Evie.

"I see the simple living hasn't run your fancy-ass out of town yet."

I stiffen beside Evie and shoot Olivia a glare. Daniel smacks his sister's arm. When I turn back to Evie, she wears a genuine smile that makes her eyes glow.

"Not yet. But not from lack of trying." Evie doesn't waste time as she sits in the empty chair beside Olivia. *Great, there goes my idea of putting distance between the girls.*

"Geneva's slowly winning Melvin over. Who knows, Olivia? This one may have the stamina to put up with your attitude," I say, trying to smooth things over as I settle in the seat across from Evie and next to Matthew.

"Doubtful. Anyone who overloads old farmhouse breakers doesn't belong around here."

What the hell, Olivia? I rush to my girl's defense, but she cuts me off before I can speak.

"Living in an old farmhouse is an adjustment, but I'm a quick learner. I can hold my own."

"Hmm, I bet you can." Disbelief coats Olivia's side glance, but she shakes it off as if remembering her role of being a team bitch. She didn't earn her Ice Queen title for nothing. "Still, there's almost no privacy in a small town. Hope you're ready."

"Pay no mind to my sister-in-law. I'm Jeanette Berge, in case you forgot. I'll be the group's buffer, considering I was once an outsider like you."

Evie smiles, but it's cut short by Olivia.

"There's a difference, though. She'll be gone as soon as Matthew fixes her car."

"Which will be done next week," Matthew says.

Olivia continues as if Matthew hadn't spoken, "And you"— she points to Jeanette—"are one of us."

Irritated by Olivia's condescending tone, I go to speak, but Evie's breath draws short, interrupting me again.

"Wait, Olivia Berge? As in the photographer who took those amazing photos hanging in the office and back at the motel?" Excitement laces her tone. She's genuinely shocked.

"Yeah," Olivia draws out, eyebrows narrowed.

"They are amazing. Those photos captivated my attention the moment I opened the door to my motel room. They really are statement pieces."

And just like that, Evie manages to thaw the Ice Queen. I don't know how she does it, other than by being her true self.

"What would you like?" the waitress asks. She turns to Evie and hands her a menu. "I know you don't know what we have, but you'll find the vegan options here."

Evie looks startled. "Oh, well, thanks." She scans the limited options and smiles. "I'll take the black bean and broccoli buddha bowl."

"Excellent."

"As I said, small towns, total lack of privacy." Olivia smirks.

"You're not wrong," Evie agrees.

"Don't be warning the new girl away. She charmed, Gramps," Ethan says when he arrives. He settles into the other seat next to Matthew.

"Did you get Melvin taken care of?" I ask to deter the conversation away from Evie. He isn't wrong though. She has wormed her way into the old man's heart and got him to open up. She has a gift with people.

"He's settled for the night with his supper." Ethan turns to Evie. "Thanks again for getting out of him what happened. I've moved everything to a lower shelf."

"No problem, but I think a proper meal service would be beneficial. I'm going to look into what options are available around here."

"Thanks, I'd appreciate that."

"So, when did you two get married?" Evie asks, pointing to Daniel and Jeanette.

Jeanette looks at Daniel with an enduring smile, and a pang of jealousy hits my chest. I want that so much. My gaze flicks to

Evie. I almost had it, but I have a knack for choosing the wrong kind of girls. Ones that never stay.

"Three years ago," Jeanette says.

"So, I take it you're not from around here. How'd you meet?"

"We met in college. I'm from northern Indiana."

"Tell her about your texting story," Ethan says with a laugh.

Daniel groans. "Not that story again."

"Yes, it's classic," Ethan says.

"Uh, oh. Sounds like a story. You have to tell me now." Evie's eyes shine as she takes in my friends smiling at each other.

"Let's just say I was skeptical of Daniel when we first met." Jeanette shakes her head.

"I had gotten a new phone number for, uh, reasons," Daniel says.

"Reasons being you couldn't keep your dick in your pants and picked up a stalker," Matthew jokes, earning him a playful glare from Daniel.

"I was lost before Jeanette came into my life." Daniel wraps his arm around his wife's shoulders and plants a kiss on her temple. He leans forward, looking around the girls, and directs his attention to Evie. "I finally convinced her to go out with me and took her to an expensive restaurant. Halfway through, I received a rather promiscuous text."

Evie's eyes widen. "Some girl sexted you during your first date? Was it the stalker?"

"Not mine. Although, I didn't know that at the time. The message read, 'This is all yours later tonight, baby'." He grimaces before continuing, "Then, a picture of a dick popped up."

"I didn't know what to think." Jeanette snorts.

"It took some fancy explaining to make her believe that was from a random dude texting whoever had the phone number before me."

"Oh, that's funny. Sexting on your first date."

"I thought he was either bi or closeted. I'd be okay if he were bi, but no way would I be a front if he was closeted."

Laughter erupts around the table, and I can't believe how at ease everyone is with Evie. In fact, she has that effect on everyone she meets. The only ones who seem to have a problem with her are her old boss and me. I don't know what his problem could've been, but Evie is great. Melvin, of all people, even likes her. When you thaw the two most challenging people in town, you know there's something special. She's so special people are willing to pay off strangers to have her in their life.

Evie's glance catches mine and holds. My heart rate speeds up. She intrigues me like no other. No matter what she's hiding, it's getting harder to keep her at a distance. I've tried to ensure we aren't together, but I don't think I can last. That taste has only fueled my need to have her, and when she looks at me with desire-laden eyes, I wonder why I keep holding out.

"I need to use the restroom," Olivia says.

"I'll go, too." Jeanette stands at the same time as Evie.

As the three girls leave, Matthew shakes his head. "They're like a pack."

"A sexy pack," Ethan replies.

Yes, I have to agree.

When they're out of earshot, Matthew lets out a low whistle. "Someone's about to get lucky tonight."

I narrow my eyes. "I know you can't be talking about me."

"All those looks she tossed your way? Come on, man. You're not that blind." Matthew tips his longneck bottle back, trying not to chuckle.

"You should've been in the exam room with them. I thought I would have to take up smoking after that eye fucking."

"You're out of your mind. There wasn't anything going on while working on your grandpa. That's disgusting."

"Yeah, okay. Whatever you say." Unbelievability coats Ethan's tone.

"She works for me. I have to maintain some semblance of professionalism."

"As a temp. She's moving soon, right?" Ethan points out.

"Yeah, which brings up my next point—"

"No, there's no point. I'm not saying you have to fall in love, but it wouldn't hurt to diffuse that chemistry between you. You want to bang her. I can tell." The smug look on Ethan's face fuels my anger.

"There's no way I want to 'bang her'. She's way too young for me."

"She's not that much younger," Matthew says.

"She's my sister's best friend. That would be like you"—I point to Matthew—"with my sister. Insanely unethical." I pause at Matthew's flinch. He gets where I'm coming from. "See, there can't be anything between us. In no way do I want her."

Movement draws my attention, and as soon as my eyes land on long, blond waves, I want to sink beneath the table.

"I forgot my purse." Evie shoots daggers at me and snatches her purse from the back of the chair. Spinning on her heels, she marches away.

"Damn it," I swear under my breath. For once, the guys have nothing to say. I spring up from my chair and dart after her. But what am I going to say when I catch her? Because no matter how truthful every uttered word is, they are still a lie.

CHAPTER NINETEEN

EVIE

"Evie, stop." Liam's voice booms behind me, but my feet keep moving, chewing up the concrete from the table to the bathroom. Embarrassment and anger clash together in a fuel-filled rage. How dare he talk about me like that to his friends. Who does he think he is? It's not as if I'm sitting around pining after his ass. I get his friends teasing him, but for him to use my age or my friendship with his sister as an excuse after what we did... that's despicable.

I'm not a child.

I pick up my pace and let his pleas for me to wait fall on deaf ears. I just need to escape. We've spent the last forty or so minutes eyeing each other. I thought maybe he, I don't know, felt the same connection between us that I did. There was a definite shift back at the office during Mr. Cusack's visit. I hadn't imagined that look he gave me. And his grumpiness toward me lessened a while ago. I was having fun. *We* were having fun. That is, until a few moments ago.

Maybe I *am* a child because believing the grumpy doctor

could see past the surface of a rich damsel-in-distress is nothing more than a childish fairy tale.

I almost reach the bathroom door when a large hand grips my elbow.

"Wait," he commands, halting my progression. Whipping around, I intend to glower but falter when I face him.

Damn those long legs of his for catching up to me.

Damn that defined jaw that weakens my knees.

And damn those regret-coated eyes currently fixated on my lips.

Lips that very much want to taste that mouth of his again. I sense my anger dissolving. Not wanting to say anything I'll regret, like admitting what his touch does to me, I narrow my eyes into what I hope is a glare and step back.

He sighs and erases the gap between us, his woodsy scent enveloping us. "You took what I said the wrong way."

"Really? I think you made yourself pretty fucking clear tonight *and* Tuesday night."

"I didn't mean—"

"You know what I don't understand?" I press, not giving him time to respond. I'm in no mood to hear excuses. "I don't know how you can look at me one minute, as if I'm your next breath, and then push me away at the mere suggestion of us being together. Your Dr. Jekyll and Mr. Hyde routine is giving me whiplash. So, forgive me if I misunderstand whatever bullshit you're trying to peddle."

Liam's eyes close as a pained expression crinkles his features. His fingers tighten around my forearm with the right amount of pressure to show his dominating presence, yet gentle enough that it doesn't hurt. I hate the rush of heat that shoots straight to my core. This entire scenario shouldn't be a turn-on, but damn it, there's no denying how soaked my panties are right now.

Why does he have this effect on me?

His eyes reopen to the most profound jade I've seen in them yet. They grab hold and pin me to my spot. I barely breathe as desire flickers through his irises, only to be doused by the ever-present reasoning. I steel myself for the onslaught of excuses for not being with me, as if the mere thought is such a horrendous concept.

"What I like... my preferences..." He shakes his head, as if that would help clear his thoughts, but I don't understand what he's trying to say. Irritation flashes in his eyes as he growls, "You and I being together is a bad idea."

"Why?" I toss my free arm in the air. "What makes it so horrifying?"

His jaw tics. No matter how angry he may be, the confusion lies heavily in his hardened gaze. Laughter trickles into our bubble, snapping our attention back to the bar. Realizing we're about to be outed, Liam nudges my arm and drags me down the hallway until my back is flush against the wall between two unmarked doors. Shadows cascade around us, cocooning us into darkness. When the two girls enter the bathroom, Olivia and Jeanette come out. I hold my breath until they're out of sight before turning back to those eyes boring into me. I want to attack those lips and claim them as mine, but I'm still furious. We won't be attacking anything if he doesn't explain to me why we can't relieve this sexual tension between us.

"Why is the thought of being with me so horrible?" I ask again.

"I don't think being with you would be horrible."

"Then, what? Because something is preventing you. I know you feel whatever this pull is between us. It can't just be me. *What* is it?"

He slams his palms against the wall, caging me in. His body towers above me, chest heaving. His voice comes out low and gravelly as he says, "If we caved, it could never lead to anything."

Ouch.

Even though I know that to be true, I didn't expect the pang of hurt hitting my chest like a direct bullet. But regardless of what the future holds, there is something between us. I feel it down to my bones. I'll be damned if I walk away from here without exploring it.

"You know what I think?" I ask but don't give him time to respond. "I think you enjoy being miserable. I think you've spent years hiding behind interning and focusing on your practice, so you won't have to face reality. Because once you do, you'll realize how unhappy these past few years have been. And if there's anything I've come to realize in this short time of getting to know you it's this—Dr. Seymour doesn't like to waste time. And *that's* what sticks in your craw the most—all the wasted time spent with the wrong woman."

The entire bar fades to the background as his gaze bores into mine.

Holy shit. Did I just slam his entire past relationship?

My mouth opens, but before I can utter an apology, he rasps, "Damn it. I can't stay away from you."

The next thing I know, Liam's hold tightens, and he shoves us into a darkened room as the words, "I fucking want you," slice the air.

His lips slam against mine as he whirls my body around and backs me against the door. The temporary blindness heightens the overall sensation, making me *feel* everything, like the tiny shivers rippling along my skin from his hands gliding along my sides. Or the way his tongue sticks out just enough to caress my lips in a soft tease. And like a sex-deprived woman, my mouth parts, allowing the tease to continue. But once his tongue finds mine, it becomes a push and pull of strokes and supple pecks. He sucks in my bottom lip only to withdraw and return for more. His hand lands on my neck, fingers gripping my throat as his thumb caresses my jaw, and holy hell, I've never been so turned on. Even his growl is sexy. I weave my fingers through his hair and gently scratch his scalp, heightening his hold on me.

"Fuck, Evie. What would you do if I stuck my dick in that pussy of yours? Would I find you wet and ready? Do you want this as badly as I do?"

I gasp, alarmed by either his bluntness or the rush of heat shooting straight to my core—maybe both. His fingers tighten ever so slightly around my neck, and *God*, I am wet for him. So fucking wet that I ache. But I can't admit it out loud. Can I?

"Is that what you want? You want my dick thrusting inside so you can ride it?"

Yes, yes, God help me, I do. But his dirty talk has rendered me speechless, so all I do is nod.

Liam clicks his tongue. "Not good enough, City Girl. I need to hear you say the words. What is it you want?"

I swallow, heart racing. I've never had to be vocal before. When I finally had sex with my ex, he was so ready it wasn't even a question. Can I even be seductive? "I-I want your dick."

"Where?"

Where? Where does he think?

God, he's going to make me say it. We're in what I assume is the janitor's closet with my crotch rubbing against his hardened bulge, and he wants me to admit what I want.

Either Dr. Seymour wants unmistakable, full consent, or he truly is dominant.

"I'm waiting," he says between sucking and kissing along the crook of my neck.

"I want your dick inside my cunt." The words come out in a rush as my cheeks heat, but they must do the trick. He wastes no time shoving the hem of my skirt to my waist and ripping my underwear off. I startle for a second. I liked that pair, but he slips his finger inside my wet heat, and all attachment to the silky material dissipates. I groan as my hips chase his thrusting movement.

"Oh yeah, you're ready." His mouth covers mine as he gives a few more pumps before withdrawing his fingers. The loss of contact is instant and causes a whimper to escape my mouth. "Don't worry, sweetheart. I'll take care of you."

The unbuckling of his belt and the drag of his zipper fill the darkness. I'd give anything to see him right now. To see his expression. Why is it always dark when we do this? The next time, there will be light. *Next time?* It is a bit presumptuous of me, but this *will* happen again. When the sound of ripping cellophane cuts through my thoughts, my center clenches from anticipation. He notices.

"That's right, City Girl. You want this, don't you?" He wedges his knee between my legs. "Spread those thighs wide for me."

The deep baritone has me obeying his command. His hands grab my ass and lift me up. I wrap my legs around his waist, my arms clinging to his shoulders. "Guide it in."

Driven by urgency, I slide one hand between us until I reach his very hard, very thick cock. My tongue runs along my upper lip as I grab hold of his length and position the tip to my opening. I can't believe I'm doing this. If someone told me I would be having sex in a closet at a bar like some sex-starved undergrad, I would've laughed in their face. Hell, I'm still partially dressed. But here I am doing just that... and wanting to fuck the doctor more than I want my reputation preserved. What would the upper crest society think of me now?

I moan as he thrusts upward and fills me.

"You okay?"

"Yes."

His mouth crashes on mine, our tongues colliding. It's as if our bodies have become one, with him filling every part of me. I wrap my arms around his neck and lift, squeezing my legs tighter around his waist. We keep this delicious pace until a shiver of awareness ripples through me.

"That's it, City Girl. Come for me."

I don't know if it's his words, actions, or how everything seems enhanced by the darkness, but I topple over as my body convulses around him.

"Oh, fuck, Evie." Liam drives into me a few more pumps until his release spills into the condom. When he slows, he holds me for a moment, panting heavily. He doesn't say a word as he pulls out of me, and I fear the return of Dr. Grump. I don't think I'd survive him ignoring me again.

"Are you going back to being cold and pretending to hate me?" I ask. I feel his warmth back away, as if he's trying to stare at me.

"Fuck no." His palm lands between the apex of my thighs, and despite how satisfied he made me, another surge of heat races through me. "This belongs to me now. And you can damn well bank on the fact that I intend to play with it often."

CHAPTER TWENTY

LIAM

Bacon assaults my senses as I descend the stairs. *Bacon?* Surely not. It has to be that Smart Bacon she was giddy to find playing Jedi mind tricks with me. Evie doesn't cook meat. At least, I don't think she does. But as soon as I enter the kitchen, I'm proved wrong as the blond-haired beauty stands in front of the stove shielding herself from popping grease. I have to peel my eyes away from her ample curves. I do not want to pop a boner while wearing running shorts.

"You're frying bacon?"

She yelps at my question and whirls around, one hand splayed across her chest, the other wielding tongs as a weapon. My gaze dips to her full C-cup tits, barely contained in her lace camisole. My cock stirs to life, pressing against the spandex. This could pose a problem. I try hard to fight the memory of tracing my tongue around those perfect pink nipples and force my eyes to look at her face before I make it more awkward between us. My actions last night after we returned home were less than stellar. I take better care of the people I have sex with afterward, but I practically ditched her after promising I wouldn't. In my defense, had I touched her again, she would've ended up in my bed, and I can't let that happen. I need to establish parameters and not let my dick take charge.

"I didn't hear you come down." Her eyes roam my body with appreciation that has me shifting my weight. We need to discuss last night sooner rather than later. We *will* be doing that again.

"I was heading out for a run. I'm surprised you're frying bacon. Doesn't that bother you?"

She shrugs. "Not so much. I know how much of a carnivore you are. I made this diet choice for nutritional reasons rather than being an advocate for animals." She points the tongs toward the island. "Besides, I have my Smart Bacon. I figured I'd break any leftover tension with food."

The corners of my mouth lift. She's direct. I like that a lot. I suppose I didn't have to second-guess my actions. She doesn't seem upset. Although, she has every right to be after I planted a chaste kiss on her forehead and left her standing in the hallway. Before anything else happens, we need to discuss what this is between us and ensure we're on the same page. Casual sex is all I can offer. I sure as hell hope she's down for that. Besides, I still need to tell her about that cryptic email. Sex is tabled until we discuss everything. I caved back at the bar. I won't have another moment of weakness like that.

"Hey, yesterday, I received..." Flames erupt behind Evie. "Shit," I yell, lunging forward and shoving her out of the way. The last thing I need is for her hair to catch fire. I grab the tongs from her hand, use them to pick up the flaming dishtowel, and toss it in the sink. As I flip the gas burner off, the smoke alarm pierces our ears. Wasting no time turning on the overhead vent, I curse and then turn off the alarm.

My entire body relaxes at the fan's low hum. Panting, I glance at Evie, who stares at the blackened bacon with tears welling in her eyes.

"Did I ever tell you why it's so easy for me to subscribe to the vegan lifestyle?" she asks.

I shake my head but remain quiet, thinking the question is more rhetorical.

"It's because I'm a horrible cook. Vegetables and grains are way easier to manage."

I belt out a laugh. This girl.

"Come here." I pull her into me. She melts against my chest as I squeeze her. "It's a good thing I can take care of myself."

We both turn to the damage, and she lets out a defeated laugh.

"Yeah, you'd starve otherwise."

"Doubtful, but why don't we go out for breakfast after I get back from my run? I'll take you to The Red Barn."

Her eyes flash to mine. The devastation marring her gray-blue hues makes my chest tighten. "That sounds good." Her eyebrows pinch together. "What were you going to say before I tried burning down your house?"

I tuck a stray hair behind her ear as the pressing email flits through my mind. No way can I tell her now. She's too upset. "Nothing that can't wait."

The soft smile she gives makes me want to do something for her. This week has been challenging. She's basically at my mercy while relying on me for transportation. An idea occurs.

"What do you have planned today?"

"More job searches, I suppose."

"Why don't we do something?"

Her eyes widen as the fog lifts, revealing the brightness she wore before *firegate* broke out. I decide right then that I prefer that look rather than one of devastation.

"Okay. What do you have in mind?"

My lips twitch. "Have you ever been fishing?"

"Fishing? As in a pole with a hook and sinker?"

I chuckle. "The exact kind."

"Uh, no, I've never been."

"How'd you like to learn? The property has an acre and half pond located on it. It'd be fun."

Her lips flatten to a thin line before she forces a rather manic-looking smile. "Sure! That sounds fun."

"All right then." I'm surprised she agreed so quickly. I half expected her to protest. "We'll pick up the bait when we're in town."

"What do we use, worms?" she guesses.

"Nah, crickets."

Her face pales. "Crickets?"

"Yeah, they're best when fishing for bluegill and crappie."

"Uh, if you say so." She mumbles under her breath, "Whatever they are."

"Oh, this will be fun." I laugh and then smack her ass. "Go get changed into fishing wear, and we'll head to town after I return."

"Aye-aye, Captain."

I shake my head and take off, wondering what I signed myself up for.

CHAPTER TWENTY-ONE

EVIE

"Right through those shade trees is where we're going." Liam parks the Gator where a path starts and points to a small clearing at the bottom of the hill. A rocky path weaves through a mixture of large maple and red oak trees. The trail isn't long but opens to a sandy shore that overlooks a pond.

"This is gorgeous." I look back at Liam.

"It's our little slice of heaven, as Gramps used to say." He flashes me a toothy smile—one I wish I could return, but I can't—not entirely. The reason lies beside my feet, mindlessly chirping away and oblivious to their demise.

When Liam waltzed out of the bait shop earlier, my stomach recoiled at the container of crickets he held. I don't think it ever settled from the way it still churns. Admittedly, I expected the little critters to be dark black like the ones scattering on the front porch, but these are lighter brown, almost gray. I've never seen this variety before, but it doesn't change a thing. I don't relish the idea of jabbing a hook through either one to catch something I would never eat in the first place.

But I'm going to try.

That's for darn sure.

I need to prove that I fit in this little town, no matter how unclear my motives are for being here. Although, I don't understand why—it's not as if I plan on staying—but it's important that Liam sees past the expensive clothes and perfectly manicured nails to the real me. Name brands and clothing labels weren't something I sought, but they were always at my disposal. They don't define who I am as a person. I am worth more than the prepaid package my mother tries to sell.

"If you grab the bait and tackle box, I'll get the chairs and poles." Liam hops from the seat and heads to the rear of the Gator. A shiver skates down my spine as my gaze lands on the mesh basket full of sacrificial lambs. *Poor guys.* My stomach does another flip.

I may have bitten off more than I can chew by agreeing to come. I don't fish. I may be from the East Coast, but the closest I ever got to slimy creatures was when I visited the aquarium.

My mouth dips to a frown. Maybe I should have backed out when Liam came in from his run and took one look at my outfit. *Talk about embarrassing.* He looked at me as if I had lost my mind.

"That's what you're wearing?"

The surprise in Liam's voice had me glancing down at my Lululemon white short-sleeved shirt paired with pale green contour-fit shorts. What was wrong with what I wore?

"Yeah," I said defensively. *"I figured we'd need something casual. And this green was the closest thing I had to camouflage."*

"We don't need to hide from the fish." His lips twitched, as if he was stifling a laugh. He pointed to my top. *"But white? Your shirt will be ruined after the first cast. I'm sure you own darker casual wear."*

That puzzled me. How could casting a line result in soiled clothing? "We'll get dirty?"

Liam didn't hold his laugh that time. "Change into a darker color. Trust me. You'll thank me later." He stepped to me and brushed his fingers along my jawline before planting a chaste kiss. My body lit in flames from the slight brush of his lips. I could have thought of a million other things for us to do today rather than fish, but I wasn't about to back down from the challenge. And since we had yet to discuss what happened in that closet, I wasn't sure where we stood.

When he came from the shower and ran his gaze along my body, which wore a tight-fitted, dark burgundy T-shirt and black biker shorts, he nodded in approval.

"Ready?" Liam's deep voice chases the memory away, but the sparkle in his eyes sends my frown packing. The man genuinely cares about me. He proved that this morning when the first thing he commented on wasn't the bacon scent but rather the act of actual frying meat. As if going out of my way had touched him. Even in his grumpy-ass state, he seems to put me first. And that does something to me.

I shoot him a genuine smile. "As ready as I'm going to be."

We trek the gravel path to the clearing, the slight breeze at our back. Once we arrive at the sandy shore, Liam lays the fishing poles on the ground and snaps the chairs open. I take in the expanse of the pond, letting the clean countryside air fill my lungs. Woods serve as a backdrop. Reed grasses and other flora line the edges of the pond. I stand transfixed as birds caw in the background. A sense of peace descends upon me. Something I haven't felt in... forever.

I turn to face Liam. "It truly is a slice of heaven."

The corners of his mouth tug to a small smile as he positions the chairs to steady them, his sleeveless shirt revealing lean muscular arms. I try not to recall how those corded muscles picked me up as if I weighed nothing, but it's too late. My mind goes there.

It's official. I can never look at those arms innocently again.

They are and will always be associated with what we did in that closet.

And that reminder makes me squirm as the delicious ache that greeted me this morning grows, reminding me I didn't imagine the entire scene. The only problem is, I woke up alone— in my own bed. He said he wouldn't turn cold and basically claimed my pussy, but he was quiet on the drive home. Then, he went straight to his room, leaving me alone in the hallway, questioning what to do.

None of that seems to matter as my gaze traces along his biceps and shoulders. When I land on mossy green eyes that hold amusement, those sexy lips slant into a knowing smile, and my cheeks heat from being busted. Liam remains silent, stepping closer to me, separated by the tackle box and cricket basket I still hold. He redirects his gaze to the clear, green water and studies the landscape for a beat. I relish his closeness and watch as a sense of bliss transforms his expression, as if cherished memories grabbed hold.

"This is my favorite spot on the property. Gramps used to bring me here all the time."

"I can see why. It's so peaceful."

He turns back to me. I expect a candid agreement, but he remains speechless as inquisitive eyes lock on mine, holding unasked questions. I get the sense he's trying to figure me out and hasn't quite gotten there. Or he's trying to find what makes me tick—at least on a social level. He figured out my sexual preferences just fine.

I am not a complicated puzzle, at least I never thought I was, but maybe I am more of an enigma than I realized. I love the city and all things associated with it, but I can see the draw to this peaceful way of living. Simplicity holds an attractiveness I've never noticed before. Then again, isn't part of the appeal of living in the city the ability to hide? There's something to be said about hiding in plain sight. A skill I've mastered well.

The moment passes, and Liam takes the tackle box from me and places it by the chairs. He picks up a fishing pole and reaches for the poor innocent crickets. "I'll bait your line for you."

"Wait," I say, clutching the container closer to my chest. "I want to learn."

His eyebrows rise. "You do?"

No, not really. What I want is to go back inside and pick up where we left off in the closet, not kill innocent insects under the guise of bait.

"Yeah." I take a deep breath and force a smile, the *I can do this* mantra repeating in my head. "I want to get the full experience."

Something dark passes through his eyes as a smirk tugs his lips. "I think you got the full experience last night."

Heat coats my cheeks. I guess we're not ignoring last night after all.

He chuckles at my reaction and motions for us to sit in the lawn chairs. "Okay, City Girl, use your left hand to pick up a cricket by holding its back."

I scrunch my nose as I peer inside the pail because, *yuck.* This is so gross. Holding my breath, which I'm sure helps, I grab one. Another chuckle escapes Liam as he mimics my actions and grabs a cricket.

"Okay, there are several different ways to bait a cricket, but this is how I learned. Take your hook and poke it through the back to the neck like this."

I gasp at his demonstration. "Doesn't that hurt the poor thing?"

He shoots me a look. "It's a cricket."

"Still."

"You want me to do it?"

"No, I'm a big girl." I swallow hard and take a few breaths before whispering, "Sorry, big guy."

My hands shake as I draw the sacrificial lamb closer and run the hook underneath its shell. Something gooey squirts out and lands on my thigh. I yelp, shooting out of the chair like a rocket. The pole and cricket remains fly from my hand and smack Liam in the face.

"Shit." Liam jerks back, throwing the chair off balance. The lawn chair topples over, and he falls to the ground.

"Oh my God, I'm so sorry." I lurch toward him, but in my haste to make sure he's okay, the edge of my sandal catches the bucket's handle. Dozens of shaken-up crickets scatter everywhere. I scream to the heavens as I jump around, arms flailing like those stupid dancing tube men in front of car dealerships.

Scurrying to set the basket upright, Liam saves as many crickets as possible. "Calm down, City Girl. They won't hurt you."

Before I protest, he grabs hold of my waist and pulls me down. I land on top of him with a thud, his infectious laughter calming my nerves.

Laughing hard, I belt out, "Who the fuck calls this fun?"

"This isn't the part they reference." His lips curve into a soft smile. I take a stuttering breath as those golden flecks deepen and darken his eyes. His hands roam along my sides, but the bulge in his pants alerts me that I'm not the only one suddenly aroused.

The question is, what are we going to do about it?

CHAPTER TWENTY-TWO

LIAM

This girl.

Every day I'm around Evie, she gets more intriguing. How is that possible? She genuinely cares for people's well-being. That empathy proves she's Ciera's opposite. How I ever compared them before, I'll never know. They're nothing alike.

Fishing obviously isn't Evie's thing, yet she was determined to prove that it could be. That determination ignites something deep inside me, and with her perfectly curved body lying on top of me, it takes everything I have not to flip her over and take her right here and now. God knows I want to. Last night, I barely scratched the surface of what I wanted to do to her body. But taking her with that email hanging overhead would be wrong on so many levels, not to mention we still need to discuss terms. *And limits.* I need to correct this before I make any more moves.

I squeeze her hips slightly before patting that glorious ass of hers. "We better get up before the loose crickets decide to attack."

Her eyes widen, and she scurries off me without pause. I laugh at how she keeps eyeing the ground, as if the crickets are staging an ambush. I stand and dust off my shorts. Now, the fun begins.

I've never been more wrong.

A few explanations and one demonstration later, I find myself staring at the low-lying tree branch decorated with fishing line. I scrub the scruff on my jaw and wonder how she could hook a tree.

"You're kind of a disaster. You know that?"

"I am not." She smacks my arm in protest, her cheeks flaming red. But damn if that sheepish smile isn't infectious. She's freaking adorable. "What do we do now?"

"Cut it down and re-rig the line."

"There's a lot more to fishing than I thought." The small amount of defeat in her voice has me smiling. Not that I like her to be disappointed, but more because she genuinely wants to learn.

"Nah, it's a labor of love. It takes practice to become a professional."

"I don't want to be a pro. I just want to cast a line without looking like an idiot."

Our gazes meet. I swear there's a hint of vulnerability rarely ever seen, at least on her, and it hits me square in the chest. Her usual magnetic personality draws people in and makes them feel at ease. This self-doubt she exudes is foreign. I sure don't like it.

"You never look like an idiot." My voice comes out low and gruff, but my words do the trick as a sheepish smile crosses her face.

"That's because I can fake it with the best of them." She nudges my shoulder. "Okay, Mr. Pro Bassman, show me what you've got."

After I rig her pole and she practices casting a few times, she gets the hang of it.

"Now what?"

"Now, we watch the bobber. We tug the line and reel in the fish when it dips."

"That's it? We just sit here and wait?"

"That's it." I place my pole on the ground and take in the surroundings. There won't be a better time than now to tell her about the email. "Hey, do you—"

"Did you—"

We pause and then laugh.

"You go first," I say.

"Did you become a doctor because you wanted to follow in your dad's footsteps?"

"I suppose that was part of it. Dad never pressured me, though. In fact, he tried discouraging me from becoming one." I laugh lightheartedly, still remembering his words. "He told me becoming a doctor is a lifelong commitment, like marriage. And when I told him I wanted to move back and take over his practice, I figured he'd be thrilled."

"He wasn't?"

"I think he was to an extent, but he warned being a small-town doctor was different. More demanding of time. He said it was a gratifying job that came with a lot of sleepless nights. People love you. They hate you. But you find your footing some-where in between." I chuckle because he was right. I just didn't realize that it would end my marriage before I had a chance to walk down the aisle. I miss his words of wisdom and would give anything to have him guide me.

"Do you regret that choice?"

Not knowing if she meant becoming a doctor or moving back, I answer honestly. "No. Not at all. I like helping people. When my grandma, my father's mom, not the one who lived here, became ill, I felt so helpless. I knew if Dad couldn't help her, no one could, but I appreciated the medical staff. Something clicked inside me then, and I knew that's how I could pay people back."

"That's beautiful."

You're beautiful, I want to say but don't. Stating terms of endearment is definitely crossing a line, and I will not fall for a girl who isn't staying. I let out a deprecating grunt.

"What?"

I can't say what's on my mind, so I blurt out the first thing I think of, "Ciera sure didn't think so."

"I assume you two discussed your plans before asking her to marry, right?"

"We did." I sense my head nodding as the memories wash through me, but they don't hit as hard for some reason. "We discussed to great lengths what I envisioned—living in the farmhouse, having two point five kids. The whole package. I thought she was on board with all of it, but this lifestyle wasn't for her." Not only did she hate country living, but she didn't even want kids. I still question why I thought she would change her mind.

A beat of silence sits between us as we watch the bobber, the topic way heavier than I intended.

"Two point five kids, huh?" she asks, amusement lacing her tone.

"Eh, more like five to twelve, but I'd take whatever."

"Jesus," she sputters. "You want a large family, huh?"

"Yes. There are fifteen years between my sister and me. I always wondered what it would've been like to have those gap years filled with more siblings."

She smiles, but her stare seems off. Distant maybe.

"How about you? Did you ever think of having kids?" And now, I'm angling for more than fish, but I want her answer.

"I never considered having children."

My heart sinks, which confuses me. Why would it matter how many kids she does or doesn't want? It's irrelevant. Yet, that niggling feeling persists because, damn it, I do care.

"I do know this," she continues, "if I were to have any, I'd have more than one. I hated growing up as an only child."

"Hence the reason to have a few."

"You don't want a few. You want a basketball team."

"Yeah, that team would dominate. There wouldn't be any stopping the Seymour effect. We'd win all the games." I can't help but chuckle at her horrified look. "I'm joking. I'd be good with two or three mini mes." *Or any, at this point.*

"Lord help us if they turn out like you." She shakes her head in disbelief.

"Hey, I'm not so bad."

"Yeah, minus the grumpiness, you're not so bad." Her eyes shine, the edges softening the longer she stares. "You're actually a good guy. The town is lucky to have you as their doctor." She takes a stuttering breath and shifts her gaze back to the pond.

Despite her earlier dig at my character, I think she means it. My stomach churns. I need to be honest with her. The longer I don't mention the email, the more guilt builds.

"Yesterday, I received—"

"Oh, my bobber," she interrupts.

"Grab your pole and hook it," I yell as her bobber disappears beneath the water's surface.

She follows the directions and gives a good yank.

"Start reeling it in."

"Oh my goodness." The line moves back and forth, causing her to laugh.

"You've got this, City Girl. Reel it in nice and easy."

The fish flops in the water, but she manages to bring it to shore. We look at the hand-sized bluegill.

"What do we do now?" she asks, smiling big.

"We're just catching and releasing."

"Not to sound like a wimp, but I'm not taking this thing off."

I can't stop the grin plastering my face. "What happened to 'getting the full experience'?"

"I think I've gotten enough for the day."

"Let me have the pole. I'll take care of it." I chuckle. My gaze dips to her smiling face, and I no longer care about the mystery email. I want her too much, and I'm tired of holding back. This girl is all mine. Starting by getting rid of this fish.

"Yoo-hoo," a familiar feminine voice yells from above.

I groan and take the pole from Evie before turning toward Mom. She stands atop the hill with a casserole dish in her hands.

"I made lasagna for dinner."

Of course she did. This is Mom's polite way of finding out the gossip. "That's nice, Mom, but Evie is vegan."

"Oh, I know. Brenda told me. That's why I made this half without meat." She beams, and I don't have the heart to point out that it still contains cheese.

"Damn, small town," I grumble under my breath. "Thanks, Mom. That was nice. We'll be right up."

I turn to Evie and sigh. "I guess it's a good thing she cooked. I don't think the kitchen can stand another one of your cooking sessions."

"Hey." She whacks my arm playfully. "I've cooked just fine these past couple of years. *Barely.* As I said, vegan is way easier."

"Okay, then. I'll head back to the house and get this ready. You two come in when you're done," Mom says.

"We'll be right there. Take the Gator back. We'll walk." I glance down at Evie, holding in another sigh. "I guess you're about to meet my mom."

CHAPTER TWENTY-THREE

EVIE

"Why am I not surprised to find out you were valedictorian?"

Confidence exudes from Liam as my question looms in the air. His mom just left, and we're finishing tidying up the kitchen. His mom insisted on doing the bulk of the dishes, but when her tongue got loose with Little Liam stories, older Liam talked her into leaving, stressing how late it was getting. I'm surprised she complied. However, the twinkle her eyes held while her gaze ping-ponged between us gave away her thoughts.

"You met my friends. The competition wasn't fierce."

I mock gasp while Liam tosses his hands up in the air defensively.

"Not saying they're not smart—they are, especially Olivia—but no one from my class took schooling as seriously as me. I wanted to attend an Ivy League school, so I had to prove myself."

"They do seem more laid back than you." I wink to keep things light, but what I really want to do is circle back to the schooling comment. I'll have to do that later because something else has been gnawing at my gut since his mom mentioned the dedication ceremony. Evidently, his father was instrumental in getting funds for an inclusive park, and the town will hold a memorial for him during the festival. They want Liam to give a speech, but he is adamant about not doing it. It's hard to understand why. Public speaking makes him nervous—that was obvious back in Chicago—but that was in front of strangers. He only needs to talk with people he adores and loves. He should say something.

"This speech the town wants you to give... why won't you do it?"

He sighs and braces the kitchen counter, hanging his head. "Don't you start on me, too."

"I'm not. Or maybe I am. I don't know. I'm just trying to understand."

He pushes off the counter and crosses his arms over his chest. Tilting his head, his eyes narrow as he glares, irritation replacing the cocky look from earlier. "I just don't like speaking to crowds."

His words have a biting tone, so I retreat.

"Okay. Fine. I get it. It's a touchy subject. Consider it dropped." I place the towel on the counter and switch topics. "You wanted to get into an Ivy League school. Did that happen?"

"Yes, I went to Yale."

Yale?

"You went to school on the East Coast and still wanted to return to your hometown?"

His body stiffens, and I want to take back the words as soon as they leave my tongue, but it's too late. The words are out, festering like a thorn lodged beneath the skin. Not only did my question sound snobbish, but it was incredibly insulting. Who am I to judge? I live in the Midwest as well. And honestly, it's not at all bad. "Sorry, that came out wrong."

"No, I get it. Living here is a different lifestyle. But I like the laid-back atmosphere and ability to relax." He pauses and lets out a disgruntled laugh. "Most of the time. Everyone knowing your business isn't so fun."

"I didn't mean to pry." Guilt for bringing up the subject and ruining the otherwise pleasant evening tightens my gut. I hate mentioning issues that remind him about his ex and why she left. Having her on his mind is the last thing I want.

"It's fine." Liam nudges his chin toward the family room. "We may as well get comfortable if I'm delving into my past."

He tops our wine glasses, and I follow him to the couch. It's the first time we've sat in here together since the night he went down on me. However, we haven't had an opportunity. He's kept himself preoccupied every evening while I stayed tucked away in my bedroom or on the front porch admiring the stars. I believed this to be the norm. That is why last night was a surprise when he introduced me to his friends. And then later, he surprised me even more.

We settle into the cushions, and I take a sip of wine, studying him. He still seems on edge.

Take a few more drinks there, buddy. You could use them.

"When I did my residency in New York City, the patients came and went, and I didn't get to connect with any of them. The only history I had of them was on the computer. Working here, I get to know my patients on a personal level." He takes a sip and averts his gaze. "They're not a number or a nameless person on a chart. Knowing their history, I can deliver a more holistic approach."

"I get that." And I do. He has a great rapport with his patients. They all love and trust him, even Mr. Cusack. But that distance in his eyes makes me wonder if there is more to the story.

"That's what I was speaking about at the conference in Chicago." A pained expression crosses his face before he raises his gaze to mine. "I'm so sorry for how that went down. I still feel bad about my reaction. Not that this in any way excuses my behavior." He shakes his head. "No matter how much I accomplish and do, I can't shake those nerves when it comes to giving speeches."

"I take it you don't like being the center of attention?"

"Never. I only agreed to the gig because a colleague I became friends with during my residency put on the conference. He practically begged me to speak on the benefits of a holistic health and social care approach. I can't apologize enough for the fallout of my actions."

I wave my hand to shoo away his apology. "It doesn't matter. You did me a favor."

"What do you mean?"

"You know about my eviction, but had I kept the job, I still wouldn't have made rent. I was down to my last hundred bucks."

"Damn, now I feel like a bigger ass. Do you still owe rent?"

"No, my landlord was cool. Not cool enough to let me live rent-free, but he said he'd call it even if I left that weekend. I still can't believe it. I thought I'd be able to find a job right after graduation, you know?"

His jaw twitches, and I swear another pang of guilt coats his features. But what would he have to feel guilty about? It's not his fault I'm not hirable.

"About that. Have you had any luck setting up more interviews?"

My shoulders slump. I've spent all week applying to places and haven't gotten a single confirmation. "I can't believe how hard it is to get an interview. At least before, I could set them up, but now it seems like I'm invisible. Not one company has responded to me."

"I think someone is sabotaging you."

My head snaps toward him. "Why would you say that?"

"I received a rather interesting email. I'm not sure if it's a direct threat, but they basically offered to pay me off to fire you."

"What?" Alarm laces my tone, but this explains so much. *And confirms my fear.* Mom denied interfering when I asked her. Sure, she could've been lying, but she acted so offended by my suggestion that I believe her. She isn't that good of an actress. But could it be... "Who sent the email?"

"The company's name is BSC Group. Does that sound familiar?"

"No. That isn't one of my parent's companies unless it's a subsidiary I haven't heard of." I take another sip, the wine suddenly bitter on my tongue. Coldness sweeps through my body like a gust of wind before an impending storm. One person comes to mind, and my body revolts at the thought. Surely not. He wouldn't. Would he? I keep my voice steady as I ask, "What exactly did the email say?"

"Here, I'll pull it up." Liam whips his phone out of his back pocket and wades through the sea of emails. Seemingly satisfied, he hands me the phone.

"I have to get to the bottom of this." My fingers shake as my voice comes out weak, but the words weren't intended to be heard. An unsettling feeling stirs my stomach as I read through the passive-aggressive email. This isn't the work from my mother or father. This level of threat and wording has Jonathan's stench all over it. Tears prick my eyes when I finish. I glance up to face Liam.

"Are you okay?"

"Yes, it just feels like an invasion of privacy." That's not a lie. I feel violated.

"That's because it is. Do me a favor. Set up a new email address and use it for applying to jobs. Make sure it doesn't correlate with your heritage," he says.

"You think they've hacked into my email?"

"It's a good possibility."

I think back to all the problems I've accrued these past few months. I used the school's email with the companies who confirmed, but after graduation, the school initiated a new policy and stopped supporting the graduate school's email address. I had to email every company and update my contact information to include my previous email addy—the one Jonathan knew. If he had hacked into my email, he would've had access to every scheduled interview, including the last one that canceled. The one where she said it was very lucrative to meet me. I had no idea what she meant at the time. Now, I'm wondering if she received a payout too. My stomach lurches.

"I think you're right. I'll try a different email and see if that helps."

Liam gives me a weak smile. "Any clue as to who the culprit could be?"

"No," I lie. I can't talk about Jonathan right now. I don't ever want to talk about him. He's someone I'd rather forget.

"You don't think it's your parents?"

"Mom denied interfering when I suspected her, and I don't think my dad would be that threatening." My eyes shift to his. "Do I need to quit? What if they come after you?"

I search Liam's eyes for answers. It sounds like he's working toward a goal, and they're holding whatever happened back in New York over his head.

He places his glass on the coffee table and pulls me toward him. "Don't worry about me. I'll be okay."

"Seriously, I can look for another job. After I pick my car up on Monday, I can look for something in that elusive town forty-five minutes away."

Liam's laughter breaks my tension, and I snuggle deeper into his embrace. "Are you kidding me? You're the best office manager I've had. No way am I letting you go."

Even though he said the words in jest, they hit too close to my heart. I don't want him to mean them, though. I'm not sure if I could handle it if he did. After a beat of silence, I switch topics again.

"Your mom seems great. It was nice of her to make a vegan lasagna."

The corners of his mouth lift to a warm smile. "She liked you."

"Yeah?"

"Yeah, I could tell."

"Because she was nice to me?" Nice doesn't even cover it. The lady went out of her way to make a special lasagna. She even topped it with cashew mozzarella. Who does that for someone they've never met?

"No, because she told me."

This draws me up short. I lean back and look at Liam. "She did?"

"Yes. Her exact words were, "I like this one, Liam. You'd be wise to keep her.""

"*Keep me?* Am I a pet?" I laugh, but it dies off as his eyes darken.

"Only if you want to be."

Jesus.

I wouldn't know what to do, but his husky voice and heady stare make me want to drop to the floor. Heat shoots straight to my core, my thighs clenching at that thought.

Fuck.

I very much like the idea—not the pet part, but offering myself to him.

Liam tilts his head and studies my face. "Does the thought of getting on all fours for me turn you on?"

My mouth parts, but no words escape. I hate being transparent, but I'm too turned on to care. I nod, my body buzzing with excitement and anticipation.

Liam's fingers clamp on my jaw as his gaze dips to my mouth. "We should set parameters."

Yes! Like safe words and stuff.

"Mmhmm," I practically purr. *Purr.* Like a freaking cat.

Oh my God, I *am* a pet.

His lips graze the crook of my neck. "I want us on the same page."

"What do you mean? You want a safe word in case the pet play gets out of hand?"

"*What?*" He backs away, brows furrowed.

Uh, did I read him wrong? "A safe word. I never did anything kinky like pretending to be an animal."

He chokes as humor dances in his eyes. "I'm not into pet play. Wait, are you?"

"No." I wave my hand, as if he's being silly. Because I'm not. I just like the idea of being on my knees for him, pleasing him. I'm not quite sure where this comes from, but it's something I definitely want to explore. "I didn't know what you meant by setting parameters."

"I just meant I can't offer anything long term."

"Oh." My cheeks heat. Yeah, I should've realized that. But who can think straight? It's impossible with his lips brushing against me.

"Is that okay? If we continue this route, we have to leave feelings off the table." His other hand slides up my inner thigh, sending shivers down my spine. My nipples tighten against the silky fabric of my bra. His eyes are practically jade as he stares at me.

I nod. "I'm not looking for anything permanent. I'll be leaving soon. It's just sex." I suck my bottom lip in a fraction, repeating the *it's just sex* thought in my mind. That isn't a lie. I don't expect this to be anything more than casual sex.

"God, you have the perfect set of lips." Then, he shoves his thumb inside my mouth, causing me to suck it. "I want to fuck this pretty mouth of yours, but that will have to wait. I need to taste you again first."

His lips replace his thumb, and the moment sweeps me away. This is really happening.

I turn so my body is more aligned with his and weave my fingers through his hair. I want this. I want more. Last night was just a taste of how we could be together, and right now, I want the entire course.

As his lips massage mine, I set out to explore, running my hands along those defined shoulders and biceps. His fingers dig into the back of my skull as he deepens the kiss. I palm along his pecs, the taut muscles hardening beneath my touch.

Another purring sound escapes as the ache between my legs grows.

He pulls away, and a whimper escapes my mouth from the lack of touch. We sit there panting, his stare bold, as if he is assessing what he wants to do to me. My body alights with desire, but the pensive expression burrowed in the lines between his brows makes me wonder if he's holding back. What did he say when we had dinner that first night? He has particular preferences and likes to be in charge. Yeah, that's it. Every fiber in me wants to know about those desires.

"When we first talked, you told me you had certain preferences."

His breath hitches. "I don't expect you to comply."

Disappointment like I have never felt sweeps through me. I don't understand where this need to please him comes from. I've never had this strong desire before, but I don't want to miss anything with him. Not now.

"Explain what you like."

He tilts his head and studies me, as if contemplating whether or not to tell me. "I don't know..."

"Please." I clasp his shirt.

He still eyes me warily, but I see the moment he caves. "Everyone has different likes, but what I prefer is referred to as a bedroom submissive."

My already tightened nipples press tighter against my bra as another surge of heat shoots through. Why is that so freaking appealing?

He must read my expression because his shoulders relax. "For instance, I like bondage. Nothing hardcore, just blindfolds and handcuffs. I'm not into impact play other than an occasional swat to the ass."

I squirm in my seat, wanting this pressure between my legs released.

His fingers work small circles on my thighs as he continues. "But here is where I lose most people. I want you kneeling in front of me, ready for orders."

Jesus, take the wheel.

I remain speechless, absorbing everything he's saying. My wanting-to-please side kicks into overdrive, where the feministic side wants to reject the idea on principle. No matter my preconceived notions, there is no denying the wetness between my legs. Don't I deserve to see where this leads? To explore something that my body responds with such fervor?

He takes a deep breath, never breaking eye contact. "This *scenario* may not be ideal for most, but I assure you, when Master is pleased, the reward is tenfold. But as I said, we don't have to engage in that type of play."

The idea of not trying feels as if someone took my shiny new toy away. I very much want to do this. "I want to try."

His eyes search mine. When he sees what he wants, he says, "You have to communicate honestly with me. We could use the standard safe words: green, yellow, and red. Red tells me to stop, but say yellow whenever things get to be too much and you need to pause and regroup. Do you understand?"

"Yes."

He raises his chin, his facial expression hardening. "While in this scene, you will address me as sir."

Holy hell. I'm actually agreeing to this.

"Do you understand?"

"Yes, sir."

A small smile ghosts his lips, which pleases me beyond my imagination. "We'll take it easy tonight."

"Okay." I realize my mistake the moment his eyes darken. "I mean, yes, sir."

"Stand in front of me."

I comply, and he swipes my shorts and underwear off in one sweep. I step out of the crumpled clothes, and he stares at my center, as if he has just discovered the world's seventh wonder. A delicious growl escapes his mouth.

"Get on your knees."

CHAPTER TWENTY-FOUR

EVIE

I gape upward at Liam, not used to someone being so commanding during sex. It's safe to say my sex life has been so vanilla that I could be vanilla Pudding Pops's spokesperson.

Thwack.

Heat splinters my ass cheek and shoots straight to my toes.

To. My. Freaking. Toes.

I drop to a kneeling position, eagerly waiting for what comes next.

"Don't look at me. I want your eyes trained on the floor with your hands behind your back."

Excitement lurches through me as I comply. I would've thought being in this position would make me feel intimidated and vulnerable, but it doesn't. Instead, this sense of wanting to please him feels gratifying. What does that say about me? From the way my body hums with eagerness, I don't think I care.

"When we enter into this type of play, this is the position I want to find you. Is this something you can do?"

I nod as he shifts, tracing his fingers along my chin. He takes in a pleasurable breath, as if satisfied by my eagerness.

"So obedient. Now, be a good girl, and turn around and spread those legs for me. I want to see your pretty pink pussy from behind."

I shudder from the harshness of his words. Who knew I liked dirty talk? Or better yet, who knew I wanted to be commanded? Jonathan never talked during sex. He also never got me off with just a stroke of his tongue. He barely got me off at all. I spent far too many nights feeling unsatisfied. I have a feeling that won't happen with Liam. But I also never made myself this vulnerable before.

Liam kneels on the floor behind me, and his hand connects with my ass again, but this time he follows it by running a palm over the area to soothe the sting.

"I said to spread them." He nudges a knee between my thighs as I comply.

Not sure of his intentions, I glance over my shoulder at him.

"Look forward," he commands.

My fingers dig into the rug as apprehension sweeps through me. What am I even doing?

"Relax, City Girl." He flips onto his back and pulls my hips down. Once his mouth meets my center, all worries slip away—the threatening email, the vulnerable position I'm currently in, and the fact that I like my ass smacked. None of it matters. Why? Because this guy knows how to work his way around a woman's most intimate parts.

Maybe I should be embarrassed about having my backside exposed with him underneath me, but I'm not. Liam is too good. There's nothing dirty or shameful about this. I feel like a freaking shrine he cherishes. And every moan he emits as he drags his tongue along my cunt serves to amplify those feelings. I swear he enjoys this as much as I do, which says a lot considering he's pretty damn addictive. But when he plunges a finger inside and draws my clit into his mouth, I come hard and fast without warning. His other hand digs into my skin as I ride his face. He releases his hold and scoots from underneath me as I come down from the high. Panting, I turn to look over my shoulder. He's sitting on his haunches staring at my center with such adoration and heat that I can't help but whimper.

"You should see how good you look right now with your glistening heat waiting for my cock." He leans to where he hovers over me. We're not touching, but I feel him everywhere. With his mouth against my ear, he asks, "Is that what you want? You want my cock?"

Tingles race across my skin. I just had a mind-blowing orgasm. How can I want more? But here I am on my knees, legs spread, and practically begging to be fucked.

He grabs my hair again and tugs until my back slams against his chest, his words demanding. "Do you?"

"Yes," I cry out.

He tugs slightly harder. "Not good enough."

"Yes, sir."

"Lean on the couch." Never letting go of my hair, he guides me to where I face away from him and pushes my upper body into the cushions—not forcefully, but commanding all the same. He wedges his knees between my legs and spreads them farther apart. I want to whimper when his hands leave my body, but the sound of his zipper causes a satisfying surge. The same anticipation I felt whenever I got ice cream. Like I'm about to get a prize.

After donning the condom, he places his hands on my hips and plunges into me in one swift movement. I yelp from the surprise, followed by another whimper. My entire body is overcome with sensation. No matter how good everything feels, I want more.

"Can you take it?" he practically growls beside my ear.

My "yes, sir" comes out more tortured than I meant it to be, but he shocked me with how quick and dominating he took me. It was almost as if he had claimed me. No complaints here. His dick feels fantastic deep-seated inside me.

"Good. Because you feel too fucking good to stop."

"Don't stop," I manage to say.

Then, he moves. And oh God, does he move. The next moments become a rhythmic bliss of withdrawing and thrusting. My hands grip the couch cushions, and this need for him to claim me runs strong. I don't know where it comes from. I've never felt this way during sex before. I could get addicted to it. To him. That thought is scary because I don't know which is worse: the fact that this arrangement is temporary or that I don't want it to be.

His thrusts increase not only in speed but intensity too. It's as if he has a point to prove. He had warned that he liked it rough. I wasn't sure what to expect, but this far exceeds my expectations.

"Be a good girl and rub your clit."

I look over my shoulder and drink him in. His mouth hangs slightly open. Lines of concentration etch between his brows as the golden flecks of his irises glow with savage fire. Goosebumps prick along my skin as his touch burns into my flesh.

He practically barks, "Look forward."

A sting lights my ass, but the escaped whimper is more from not understanding why he doesn't want me looking at him. I face the cushions again, wondering if it's a dominant thing, like his way of maintaining control. I don't ponder the reasons long because what he's doing to me feels good. So good that I'm close to tipping over again.

"I said rub your clit for me."

That dirty mouth of his.

This time, I obey and slip my fingers down my stomach. A shiver races through me once I reach my clit.

"Yes, that's it. Now, rub."

I rub in a circular motion against the swollen bundle of

nerves. Sensations shoot across every nerve, causing my back to arch and my taut nipples to brush along the cushions.

"God, you look so damn sexy."

"I don't think I can last much longer." I'm working on sensory overload.

"Hang on a little longer." He repositions himself to where he lays on my back, shifting the angle inside. It feels deeper and fuller, as if he fills every compartment my body offers. Holy crap, this position is a game-changer.

"Yes, right there. Don't ever stop," I say through my pants, my stomach tightening.

He brings his mouth to my shoulder and presses open-mouthed kisses along my skin as his hands dig into my hips. I'll probably have tiny bruises splayed across each hip, but I don't care. This feels too incredible. He pumps faster, and my world bursts in a downpour of fiery explosions. I scream his name so loud I fear the neighbor miles down the road can hear. He doesn't seem to mind as I convulse around his dick and ride my orgasm. He thrusts one final time before collapsing onto my back. With our sweaty bodies intermingling, I smile, not caring if he ruined me for all the other men. Because, holy crap, the few one-night stands I've had were nothing in comparison.

"That was amazing," I say, panting.

"Mmhmm, agreed. You're so damn addictive." He playfully slaps my ass before dropping another kiss on my shoulder. "Be still. I'll go get a towel to clean up."

When he comes back, I stay quiet as he washes my backside. My thoughts race laps in my mind. I'm not sure where we go from here. He's still my boss. Still Ansley's brother. Still temporary.

We get dressed, and I follow him up the stairs. When we reach the hallway, he turns and pulls me into a hug.

"Was that too much for you?" His voice is pensive as he asks.

I shake my head. "No, I liked it." Which is the truth. There isn't any use lying to him or me. He gave me just enough commands along with praise to satisfy my needs. He plants a chaste kiss.

"Thanks," he murmurs against my lips. Then, he exits into his room, leaving me alone in the hallway, dazed and confused.

It's just sex.

Isn't that what I said? He can't offer anything long term, and I'll be leaving soon. That's the arrangement. But then, why does his walking away make me feel unsettled? I stare until the door closes behind him, and a thought occurs.

I still haven't seen him naked.

CHAPTER TWENTY-FIVE

EVIE

"You missed your plane again." Mom's voice rings in my ear as I stand outside Matthew's building, my gaze drifting to the cloudless sky. I mentally count to five. Losing my temper with my mom won't work to my advantage, but for crying out loud. When will she get it through her head that I'm not coming home? Not now. Not ever.

"Mom, you need to come to terms with the fact that I'm not coming home. You should donate the amount you're spending on tickets. There are way better causes for that money." It is the second wasted ticket she's purchased.

"I don't understand why you're wasting your time in that small town. There isn't anything there for you."

"You wouldn't understand," I mumble. Any explanation would be futile. Mom can't comprehend the need to accomplish things independently or fathom wanting to help people tackle the issues they face. Take, for instance, Mr. Cusack. He was trying but failing at a simple domestic chore like cooking supper. After a few phone calls, he now has a program that delivers nightly meals. He would've never gotten that done on his own. This particular instance may not be my dream to help underprivileged children access healthcare, but it's still helping. I still get gratification from making a difference.

"You're right. I don't understand why you won't come home and get married. You need to take your rightful place."

I bite back the insult on the tip of my tongue because the last thing I want is to discredit her life. She chose to be a hood ornament and is perfectly content with that choice. I respect that. I just wish she would show me the same respect.

"Despite what you think, I actually like it here."

She scoffs, as if I never said anything. "Jonathan came to the house yesterday, asking about your return. He'd take you back if you apologized."

I suck in a breath. Mom never brings up Jonathan. She knows our breakup was ugly. She can't honestly believe mentioning him would lure me back. His name alone makes me want to run farther away.

"I have nothing to apologize for," I say through gritted teeth. "I can't believe you'd suggest such a thing." Frustrated, I kick a small pebble and watch it skid across the parking lot and onto the sidewalk. My stomach churns. It's bad enough that my relationship with my parents is strained, but to suggest I get back together with my ex—the very one who hurt me—is incomprehensible. What is she thinking?

She has me so riled that I back up and stumble when I hit something hard. Not something but someone. I whip around to apologize, but the guy just grunts. He pulls his baseball cap lower over his unruly hair and pivots away. *Weird.*

I pull my focus off the stranger and shift to the more pressing matter. "Mom, I'm going to ask one more time. Did you interfere with my interviews?"

She lets out an exasperated gasp. "I told you, no. As tempting as it sounds, I wouldn't do that."

"Do you think Daddy did?"

"He's many things, but he wouldn't stoop to that level."

I almost laugh. I'm pretty sure Dad would indeed stoop to that level. He has done some despicable things in the name of "business." I take a deep breath and ask, "Have you heard of the group BSC?"

"Hmm, I believe that's one of Jonathan's subsidiary companies. Why do you ask, dear?"

"I read a news article about our hometown that mentioned the business," I lie. I'm not diving into the truth. The last thing I need is Mom to run and tell Jonathan I'm onto him.

"See, even fate is pushing you home."

"Doubtful."

"You need to come back soon. Your father isn't feeling well."

"Why, what's going on?" Instant guilt pricks my skin and gnaws at my conscience. I don't want anything to be wrong with Daddy. We may disagree on what I'm doing with my life and the direction I want to take, but he's still my dad.

"It's his chest. The doctor isn't overly concerned but wants him to slow down. You know your father."

Yes, of course. Dad's motto is business above everything else —including family, health, and *me*. God, I don't want that lifestyle. But as much as I feel torn between not dropping everything and checking on him myself, I can't help but feel skeptical. There's a small part of me that doesn't trust her. She'd say anything to get me to come home. I'd feel horrible if there was any truth to her words. I'd feel even worse if something happened to my dad.

The will I've spent the last four years holding on to so tightly starts to resolve, and I feel myself caving. Pinching the bridge of my nose, I say, "I'll see what I can do."

"I'll book you another flight for tomorrow."

"No, Mom. I'll book it myself. I'll come home when I can. I

have commitments to attend to first." *Like setting up job interviews that no one from back home will learn about.* The last thing I want to do is blow my chance at freedom. Besides, Mom sounds a bit too anxious, which makes me doubt her even more.

"Geneva Madeline Thornhill, you can't possibly like it there."

"I'm not sure how you formed this opinion, but this town isn't a bad place to live."

"In the middle of nowhere surrounded by those mediocre people?" Disbelief oozes from every syllable.

"Yes, as I said, I *like* it here. The people are genuinely nice." I need to end this conversation and get my car before I tell her what I actually think about the people back home. "I have to go, but I'll let you know when I can come to visit."

"Make it sooner rather than later." She hangs up instead of saying goodbye like a normal person.

I clutch the phone tighter and let out an aggravated sigh. Who is she to judge the people living here? I've witnessed countless people going out of their way to help each other. You don't find that in Mother's inner circle. They've made stabbing you in the back an art form. Living here isn't bad at all. It's actually nice. I pause. The truth behind those words hit me like a sledgehammer.

"Aren't parents' fun?"

I start and spin to face Olivia. Caught off guard, I take a few breaths to gather my wits. She's beautiful in a marigold pantsuit outfit with her long dark hair tucked into a bun. She looks powerful and a little intimidating.

"Yeah. They're a real blast."

"I take it they want you to move back home?"

I can't tell if it's genuine concern in her question or hopefulness. She warmed up to me back at the bar, but there was still an edge of wariness. It's as if she hasn't made up her mind whether to like me or not. Or maybe she's being friendly for Liam's sake. I don't know why she bothers. It's not as if we're an actual couple.

"Ever since I left for college, Mom's plan for me was to marry rich." She has been trying since I hit puberty, but I won't open that can of worms.

"You're certainly not going to find Mr. Moneybags in Sugar Creek Falls." Her tone is defensive, challenging almost. "Not the kind of money you're used to."

"Good thing I'm not looking for one, then."

That almost earns me a smile.

"I couldn't help but overhear that you're still interviewing?" It's more of a statement than a question.

"Yes," I answer slowly.

"Does Liam know this?"

I study her for a moment. She's good at hiding her emotions, but I see the defensiveness in her eyes when she says Liam's name.

"Yes, but I don't see why that's your concern."

"Liam's been my friend for a long time. All he wanted was to become a doctor, settle down, and raise a family." She crosses her arms over her chest and shakes her head, her features darkening. "Not that he wants anyone from this town, but I sat by and watched one city girl destroy him. And while I'm not surprised he picked up a stray, I won't sit by quietly while another transient girl tries to hurt him again."

I cringe at her words. They slice through me. Although, I don't understand why they cut so deep. I knew Liam was crushed when his fiancée left, but hearing he was devastated makes it ten times worse.

Her insinuating that I'm a stray ticks me off. I am not a helpless animal. Well, for the most part. I did need shelter and food. The nurturing was a bonus. And she's right. Our time comes with an expiration date, but we're adults. We know what we're doing.

"I have no intentions of hurting Liam."

"Then, I suggest not getting involved with him."

My eyes narrow. What I thought was concern over a friend seems deeper. More personal. "What we do or don't do isn't your concern."

"Liam is always my concern."

And there it is, a slight crack in Olivia's Teflon armor. Why hadn't I seen it before?

"You like him."

Her eyes grow wide. "Of course I do. Liam's a lifelong friend."

"No, I mean you *like* like him."

She blinks and turns her head away. "You don't know what you're talking about."

But I think I do, and she doesn't want to admit it. I don't press her. It's irrelevant what happens anyway. "You know I'm not staying. After I leave—"

"I've known Liam for over thirty years, and aside from high school dances, he never dated anyone from town. Trust me, there's nothing there between us. Not once has he looked at me the way he looks at you. Heck. He didn't even look at Ciera that way, and he put a ring on her finger. There will never be anything between us. I know my worth." Our gazes connect, and her chin rises defiantly. "The guy I'll spend the rest of my life with will know it too. Otherwise, I'm better off being single."

There is a story behind her statement, but I don't pry. It's not my place. But she's wrong about a special look toward me. If he has anything in his eyes, it's lust. That was made abundantly clear last night. And I'm okay with that, *I think*. I doubt she knows the true reason he never dated anyone from town. My insides heat at being privy to such an intimate detail.

"Everything okay out here?" Matthew's question carries across the parking lot.

Olivia is the first to break our staring contest as she turns toward a fast-approaching Matthew.

"Everything's great. Thanks again for the oil change. See you on the fourth." She walks over to a red Mini Cooper and hops inside. Matthew and I stand there, watching until she backs away.

"She's very protective of Liam." He shrugs. "Has been ever since grade school."

Yeah, because she is hung up on him. I flash him a smile, refusing to show how affected I am by her. "I get that. Liam's lucky to have such loyal friends."

"I've got your car ready to go." He takes off toward the shop's entrance with me by his side. "Are you ready for the party?"

"Party?"

His head tilts with a questioning look. "Yeah, the Fourth of July party. Liam hasn't mentioned it?"

"No, not yet."

"It must've slipped his mind." He walks behind the counter and grabs my invoice and keys. "The bill comes to five-hundred and eighty-seven dollar and thirty-five cents."

My brows furrow. "Is that all?" I came fully prepared to negotiate payment terms as the original estimate was in the thousands, but I have enough to cover most of the bill from my one paycheck. My eyes rise to Matthew's. He shifts on his feet.

"Yeah, I, uh, used aftermarket parts. It cut the price way down."

"I thought we were waiting on parts from the factory?"

"The aftermarket factory," he quips.

"Oh." I lay three hundred dollars on the counter. "Well, I can cover the rest after the next paycheck, then."

"I trust you."

A sense of pride washes through me. As flippant and careless as I've been with money in the past, it does something to me to have someone trust me enough to give me credit. I swallow past the lump in my throat. "Thank you."

"You're welcome. Don't forget about the fourth. We have a potluck and cap the night with a firework show." He winks as he hands me the keys. I think Mr. Tillman is a huge flirt.

"Let me get this straight. It's a bunch of drunk guys shooting off fireworks?"

"Sounds about right," he says through a laugh.

"I can't think of a better time." *That is, if I'm even invited.* Liam has yet to mention going. But what can be better than spending an entire evening with a scorned, unrequited love friend? Lord help me.

CHAPTER TWENTY-SIX

EVIE

"Is something wrong with the internet?" I'm sitting on the porch swing, trying to pull up my email, but my phone won't connect. I need to check for responses to my applications. I'm most excited about a job with the Marion County Health Department. If things go well, I can visit Ansley while I interview. It's been a week since I picked up my car, and I've yet to drive it anywhere.

"I forgot to tell you I changed the password."

"You did?"

"I thought over what you said, and you're right. It's past time. The new code is Firegate 1." He sits beside me and tosses an arm over my shoulders. I curl my legs up and snuggle against him. "Any particular reason for that?"

The corners of his mouth lift. "See, this master chef almost burned down my kitchen."

I punch his side playfully. He starts chuckling and holds me tighter.

"But now you'll have a reminder of me."

He plays with the strands of my hair as he casually asks, "That's a bad thing, why?"

Because I'm not staying.

I redirect my attention back to the night sky and the blanket of stars that somehow seem comforting. "I guess it's not."

Liam's mood has been more playful this past week, and I'm here for it. He hasn't shut me out. It's been the opposite. We're inseparable between working together and living under the same roof. And we have sex. Lots of sex. I think we've christened every room in the house but the bedrooms. Everything is great except for two things: I still haven't seen him naked and we never sleep together.

It's just sex.

That reminder is why I can't put energy into things like him changing his Wi-Fi password or wanting me to snuggle against him.

Or when I introduced him to the many different ways of cooking tofu. I figured his ex-fiancée had shown him, but he said he never had any interest before. I didn't know how to take that statement.

And I certainly can't read too much into the most noticeable change—him dropping Geneva for Evie. *Finally.*

It's strictly physical. Nothing more.

And yet, I'm curious.

"I've never asked, but why did you start calling me Evie?"

His sigh cuts through the still night. He sounds weary, as if the explanation is exhausting. "I tried hard to keep it platonic between us. I figured I'd stand a better chance if I didn't get personal." He squeezes me tighter. "I was wrong. You're too irresistible."

Thump, thump. There goes my heart.

Whatever you do, Evie, do not fall hard for this guy.

It's just sex.

I don't respond and continue to stare at the twinkling stars. "I love the night sky out here. You could get lost in it."

"The stillness makes it easy to disconnect from the world. I needed this after that last year in the city."

I wait for him to elaborate, but he never does. Instead, we sit in comfortable silence while the sway of the swing lulls us into peaceful bliss. After some time, I pull up the settings on my phone.

"I better change the password and check my email. I'm waiting to hear back from the Marion County Health Department." When I saw the job opening at one of their branches in Indianapolis, I wasted no time filling out the application.

He remains quiet while I punch in the code. Once I connect to his Wi-Fi, I open the new email address and gasp. "Oh my God, I got an interview."

The hand playing with my hair falters before he says, "That's great. When is it?"

"It's for this Friday, but don't worry. I won't have to leave. It's a phone interview, and let's see..." I scan the rest of the information. "Okay, it looks like I'll have to conduct an in-person interview if I get a callback," I respond accordingly and turn to face Liam. Those mossy green eyes bore into mine. Although he wears the same smile as me, I feel off. It will be hard to leave if I get the job. But this is my dream job. It's exactly what I want to do. Shouldn't I be more excited? I shake off the unease. Of course this is what I want. It's just late, and I'm tired. We had a busy day.

"Before I forget, my friends have a get-together every Fourth of July. We've done this since high school. I haven't been to one since my residency, so I'll be going. I wanted to warn you ahead of time."

I don't mention Matthew had told me when I picked up the car. But I'm confused. Is he telling me because he won't be around or because he wants me to go? "I'm sure I can find something to keep me busy."

"What? No, I meant we'll go together. That is, if you want."

"Oh. Okay."

"Sorry, I wasn't clear. You don't have to go."

"No, that sounds like a good time. Are we supposed to bring something to eat?"

"I'll take care of that, but you may want to pack something specifically for you. I'm not sure what food choices you'll have."

"Sounds good." I lean back into him and smile. This, whatever it is we're doing, may be temporary, but it feels very real. As real as the peacefulness of sitting under the star-filled sky. City lights or starry nights? It's getting harder to distinguish which one shines more.

CHAPTER TWENTY-SEVEN

EVIE

"Happy Fourth!" Ansley's enthusiasm rings through the phone and makes me smile even though festive doesn't quite cover my mood. Cheers erupt from Ethan making his third bag in the cornhole game, decimating Liam's pathetic attempt at playing. I hold the phone closer to my ear and step from the crowd, walking toward the backyard. We're at Daniel's and Jeanette's farm, and the area is massive.

"You should be here instead of celebrating by yourself." I think about tossing my half-eaten apple but hang on to it as I enter a fenced gate into what I guess is a chicken coup. They must be resting for the night in the barn because all I see is a doghouse. I lean against the fence and focus on the pasture behind the red barn. It's picture-perfect, with grazing cows and the sun dipping in the west.

"I wouldn't be by myself if you came to visit."

"Better watch what you wish for because I'll be there the second week of August."

"Wait, what?" Scuffling sounds crackle in my ear, as if she's sitting up. "Are you serious?"

"Yes, I got a second job interview."

"Hell, yeah. We can be roomies again when you land the job."

"Let's not get ahead of ourselves. You know my track record."

"Eventually, something has to give. Positive vibes, girl."

"Yeah, I do have a better feeling this time." I haven't told Ansley about Jonathan's interference. That's too long of a story to tell over text or a phone call. My confidence improved after learning it wasn't entirely my fault for not landing the initial interviews.

"Have you told my brother yet?"

I hesitate, swallowing past the lump in my throat. It's not as if I wanted to withhold information. I just wasn't sure how best to approach the topic. We've gotten close these past few weeks, and I've broken down some of his walls. I've yet to knock out the last layer that surrounds him like an armored tank. Even when we have sex, he still guards himself. He won't let me look at him. We've fucked plenty of times, and I've yet to see the guy fully naked.

And that bothers me for some reason.

Hence the reason I'm in a sour mood. The moment I think there is more between us, he acts insensitively, especially after we fuck, which is how I should refer to it. What we do is undoubtedly not lovemaking.

He must be pining after his ex-fiancée more than I realized. He is on the rebound, after all. But considering I've known men with food in the refrigerator lasting longer than their grieving period, I figured he'd be over her by now. It's been just shy of six months.

"Not yet. Your brother knows I had an initial interview, but I haven't told him about the call back yet." A rustling sound piques my interest, but I don't turn to look. I'm inside this pen, safe and sound.

"Don't worry about him. He'll find someone to replace you."

Replace me.

I don't like the way that sounds. I don't want to be replaced.

"I'm not worried—" I yelp from the peck at my hand as dark feathers catch my peripheral. My phone flies out of my hand. The bird charges at me again. I do the only thing I can at that moment and scream.

"Hey, hey. Back away." Matthew claps his hands, making all sorts of weird noises. "He's after your apple."

Once Matthew's words register, I toss the half-eaten apple at the monster and hit the thing in the head.

"Shit." Matthew starts laughing and picks up the fruit. "Here you go, buddy." He turns to me. "Get out of the pin. I'll lure him to his house.

Matthew leads the turkey to the doghouse, which must serve as a turkey house, while Liam and the rest race up to me.

"Are you okay?" Liam asks, his gaze roaming my body, as if he's assessing for damage. He grabs my hand and exams it, but the bird's beak mainly got the apple.

"I'm fine. He scared me more than anything. I didn't realize that was a turkey pen."

"You have to watch where you're going, City Girl," Olivia snickers, but the sparkle in her eyes lets me know she's kidding.

"Mommy, Tom Tom attack the city girl!"

Everyone starts laughing at Daniel's and Jeanette's three-year-old son. "She's fine, honey. That's why we tell you to stay in the yard, not the pens." She shoots me a knowing look.

I suddenly feel like a scolded toddler.

"Why were you out here?" Liam asks, concern still coating his features.

"I was talking to your sister." I pat my ass, as if I had stuck it inside my dress's nonexistent pockets and glance over at the pen. Matthew stands there with my phone next to his ear. A hint of regret flashes across his expression before he reels it in. He scratches the back of his head and rests his hand on his neck a beat, looking at the phone.

"Everything okay there, Matthew?" Liam hollers.

His head snaps up, and he walks over to us. "Yeah, I told Ansley what happened. Tried convincing her to come back."

"Yeah, I wish she'd visit more. If I knew the asshole who hurt her, I'd beat his ass."

Matthew's back straightens.

Hmm. Interesting.

"Did I overhear you say you have an interview?" Matthew asks.

I cringe. So much for telling Liam on my own time.

Liam's head snaps toward me. "You got the follow-up interview?"

"Yeah, I was going to tell you later tonight. It's not until the second week of August."

His face is stoic, and I wish I could read his expression.

"Good luck. I'm sure you'll be glad not to work for this grump," Matthew says jokingly.

I laugh, but my heart isn't in it. "He hasn't been too bad." My gaze slides back to Liam's. He stands there emotionless, as if knowing my absence won't affect him.

It's just sex.

I repeat my earlier statement to gain clarity. It's silly of me to expect anything different. Besides, the sex is phenomenal. Who am I to complain?

It's just sex—really, really good sex.

"Okay, City Girl, enough of these men monopolizing your time. Come hang with us." Jeanette threads her arm through mine and tugs me away. I glance over my shoulder at Liam. He still stands there with that damn stoic expression. *Okay, then.*

CITY LIGHTS STARRY NIGHTS   193

"What's this I hear about you leaving?" Jeanette asks when we're away from the men.

"I have an interview next month in Indianapolis."

"Are you sure you can't stay in town? We need you."

This time, my laugh is more genuine. "What do you mean? I haven't done much since arriving in town."

"You keep Liam happy. That's not a small task."

"I'm not sure about that."

"He's been in a funk ever since Miss Highfalutin left. These past few weeks, Liam has seemed happier. Plus, I like you."

"It's nothing serious." I glance over at the man in question. Warmth spreads through me the moment our gazes connect. Is that what I want? I shouldn't let my mind entertain those thoughts, and yet... Maybe his stoic expression is because he doesn't want me to go. No, that can't possibly be true. I pull my gaze back to Olivia, who meets mine with a smirk.

"Uh-huh. Nothing serious."

"It isn't," I insist, but I can't help but laugh.

"Sure, that's why he paid for your car parts," Jeanette says with a snort.

"What?" I rear back. I know the rumors in this town take off like wildfire, but I hadn't expected my car to make the rounds. "I paid for the parts."

"Well, sure. Matthew said you paid for part of it, but Liam covered the majority. He's generous, but he wouldn't have done that if he didn't like you." She winks as if I should be grateful. I'm anything but.

Olivia's gaze ping-pongs between us. "You seriously didn't know?"

"No, I had no clue he did that for me."

"I'm sure he thought he was helping." Olivia tries to reassure me, but she's sharp. She senses something's off.

I fake a smile when I feel anything but joyous. I feel crushed.

I thought I was doing something on my own without help. That was a lie, just like everything else in my life. Will I ever be able to take care of myself?

I glance over at Liam. I don't give him a flirtatious look when I catch his eye. I don't give him any kind of look. I just give him the same courtesy he shows me.

CHAPTER TWENTY-EIGHT

LIAM

"When are you going to spill the beans about Evie?" Ethan asks when the girls are out of earshot.

"What's there to tell?" I ask, eyebrows drawn together. Seriously, what is this? Why are my friends so obsessed with my love life?

"You're obviously getting some. You've been a hell of a lot happier," Matthew chimes in.

"We're in our thirties. The days of kiss and tell are way over."

"Here's to that," Daniel says, clinking our bottles together.

"You're just sticking up for him because Jeanette would have your balls in a vice if you talked about your sex life," Ethan says through a laugh.

"That's no shit." Daniel mock shudders. My shoulders shake with laughter, despite being the brunt of their joke.

"Are you going to be good if she gets that job?" Matthew asks, his tone more serious.

I shrug, as if it's no big deal, and take a draw of my beer. No way will I admit learning about her second interview threw me for a loop. I'm not sure I like the idea of her leaving, but there's nothing I can do about it. She can't accomplish the things she wants to achieve by staying here. I learned that lesson. I got the heartbreak to prove it. However, I haven't thought much about Ciera these past few weeks. A different woman has my attention. One that looks damn good in her flowing sundress that shows off those luscious curves and sun-kissed skin.

The thought of Evie is like a magnetic pull drawing my gaze across the yard. I can't seem to help myself. There's nothing wrong with checking on her. I'm only doing a well check. What if the girls are mistreating her? As if on cue, the girls' laughter drifts over to us. That sound, along with the genuine smile Evie sports, relaxes me. Heck, even Olivia boasts a rare smirk.

The slight breeze blows her blond locks from her face. She's so beautiful. But it's more than that. It's the way she makes everyone around her feel better about themselves. I go to turn away, but her shoulder strap slips, revealing the fleshy side of her breast. I bite back a groan. The exposed skin shouldn't distract me, but I find myself wanting nothing more than to peel the dress off and suck those breasts. Sex between us has been phenomenal, despite the barrier I've created. She will leave eventually, so to keep from getting involved emotionally, I never have her look at me. When we have sex, it's either in complete darkness or some variation of doggy style. I don't want to cross that line.

Evie tilts her head back in laughter and glances this way. When her eyes meet mine, I give her a devilish smile. As if reading my mind, she gives me that sexy look she gets before we have sex. I wish the sun would set already so we could get the fireworks over with. I'm ready to have her all to myself.

"Sure, tell me again that you want her to leave," Matthew says, snapping my attention back to them.

"Okay, I admit it. I don't want her to go. That still doesn't change the fact that she will." That sentiment only strengthened after receiving another threatening email from whoever wants her back. She obviously can't stay here.

"Give our man a break, Matthew. He's having fun without the worry of getting cat scratch fever," Ethan says, his lips twitching.

"You got a cat?" Daniel asks. We all know Matthew's distrust of cats after trying to tame a feral calico cat back when we were fourteen.

"No." Matthew shoots Ethan a glare.

"Why are you worried about cat scratch fever?" I ask, intrigued.

"Show him," Ethan goads.

"I'm not showing them." Matthew shakes his head. "It's not that big of a deal."

"What are you hiding? Is it something I should look at?"

"No. I'm fine."

"Just show him," Ethan repeats.

"Maybe I should look. Your lymph nodes do seem swollen." I'm messing with him, but it's worth it. I almost lose it when his eyes widen.

"Seriously?" Matthew lifts his shirt as he twists to reveal his back. "Do they look okay?"

We gape at the claw marks marring his back for a beat before bursting out in laughter.

"What did you do?" Daniel asks.

Ethan laughs harder while Matthew gives him another glare.

"You may as well tell us." I wave to his back. "We're already thinking the worst."

"I went to The Pump House the other night and may have tied on a few too many. Well, Katrina was there, and we started doing shots."

We groan.

"Stop. You voluntarily talked to Katrina?" Daniel asked.

Katrina and Matthew have dated on and off. They are as compatible as oil and water. The choices around here are limiting unless you're willing to drive over forty-five minutes. That's another reason I had no desire to date until I met Evie.

And once again, my eyes stray to her. But instead of the intriguing gray eyes staring back at me, they look confused. And a little angry. Why is she upset? I scan the girls' faces, but they don't seem to be giving her a hard time. Evie doesn't look upset with them. She seems upset with *me*. What did I do? I move to go over and see what upset her when my phone pings with a text. I glance at the screen and cringe. It's as if my earlier thought summoned the devil.

Ciera: We need to talk.

Since there isn't anything I need to say to her, I ignore the text and glance back at Evie. Her smile seems forced, but she looks okay otherwise. I settle back in my seat and finish listening to Matthew's story.

"So, after we returned to her house, our drunk asses didn't make it to her bedroom. We started banging on the floor. As soon as I slid into her, the damn cat jumped from the shadows and landed squarely on my back. I popped up so fast that the cat clung for dear life. Damn, those claws hurt. I never deflated so fast in my life."

The guys roll with laughter from Matthew's story, but my mind is on Evie and what we're doing. Matthew is content to stick with one-night stands, but I'm not. I'm over the single life. I don't want freak accidents that make great stories. I want the entire picture: the wife, the kids, and the fucking white picket fence. But I don't want it with just anyone.

My gaze strays back to the blond with mesmerizing gunmetal

eyes. I want her. And not for just the night. I want her every night. *Damn it.* I don't want her to leave.

No matter what the earlier email I received threatened, I don't want to lose her. I'll tell her tomorrow about the email, but not tonight. Tonight is about us.

And as I hold her during the firework display, all I can think about is getting her back home and showing her exactly what I want. I don't notice how stiff she feels in my arms. With my mind trying to come to terms with letting her go, I miss how quiet she's been. All I can think about is how crushed I will be when she leaves.

I wouldn't dare hold her back from pursuing her dream, but Jesus, I don't want her to go. Even the fact that she doesn't want kids—something I've always pictured—can't shut down my feelings.

After the last rocket shoots across the sky, I whisper in her ear, "Let's go home."

She nods, and I can't get us there fast enough.

CHAPTER TWENTY-NINE

EVIE

I'm not sure when the shift came, but something about Liam changed. I felt it when he held me during the fireworks. He didn't hide that we are together, which is something I thought he'd do. But that doesn't negate the fact he lied to me.

Driving home from the party, I bite the inside of my cheek and contemplate if I should say anything. I don't want to start a fight, but I can't let this go.

"Before I forget, I wanted to warn you to be careful. The guys were talking about some strange stranger lurking in town. We think he's either with the construction crew or maybe scoping the area out for the festival. We get a lot of foot traffic leading up to the festival, so I doubt he's anything to worry about, but Matthew saw him loitering by his building."

I nod, acknowledging his warning. I wonder briefly if it was the guy I bumped into, but the man seemed harmless. Besides, how would I know who is a stranger in this town or not? There are more pressing issues to address.

"Speaking of the garage, did you pay for my car repairs?" I study Liam intently, half-expecting him to lie.

His sigh cuts through the heaviness. "Did Matthew tell you?"

"No, Jeanette."

"Matthew has a big mouth."

"I think the bigger question is, why didn't you tell me?"

"I didn't want you to find out."

Well, he's undoubtedly telling the truth.

"That's not a good enough reason. Why would you do that?"

"He was going to put junkyard parts on to save money, but I told him not to."

"You didn't even know me then. Why would you care?"

"Because you're my sister's friend. I didn't want inferior parts on your car. Who's to say those parts wouldn't break down the following month."

I bite back my frustration because I see his point. He was looking out for my well-being. But I don't want to be reasonable right now. I wanted to do something on my own. "That still should've been my choice."

"You deserve the best."

"The best." I scoff. I've had nothing but the best my entire life. "I drove an Audie before selling it off and buying this. It wouldn't hurt me to get knocked down a few times."

He pulls into his driveway and kills the engine. That muscular jaw tics. Turning to face me, he practically growls, "You need to quit seeing yourself as a spoiled rich kid. You're *nothing* like that. I offered to help before I knew you because that's who I am. It had nothing to do with pity. I just wanted you safe. I could never forgive myself if anything happened to you."

"While I appreciate your concern, people always place after-market products on their vehicles. I am not your pet project." I exit the truck as anger flashes in his eyes. This night took a drastic turn from where I thought it would go, and maybe I'm irrational, but I can't help it. I'm so mad. He stalks around the truck toward me.

"I don't think of you as a pet project," he spits out, hands clenching as a shiver of anger ripples through him. He steps closer, erasing the gap between us, standing tall and straight like a towering spruce. His voice lowers to a rumble. "Those weren't aftermarket parts. They were from a junkyard—a slight difference—but don't think for one second that you're not my concern. Whether you want to admit it or not, I care about you. A lot."

My chest heaves, but there is no denying the lurch of excitement zinging me. He cares about me. Isn't that what I wanted? I'm just disappointed that I didn't get to take care of myself. But taking caring for myself doesn't mean I have to do everything alone. I can ask for help. There wasn't any way I could pay for those parts. It wasn't fiscally possible.

"I'm paying you back. Every dime."

"Fine."

"Fine." My heart jolts, and my pulse pounds. His unwavering gaze bores into mine in silent expectation as the air charges with electricity. This argument sounds silly, and I wonder why I'm fighting the pull. Maybe I'm itching for a fight. If we argue, I won't have to face that I like it here. That I like him. I want to make it on my own, but I also don't want to leave him. Does he feel the same?

His eyes slam shut, and I swear I feel the moment his will crumbles.

"Fuck, I can't resist you." He picks me up, and I wrap my legs around his waist as his mouth crashes onto mine. The kiss isn't rushed, but it's demanding as he strokes, teases, and claims.

I drink in the silent assertions of his kiss as he kicks open the door to his house and carries me to his bedroom. Once we reach his bed, I unwrap my legs and set my feet on the ground.

I go to kneel but stop when he says, "Don't move."

He traces a finger up my thighs, dragging the hem of my dress along with them. Inch by inch, he raises the dress until it's up and over my head. He backs away, leaving me in nothing but my bra and underwear. Appreciation coats his features as he unbuttons his shirt, but he never takes his eyes off mine. I lick my lips as my nerves tingle in anticipation. When he unbuttons his shorts, I think my heart explodes. He never lets me watch. He never allows me to see him naked. When the shorts drop to the floor with the underwear following next, I have to fight to keep from gasping. I've felt how large he is, but damn, what a visual. My mouth parts, wanting to devour him, but he's in charge.

"You're so beautiful." He closes the distance and reclaims my mouth while his fingers work to release my bra. It falls to the ground along with the other articles of clothing. He runs his thumb along the underside of my breast while maintaining a slow, sensual kiss. He takes his time, as if committing every piece of me to memory. I go exploring myself. If he's allowing me this luxury, then I'm taking full advantage. His body quivers beneath my touch as I run my palms along his peaks and valleys.

"I want you in every single way," he rasps.

Unsure what he means by this, I remain quiet, other than the slight moans his touch elicits. He backs me up and lays me on the bed. Wrapping his fingers around my waistline, he places his lips on my stomach and presses soft kisses. I hardly notice when he slides my underwear off.

"Spread those thighs for me."

"I love it when you tell me what to do, sir," I admit. My confession causes a low groan to rumble from him.

"God, you don't even know how sexy you are."

He dons a condom and hovers over me. That earlier shift between us returns in full vengeance. I'm afraid to breathe, fearing the slightest breath will scare this moment away. I don't want this to end. Lying naked on his bed with him on top of me is more than I can ask for.

He lowers his mouth to mine, giving me one last kiss before

his lips sear a path down my neck to my shoulders. His mouth dips to suck a nipple as he palms my breast.

"I've been wanting to do this all night," he says, tracing his tongue over the hardened peak. He takes his time exploring before moving to the other side. My body hums with desire, beyond ready for him.

"I need you," I moan when he bites down lightly.

He lines his cock against my opening and holds my stare, the scent of our arousal in the air. We've had a ton of sex, but never like this. This time is different. When his eyes don't stray from mine as he plunges inside me, I know we're no longer fucking as friends. This is so much more. The problem is, I don't know where we go from here.

With his mouth partially open, intense emotion pours through his unwavering stare. I'm transfixed by the overflowing satisfaction swirling through me. The feeling holds until he pushes me to the brink, and my muscles contract around him. He thrusts a few more times, chasing his orgasm until he collapses beside me. I lazily run my fingers along the length of his back, contentment pouring from me.

When his breath catches up, he says, "I'll be right back."

He moves to take care of the condom, but as he enters the bathroom, his phone buzzes on the nightstand. Curious about who would text this late, I eye the door and strain to hear if he is coming out. When I think it's clear, I snoop and look at his lock screen. The current euphoria I am in crashes to the floor.

> Ciera: Fine, I understand you're busy. We can wait until tomorrow, but it's important. Talk to you then.

Wait, what does she mean by understanding he's busy? Had he talked to her tonight and didn't say anything to me?

I lie back down and stare at his ceiling, unsure what to think.

Was everything I thought and felt a figment of my imagination? Am I fooling myself? Maybe Olivia is right. He wants to settle down with a wife and kids, but it won't be with anyone around here, *including* me. I scramble off the bed and grab my bra and underwear as the bathroom door swings open.

"What are you doing?" He stands there naked, his glorious dick at half-mast. His body is too distracting. Unable to concentrate with him standing there looking so divine, I divert my eyes toward the hallway.

"I was going back to my bedroom." No way am I admitting I snooped.

He looks alarmed. "Is that what you want?"

"No." *Damn it*. Why did I admit that? Because I'm a fool. A lovesick fool who doesn't know any different.

"Good, because I don't want that either." Liam stalks over to me and takes the garments from my hands. "I wasn't done with you." Setting me back on the edge of the bed, he drops to his knees. "Spread those pretty thighs for me again."

Jesus, I'm weak. But if I'm going to obey, I may as well enjoy the trip into Submissionville. Who knew being obedient would lead to multiple orgasms? This girl sure never did. As he drags his tongue along my sex, I get lost in the moment. I'll deal with the fallout of a broken heart tomorrow.

CHAPTER THIRTY

LIAM

The next morning, I find myself wrapped around a curvy blond. I smile into Evie's back while my cock presses between her thighs.

"Sorry, but someone's glad to see you this morning," I say as she stirs awake. I do the decent thing and back my hips away but almost stop when a small whimper escapes her mouth.

She flips to face me, causing hair to fall across her face. I tuck the loose strands behind her ear and rest my hand on her shoulder. She closes her eyes, and I drink in her peaceful serenity. Does she realize what she does to me?

"I didn't mean to fall asleep here," she says sleepily.

"It's okay. I like waking up with you." *It's something I could get used to.*

Her eyes open, slate grays matching my green ones. "I didn't think you wanted me in your bed."

She's not wrong. I tried to keep this thing between us about sex, but I let my guard down last night. I crossed the imaginary line I drew for myself, but the reason for the line is hard to remember with her lying naked in my bed. "It turns out I do."

"What brought on the change?"

You.

"I got tired of fighting the pull." Before I do something irreparable, like confessing that I don't want her to leave, I turn away and reach for my phone to check the time. I wince at the missed text. Why is Ciera blowing up my phone?

"What's wrong?"

"Nothing important." It isn't a complete lie, but discussing my ex is the last thing I want to do with Evie in my bed. I need my morning run and a fifth of vodka to deal with her. I lean over and kiss Evie's forehead. "I do need to tell you about the email I received. I wanted to tell you earlier, but things escalated between us."

The tiny crease between her eyes she gets whenever she's thinking hard appears. "You received another one from the BSC Group?"

"Yep. The tone was more threatening this time."

Her face pales. "What did it say?"

I pull it up and let her read it.

From: BSC Group
To: Dr. Seymour

Dr. Seymour,

Since the previous email went unanswered, we assume you mistakenly overlooked our generosity. Don't worry. We'll give you one last opportunity to make the right choice and take us up on our offer. Kickstarting your campaign with this more than generous offer is your best option. We would hate for the townsfolk to discover the force driving your passion. From what we've been told, Sugar Creek Falls is a small community. The hit your practice would take if patients lost confidence in your ability to serve them would be catastrophic to your career.

We look forward to hearing your response.

The BSC Group.

She places the phone down and looks at me. "The responses are getting less passive aggressive. They obviously think they have something on you."

I close my eyes momentarily and shake my head. "That's because they do. It happened while I worked in the emergency room."

"Back in New York?"

"Yeah. The hospital board placed me under investigation for failure to treat a patient in accordance with the hospital's standards of care."

She flinches, but it's more from confusion. "But you're an excellent doctor from what I can tell."

"Thanks, but I'm far from perfect." I blow out a long breath, gearing myself up for this conversation. I haven't talked about this with anyone, not even Ciera. I was in too dark of a place after it happened and closed off. She never pressed.

I guess heavy topics aren't off the table this morning. I lie on my back and stare up at the ceiling. "We were two-thirds into a shift when a teenage female came in under duress. A quick assessment showed she was in labor. We contacted the obstetrician on call since the patient had no prenatal care, but the doctor was performing a C-section. We didn't have time to wait. The patient was dilated to ten centimeters and one hundred percent effaced. We had to move quickly."

I take a deep breath, trying to calm my racing heart. I hate reliving this night, although I've replayed it multiple times in my mind. My voice comes across as flat and unemotional as I tell the story. It's the same tone I had to use to save myself. The lawyer told me countless times not to show any regret or remorse. He feared any type of compassion would ascertain guilt. So, per his request, I became a mechanical robot, pretending nothing could touch me. No matter how strong I appeared, I cowered on the inside. That's the thing about guilt. It doesn't care who you are.

"Once we hooked the monitors up, she had a contraction, and the baby was in distress. With no time to spare, we prepped for a vaginal birth. When it came time to push, the baby had a type B nuchal cord. The umbilical cord was wrapped too tightly; I couldn't get it loose. And his color—Christ, his color was so cyanotic. I quickly clamped and cut the cord before delivering the baby's shoulders. The theory is to prevent the cord from tearing away from the placenta, but it didn't help. The baby was born with hypoxic-ischemic encephalopathy. Both the mom and baby were severely anemic. The family ended up suing. With no previous history and due to the lack of prenatal care, they settled out of court. The board cleared me, but that case still haunts me today. I keep wondering if the outcome would've been different had I done something different. So far, the baby has hit all his milestones. Hopefully, he won't suffer any long-term consequences." I won't disclose how I know that information, considering my friend back in the city could get fired for violating the HIPAA Privacy Rule.

Evie's eyes soften as she weaves her fingers through mine. "It sounds like you did everything in your power."

"Yeah, that's what the panel decided." I squeeze her fingers, surprised by the calm her touch brings. "That's why I want to open a prenatal facility where people can get proper healthcare. I would like different providers to volunteer their specialties."

"That sounds perfect. Would you open one in Sugar Creek Falls?"

I hesitate. "It would be great to have one in this small town, but it's not plausible. More people would benefit if we set it up in Terre Haute. I've found space and applied for some grants. There's also federal funding available through a new program. But it will take a lot of money to get this going."

"I like the idea."

"Yeah, well, I haven't told too many people, aside from the grant writers. I don't know how this BSC Group found out. They must think their threats have weight."

"Don't they?"

"We do live in a rural area. I will have to deliver a baby from time to time. But it wouldn't ruin my practice."

Those gray irises darken with remorse. "I'm sorry. I feel like this is my fault."

"Your fault?"

"Well, yeah. My past wouldn't be threatening your plans if I hadn't come here."

I bring her hand up to my lips and kiss it. "If you hadn't come, then I wouldn't have known the best thing to arrive in Sugar Creek Falls."

Pink coats her cheeks, but she still looks pained.

"Don't worry about this email. People who send vague threats through the internet don't follow through. They're like keyboard warriors, hiding behind a screen. It would be nice knowing who the prick is, though."

"He's an ex-boyfriend." A single tear falls down her cheek. "Jonathan Blackwall-Smith the Third."

God, even his name sounds like a pretentious prick. It makes sense why he is pushing hard for her to return home. My stomach roils. I can't imagine what she's thinking right now. With our hands molded together, I take my free hand and run my fingertips along her forearm.

"I take it he wants you back," I state rather than ask. Of course he wants her back. Who wouldn't? I'm struggling with letting her go myself.

"He doesn't want me because of some undying love. He wants the merger my dad promised him. By marrying me, he'd get everything he wants."

"Are you for real?"

"Unfortunately. Our breakup wasn't the easiest. I had him to contend with, and I had to convince my parents."

"So, your parents loved him?"

"I wouldn't jump to love, but they saw him as an acquisition."

I'm unsure what she means, so I continue tracing small figure eights along her smooth skin until she elaborates.

"Jonathan is heir to his daddy's windmill company. Since my father's business is in the oil fields, you can imagine Jonathan's vision of collaborating with renewable energy. It was a match made in corporate heaven." She scoffs. "Our parents have been pushing us together since we were kids. And I didn't mind at the time. Jonathan was the typical good-looking, rich kid that everyone looked up to in school. He had it all: looks, charisma, money, and a wandering dick."

I know exactly where she's going with this story, but I don't interrupt. I have a feeling she's held this in for far too long.

"We dated all through junior high and high school, until I caught him his senior year with the head cheerleader behind the bleachers."

"That's rough."

"I wish that were the end of it, but no. It gets worse." A shiver works through her body, and I stop myself from tensing. But if that asshole hurt her...

"My parents were livid when they found out that I broke up

with him. When I explained my reasonings to Mom, she told me that's how it is with rich men. They have their pieces on the side, and as long as he had those women, I wouldn't have to do anything I didn't want."

My eyebrows rise to the ceiling because what the fuck? Who tells their high school daughter that?

"Yeah, what the fuck, indeed."

I clamp my mouth shut, not realizing I said that out loud.

"I told her what I wanted was not to date Jonathan. And boy, oh boy, he didn't take to being dumped too well. I never could decide if it was due to his bruised ego or the fact that he wouldn't inherit Daddy's company, but he wouldn't leave me alone."

She swallows and closes her eyes. Her breathing ticks up a notch. I fight the urge to hunt this fucker down.

"He came over late one night after my parents left for one of their many charity dinners. With the house staff retired for the night, I decided to go for a swim, unaware of an impending storm. The sky opened, and I raced to get out of the pool. Instead of darting to the house, I ducked into the pool house. That's one move I regret to this day. I would've been behind locked doors had I just gone inside. It wasn't long before I realized I wasn't alone. Thunder cracked overhead as Jonathan grabbed my neck and threw me against the wall. I was helpless against his strength. He'd been drinking. I could smell the gin on his breath. He told me I was his and I wouldn't ruin his plan. Lightning flashed around us, and his eyes..." She squeezes her eyes shut and takes a shaky breath. "The look in his eyes was menacing. It wasn't lust, and it certainly wasn't love. It was just pure evil."

"Did he—"

"No. I kneed the bastard in the balls, which released his fingers from my neck. I tried to run away, but he grabbed my left ankle. I fell to the ground and tried to scramble away, but I wasn't a match. He pinned himself over me and told me he could do whatever he wanted with me."

Oh, God. I practically did the same thing when I made her submit to me. Not once had she ever seemed like she didn't like it. Not once.

"I get rough during sex. If I had known..." I can't finish that sentence, but I would never have acted domineering.

"Don't," she's quick to add, "that's the twisted part. I like it when you demand things from me in bed. I get off on your commands."

My dick jumps to life at those words. *Down boy. This is not the time.* "That explains your hatred for storms."

"It puts me back in that vulnerable spot."

"How'd you escape?"

She bites her lips and closes her eyes again.

"Evie, how'd you escape?"

"He could tell I wasn't put off by having him control me. It's not that I wanted him, but"—she turns her head away—"I'm not proud."

"So, you..." I let my question hang because what she admitted was heavy. And I'm not sure I could stomach hearing she allowed him to touch her.

"The second he let his guard down, I grabbed the nearest object, which happened to be a vase that got knocked over from our struggle, and smashed it on his head. Then, I ran inside the house and locked the doors."

"Did your parents press charges?"

She scoffs. "They were more upset over the broken vase and their busted business deal."

"What?" Who are these awful people? And how did this caring, bundle of sunshine come from them?

"As I said, they still want us to get together. Business before family and all that."

"Jesus. No wonder you wanted out."

"I made the right choice."

Damn, she has been through a lot. After hearing how everyone dictates her life, I couldn't ask her to stay, no matter how badly I want her here. It wouldn't be fair.

But I don't want her to go.

Why do I keep going back to that thought? Maybe because it's true and I can't tell her. There are too many factors preventing us from being together. She doesn't want kids and likes living in the city—the opposite of what I want. I won't make someone stay with me ever again, but I want to do something for her. She deserves a good time before she leaves and one good date to remember me. "I want to take you out to eat before you leave."

"To the Wagon Wheel?"

"No, a nicer place. I thought about Stables in Terre Haute."

"Hmm, the elusive city. What does one wear to such an establishment?"

"Whatever one wants."

"Seriously."

"Casual. It's a nice steakhouse, but there isn't a dress code."

She places her hand on her chest in a mock surprise. "You mean to tell me the carnivore picked a steakhouse?"

"Shit, you're right." How could I be so insensitive? "I could look and see if there's a vegan restaurant."

She flips to her side and places a finger on my lips. "Hush. It'll be fine. I'm sure they'll have something I can eat."

I glance down at her. This woman takes things in stride, where Ciera would've flown off the handle. Evie is way more mature than my ex, who is fifteen years older. It hits me like a bad review on Yelp. Evie is only twenty-two. A fact I often forget. Wouldn't she rather party it up? Here I am offering to take her out to eat like some old, retired couple. What the hell is wrong with me? "We don't have to go out to eat. We could go dancing or whatever."

"Like clubbing?" A hint of surprise underlines her tone, but I can't tell if it's good or bad.

"Something like that. I'm not sure what the nightlife scene is in Terre Haute anymore, but I'm sure we can find somewhere to dance."

"God, no. I know I'm young, but loud music piped through an overhead system drives me crazy."

I chuckle. "Hmm, I should stop calling you City Girl. You're not living up to the reputation."

"Oh yeah?" She moves quickly, surprising me by getting on top and straddling my thighs. "I might've been awkward as fuck out on the farm, but I know how to ride this." She grabs my dick which is more than ready to go. For once, I don't mind her taking the reins.

"By all means, City Girl, show me what you got."

CHAPTER THIRTY-ONE

EVIE

"Hello," I call out as I stand outside the clinic's back door. I scan the alleyway but don't see anything out of the ordinary. I swear I heard a commotion while grabbing supplies from the stock room. Rachael and Liam are on their monthly rural checks, so the clinic has been relatively quiet. Maybe too quiet.

I step back inside and secure the door. Liam should invest in an alarm system. Perhaps one with cameras. Shaking my head, I duck into the supply room and grab the alcohol bottle and bag of cotton balls I abandoned on the shelf. I need to add these to room three and then call it a day. I step into the hallway, and a shriek leaves my lungs at seeing a figure standing near the bathroom.

"What are you doing here?" I ask, clutching the alcohol bottle. If he steps closer, I'll chuck the bottle at him as I did with my apple to Tom Tom. I still feel bad about that. The turkey wasn't doing anything wrong other than wanting the fruit.

Focus, Evie.

"Sorry, ma'am. I just needed to use the bathroom. I yelled out when I arrived, but nobody was around."

My eyes narrow. There's something familiar about the guy. I

swear I've seen his unruly hair before, but I don't remember the untrimmed beard. However, those deep-seated eyes are a little too narrow to forget. I know I've seen him before, but I can't pinpoint where.

"This isn't a public restroom," I state, even though I have no idea if it is or not. I'm sure Liam wouldn't mind a nonpatient using it, but I'm here alone. It's not as if I have self-defense skills.

"Understandable."

"Did you need to make an appointment?"

"No. I thought I did, but I got everything I needed." He points a thumb over his shoulder to the bathroom.

"I'll be on my way." He pulls a faded blue baseball hat out of his back pocket and places it on his head. With a dip of his chin, he spins on his heels and saunters away. It clicks to where I've seen him. He's the guy I plowed into when I picked up my car.

What is his game?

When the door shuts behind him, I dash over and lock it. I'm not sure if it's a coincidence running into him again or not, but I'm not taking a chance.

I quickly scan each room, but nothing looks out of place. Shaking off the unease, I replace the alcohol and cotton balls in room three. I step back into the hallway right when Rachael walks through the entrance, followed by Liam.

"Oh, you're still here. I thought you left since the door was locked." Liam greets me with a smile, something I haven't gotten used to, as his feet chew the distance. He leans down and brushes his lips against mine. "Glad you're still here."

My eyes widen. I can't believe he did that in front of Rachael.

"Don't look so shocked, honey. I knew it was only a matter of time." Rachael chuckles as she places the charts on the desk.

"Why does everyone say that?" Liam asks.

"Because it's true. Everyone within a twenty-mile radius can tell you have the hots for her." Rachael rolls her eyes. My cheeks heat as she turns toward me. "Was everything okay?"

"Yeah, I restocked the rooms. You can find tomorrow's schedule on your desk. I put a call out to the company for the updated software program. They'll have a quote ready in about a week. Other than the creepy guy using the bathroom, everything went well."

Liam jars backward. "What creepy guy?"

"I'm not sure, but I've run into him before. I'll point him out if I see him again."

"The festival is a couple of months away. It's about time for the early birds to scope things out," Rachael says, clearly not as concerned as Liam.

"Hmm, I don't like it. You'll be at your interview during the next rural check. I don't want you by yourself again." He points to Rachael. "That goes for you as well."

"Aye-aye, Captain." She pulls her keys from her purse. "I'm taking off. See you two tomorrow."

When she exits, Liam turns back to me with a twinkle in his eyes. "We have cause to celebrate."

"Oh?" I ask, intrigued. "What for?"

"I secured a major grant, and the federal funding came through for the clinic. I'm making some calls tomorrow to see what the next steps are."

"That's fantastic. I'm so excited for you."

"Thank you. It feels good to make some progress on this." This is the happiest I've seen him. I want to bottle this moment up because of its rarity. "I just have a few things to do on the computer. Then, we'll leave."

"It's Thursday. Are we meeting the gang at The Pump House?"

"Only if you want. We just hung out with them on the fourth."

My mouth curves into a grin. "I think we should be social."

"Fine." He leans down and kisses my nose. "Let me take care of business, and we'll take off. Just don't mention we're going to Stables next Friday."

"Why?" I ask as he walks away.

He looks over his shoulder. "Because I don't want anyone barging in on our time."

As he continues down the hall, I try not to smile like a giddy schoolgirl. Who would've thought this grumpy man could treat me so nicely?

CHAPTER THIRTY-TWO

EVIE

Jonathan: Tick tock goes the clock.

My hands shake as I slip the phone into my purse and take a deep breath. Despite his unoriginal threat, I refuse to be intimidated. It's date night, and Liam and I are standing by the hostess's desk, waiting to be seated. I didn't dress in my black, side-slit, wrapped neckline dress and red stilettos just for some jerk to ruin the evening.

"Everything okay?" Liam asks, eyes trained on my purse.

"Everything's perfect." I flash him an assuring smile, but the glint of approval in his eyes as he peruses my body calms my nerves.

"I'd say." He pulls me closer to his side, his hand spanning along the side of my hip. "I know I said this earlier, but you do look ravishing. Waiting to get you alone and peel this dress off will be torturous."

A shiver races down my spine, the idea rendering me speechless.

"Mmhmm, let's see." He slowly traces the tips of his fingers down to my thigh and up to my waist. "I'm picturing you wearing nothing but those shoes while down on all fours, with your knees spread and that juicy cunt of yours hiked up, ready and willing."

Good grief. A girl can get drunk off his dirty talk.

The hostess clears her throat, and my face flames red. I hope to God she didn't overhear what he said. A soft chuckle escapes Liam, but me... I am so mortified I can't even look her in the eyes as she seats us.

"Pierre will be your waiter this evening. Enjoy your meal."

"Thank you," I say as she places the menus on the table and skitters away. Yeah, she so overheard. Tucking my mortification away, I glance around the restaurant and soak in the atmosphere. The dim lighting, along with the dark stained wood and brick exterior walls, sets an intimate mood. A grand staircase welcomes guests as they enter and leads to a banquet center, but we appear to be sitting in the old stalls. "This place is incredible. Did this building really used to be a horse stable?"

"Yeah. Pretty remarkable, huh? They restored the building in the late nineties. A lot of the décor came from historical buildings around town."

"It has an elegant, yet rustic feel. Thanks for bringing me." My gaze makes its way back to his.

"The pleasure's all mine." The intensity in his eyes causes me to pause. Oh, how I wish I could read his thoughts. Although, by the way he drinks me in, I can guess.

The waiter arrives and introduces himself. He fills us in on the specials and asks for our drink order.

"Tonight is a celebration," Liam says, looking pointedly at me. "She's going to smash her upcoming interview."

I force a smile as the waiter wishes me luck. Shouldn't Liam's encouragement make me happy? This job is what I want. I leave for my interview in two days, and we haven't discussed my leaving other than the quick mention about staying with his sister. Sure, we've been busy between the patient load and our nightly escapades, but we could've carved out time to discuss our situation. It's not as if I sleep in my own bedroom anymore. Still, with him acting all couple-*ly* like, not once has he told me he'd hate to see me go.

"Would you like to try a bottle from the wine collection?" Pierre asks, pulling me out of my spiraling thoughts.

Liam's eyes flick to mine. "Is the cabernet okay?"

"That would be perfect."

After the waiter offers his suggestions, Liam chooses a bottle from Napa Valley, and we settle back into our chairs.

"Is this where you bring all of your dates to impress?" The question comes across as teasing, but I am genuinely curious. Thoughts of him sipping wine with his ex-fiancée infiltrate my mind. He has not told me about her texts. I want to know if he corresponds with her, but do I have the right to ask? We aren't exactly in a relationship for the long haul.

So, why do I want him to ask me to stay?

"No. You're the only one I've ever brought here." The intensity in his voice surprises me.

"This is your first time being here?" I find that hard to believe. He's too knowledgeable about the place for that to be true.

"No. My parents would bring us here for special occasions." His features soften as he glances around the area. I imagine this place holds a lot of happy memories.

I reach across the table and weave our fingers together. "You know, it's not too late to commit to speaking at the dedication ceremony.

The contentment resting in his features vanishes like the profit in a bear market. "Don't start. I honor my dad every day by showing up to work. I don't need to speak about my dad's legacy when the entire town knows he was a stand-up guy."

Sorry, Mrs. Seymour. I tried.

She came into the office the other day and asked me to coerce Liam into committing. I told her I didn't wield that kind of power. She said I have more power over him than I realized. I hoped she was right, but not about the ceremony. If the man commits to anything, I want that to be me. So far, she has been wrong on both counts.

"Fair enough."

The waiter picks this moment to pour our wine. Once we place our order, he leaves. I sip the cabernet and hold back a groan. I haven't had wine this smooth in forever. Well, since I left the house on Charleston Bay. A hundred-dollar bottle of wine isn't easily obtainable when you're on a shoestring budget.

Liam leans back in his chair and asks, "Are you looking forward to your interview?"

I guess we're going there.

I take another sip, buying myself time. How do I answer? The truth will scare him away. I had every intention of getting away from here until the reality of leaving Sugar Creek Falls for good became real. Damn if this small town didn't come up and wrap around my heart—sort of like the grumpy doctor sitting across from me with skepticism marring his expression. It's almost as if he doesn't want to hear my answer. Or he's ready to pounce if I say the wrong thing. The trouble is, I don't know what he wants to hear. I place the wine glass down but don't let go of the stem.

"Sort of. I'm anxious, though."

"You'll do fine."

"How do you know?" I laugh.

"I hired you, didn't I?"

"You hired me without conducting an official interview." I raise the glass back to my lips and peer over the rim. "I think that's called desperation."

"Yeah," he laughs, "but I've worked with you. You're a hard worker."

I feel my cheeks blush at his compliment. "Thank you, sir."

His eyes dilate as he looks at me. Then, he shakes his head, as if to refocus, and asks, "So, what made you decide to work for the public health sector?"

"I want to help underprivileged people obtain access to healthcare." I pause. That's my cookie-cutter answer, but I feel the need to elaborate with Liam. I've never told anyone the actual reason behind my career choice. "I'm sure by now you realize how privileged I've been. I grew up with a nanny."

"No, not you." Now, it's his turn to tease.

"It's true." I tilt my head and get a faraway look. "Miss Carmichael, my nanny, took care of me. Anything my mom wouldn't let me have, like ice cream, Miss Carmichael would sneak it in for me."

"You're not lactose intolerant?"

"No. At least, I wasn't at the time. Mom wanted me on a strict diet since I was shorter."

Liam's stare becomes baffled.

"One is more likely to pack on pounds being vertically challenged," I explain. When he still doesn't seem to understand, I repeat the phrase Mom always stated, "Men want trophy wives by their side, not curvy consolation prizes. That's what the side pieces are for."

"I beg to differ." His features harden, and his grip tightens around the wineglass, but I won't explain further. I don't want the focus to shift to my mother's misgivings. That conversation is for another night.

"Anyway, Miss Carmichael missed a couple of weeks of work during my freshman year. I remember being so angry. Mom was constantly nagging me, and I needed an escape. When Miss Carmichael returned, I told her she should be fired for insubordination." Tears well in my eyes. "What she told me next has stuck with me to this day. That was when something inside of me changed. One of those life-alternating moments, you know?"

"What'd she say?"

"First, she apologized. *Apologized.* As if my spoiled ass deserved it. Then, she said she took her daughter to the children's hospital in Delaware. I asked her why she took her so far when we have an excellent one in Philly." I laugh humorlessly. "It turns out that was the closest place that accepted non-insurance patients. I realized that day how privileged I was. Then, I got angry. How could my parents employ people to take care of their only daughter when they didn't take care of them? *Mother* simply stated that's what they signed up for. As if it's their fault for wanting to work. It made me sick." My voice cracks as a single tear slides down my face. I quickly swipe it away, but as I raise my gaze to his, I'm startled by the war of emotions swirling through his stare. He looks almost defeated.

"You owe it to yourself to go to this interview."

I swallow past the disappointment lodged in my throat. Why had I thought he'd ask me to stay? "Yeah, I plan on it."

My purse buzzes, which I ignore. I should've turned the stupid phone off.

Liam nods at it. "Do you need to check that?"

"No."

"What if something's wrong?"

"Your sister is the only person who texts me." Ansley and my ex-boyfriend, that is.

"It could also be your parents. I know they aren't the best, but you should make sure everything is okay," he says, voice softening. Dad's issues come to mind. I haven't mentioned Dad's ailments to Liam, partly because I don't believe my mom, but I get where he's coming from.

"Fine." I snatch the phone from my purse, but I still after unlocking the screen.

> Jonathan: Quit playing games. I know where you are. Take the damn flight home.

"What does he mean by flight?" Liam's mouth forms a straight line. "Has he been texting you?"

"My mom has booked flights for me every Monday since my arrival."

His eyebrows rise. "Seriously?"

"Unfortunately. She thinks I'm wasting my time here. I'd be better suited back home marrying a pocketbook. Or..." I wave my hand over my phone to indicate Jonathan. I don't want to say his name out loud too many times. He may pop up like *Beetlejuice*.

Anger flashes in his eyes, but I somehow think it's directed at me. "You haven't mentioned any of this before."

"I didn't think I needed to tell you."

"Why wouldn't you?"

I don't like his accusatory tone and go on the defensive. I'm not the only one keeping secrets here. "That's my business."

"We've been fucking. Your business is my business."

"If you're going to be an ass about it, let's be honest." I straighten in my seat. "When were you going to tell me about your ex-fiancée texting you?"

The fight leaves his face, and he crashes into the back of his chair. "You know about them?"

My stomach sinks. I knew of one and assumed a few. How many have there been?

"Yes."

"I haven't responded to any of them. I have no idea what she wants."

"Don't you think you should see if anything's important?"

"There's nothing from her I want."

That makes me feel somewhat better. I sigh heavily. "I've received a handful of texts from Jonathan ever since graduation. Like you, I never respond. There is nothing I want from him either."

He runs a hand down his face, and all traces of resistance vanish. "It looks like we keep running from our pasts. Maybe it's time we run toward our future."

I agree. But the problem is, what future do we want?

CHAPTER THIRTY-THREE

LIAM

Thwack.

Thwack.

Thwack.

There's something about hitting inanimate objects. Or in this case, the floor nailer. It's rather freeing to release this frustration—even though the only person I have to be angry with is myself. Regardless of the fact that the dominant in me wanted to will her to stay, the only choice I had was to let her go. Asking her to stay would be my most selfish act. I wouldn't be better than her parents or ex-boyfriend.

"Why don't you ease up a little? I won't have any flooring left at your current rate."

I look at the floor nailer in my hand and the hardwood flooring. Noting the planks are fine, I turn my glower toward Matthew. It goes unnoticed. Perched on a ladder, he directs his focus to the overhead chandelier he is installing.

"You have to swing it hard," I protest.

"Yeah, but not so hard the planks splinter."

I let out a frustrated growl. "You want to do this yourself?"

"Easy. What the hell is wrong with you? You've been grumbling ever since you walked through the doors."

I give another grunt, which only proves his point. I'm laying the flooring down in his mom's office while he works on finishing touches. Completing the project is imperative with the festival kicking off in a few weeks. People will trickle into town next weekend, and the motel will be at full capacity. Between the motel occupants and the fees collected from the parking behind the property, Matthew's family makes enough money to carry them through the entire year. His mechanic shop is a bonus. I've often teased they could bulldoze the motel, turn the lot into more parking, and double their profits, but the motel keeps his mom busy.

"The office is coming along. I should finish the floor today." It has been a team effort. Once the electricians rewired the office, Matthew and Ethan replaced the drywall. Daniel built the cabinets and counter while Olivia and Jeanette painted the office a cool light gray with silky white trim. My contribution is to finish the flooring Matthew and Ethan started.

"Don't change the subject. Does this mood have something to do with Evie leaving today?"

"Why would you say that? I was in a great mood until you started harping me about feelings and shit."

"Jesus. You're the smartest dumb guy I know," he chuckles.

Thwack.

Thwack.

Thwack.

"Ignore me all you want, but at least admit to yourself that you don't want her to move."

I stand and stretch my back, wiping the sweat from my brow. "It's not as if we're a couple. We're messing around. She's free to do whatever she wants."

"And you're sure you know what she wants?"

"Of course I do. It's always been Evie's goal to move back to the city." I grab another plank and line it up against the board on the floor.

"If that's what you say."

I rub my chest, ready to lash out at the judgment in his tone. "What do you mean? She said from the beginning that her stay was temporary."

"That woman from the fourth didn't seem keen to leave. That hasn't changed in the last month, just saying."

"We're not a couple," I reiterate, even though part of me knows he's right. We look like a couple. We live together. We fuck. Although, what we've been doing is more than fucking. I let her in. I tried to keep a distance between us. I thought not looking in her eyes during sex would make it less intimate and keep me from getting close. *Keep me from falling for her.* Jokes on me. It didn't work. She somehow burrowed herself into my soul. And now... Now, I'm left laying the wrong kind of wood.

Thwack.

Thwack.

Thwack.

"Okay, we're changing jobs." Matthew climbs off the ladder and takes the floor nailer out of my hand. "You finish hanging the light fixtures, and I'll tackle the flooring." When I step toward the ladder, he adds, "Just admit you don't want her to leave."

"For fuck's sake, we're not a couple." I climb up the ladder and start attaching the globes. I'm not sure placing glass in my hands is better, but so be it.

"Bro, you're more upset over her than you ever were with Miss Snooty Patootie."

Matthew never warmed up to Ciera. None of my friends did. After seeing how easy it is to be with Evie, I wonder what I ever saw in her. She was complicated as fuck. Still, I was going to marry the woman. There had to be something there.

"Ciera was my fiancée. I think that merits more heartbreak."

"Hmm, agree to disagree. I think you mourned the lost concept of what you wanted. This time, you lost the girl."

"The lost concept of what I wanted? What does that even mean?"

"It means you mourned over the family you've always wanted, not the girl."

I finger-tighten the screws in the delicate glass, careful not to overtighten. Is Matthew right? When Ciera left, all I could think about was the loss of family. As if she was my only chance at having the family I wanted. Or basketball team, as Evie put it. I laugh at that thought, but it comes out a little manic and earns me a side glance from Matthew. My face feels tight as I remember the look on Evie's face when I said I wanted five kids. It was priceless. Except, she said she didn't want kids. At least, not anytime soon.

"You didn't ask Evie to stay, did you?" This comes out as an accusation more than a question.

"I can't choose for her. Evie has to decide to stay on her own." No way am I forcing someone to live here again. Been there, bought the heartache.

"But how is she going to know staying here is an option if you don't tell her your feelings?"

I grumble and move on to the next globe. If I pour my soul out and she walks away willingly, the tiny bits left of my heart will shatter. There won't be any shards left to put back together.

But she'll leave for sure if I don't tell her.

Damn, Matthew is right.

Huh, I never thought I'd think those words. I climb down the ladder to grab another globe and miss a wrung. Catching myself before I fall on my ass, I glare at my friend.

"She's only twenty-two. She doesn't want kids," I say to

defend my choice. "That defeats my entire purpose for wanting to get married."

"Is her not wanting kids a definite?"

I try to think back to what she said, but her exact wording evades me. "I'm not sure, but she's young. She won't be ready anytime soon."

"Her age isn't a factor here. The couple involved are the only ones who need to worry about age," he says defensively. Dating younger women has always been a sore subject with him, which is strange. I've yet to see him with anyone younger.

He lets out a frustrated breath. "So, what you're saying is, if she doesn't ever want any kids, it would be a deal breaker? You could never be with her?"

I ponder what he asked. What if she never wants kids? Could I still be with her? I know I love spending time with Evie. I love how she makes me feel. I love how she lightens a room and puts everyone at ease. She has a certain glow about her that makes me happy. I love...

Damn, I love her.

Kids or no kids, it's hard imagining life without her.

"No, it wouldn't. But that still doesn't change the fact she needs to decide what to do." She has to decide on her own. People have dictated her next move her entire life. Hell, they told her what to say, eat, wear, and think. It's no wonder she got away from there. Her light would dull living that lifestyle. I can't be the one telling her what to do. She has to choose, but I need to tell her I love her.

Okay, maybe not start with love. I don't want to scare her away, but at least tell her I have strong feelings for her. She deserves that much. When she comes back from her interview, I'll confess my feelings. Then, it will be up to her to decide what she wants to do.

Relief washes through me. I feel settled for the first time since

Evie left. Maybe the situation isn't as dire as I made it out to be. Right as I start to finger-tighten another screw, the front door swings open.

"We're not open yet..." Matthew's voice drifts off.

Curious about the newcomer, I pull my gaze away from the globe, and it lands on the last person I expected to set foot in Sugar Creek Falls.

But I'm not fixated on the woman. I can't stop looking at the hand rubbing affectionately across the tiniest baby bump. Her lips form a tight line when I finally direct my gaze back to Ciera's.

"We *need* to talk."

CHAPTER THIRTY-FOUR

EVIE

"For a girl who just nailed her interview, you don't look so happy." Ansley settles into the wrought iron chair outside a vegetarian restaurant in downtown Indianapolis. The noon sun beams around us, but the restaurant's canopy extends far enough to protect us from the rays.

I shoot my best friend a tight smile. "I'm happy. I'm back in the city with my bestie. Nothing could top this." *Except, maybe some quietness.* Granted, downtown Indy isn't as loud as Chicago, but it doesn't lack the ever-present horns and screeching-brakes sound.

Or the constant crowds that are clamoring for attention.

I sit back in my chair overlooking the street and sip my bottle of sparkling water. I'd opt for wine, but I had decided to drive back today instead of tomorrow.

"I call bullshit. You aren't your usual upbeat self. What gives?"

As she asks the question, someone skateboards past us, singing at the top of their lungs, oblivious to how off-key they are.

Annoyed by the intrusion, I ask, "How do you even think with this constant noise?"

"Oh, no." Her face grows solemn as her shoulders slump.

"What?"

"The town's clutches grabbed hold of you and inducted you into their cult." She grabs my shoulders and pretends to shake me. "Give me back my best friend."

"Stop," I say through laughter. "They have not."

She settles in her seat. "Oh, I think they have. Just look at the facts."

"What on earth are you talking about?"

"You were just offered your dream job and told them you'd think about it."

"That's just good business sense," I point out. "It's not good to appear too eager."

"Okay, but you're still not excited like usual. What do you really want?"

I shrug and blow out a breath, unsure how to answer. I want to prove that I don't need my parents' money. I don't need to be a debutante to survive. When they cut my funding, I didn't crawl back home as they anticipated. Sure, it hasn't been easy, but I didn't break.

This new job offer is what I dreamed of doing—helping families obtain insurance or proper funding. Sugar Creek Falls is too small for me to set that up. What happens after I move here? Will self-satisfaction come then? Knowing I have the job to obtain that goal isn't bringing the gratification I thought it would.

Maybe my priorities changed. Liam pays me a decent salary —enough to cover rent and expenses. What keeps me from moving out of his house? That is the question I need to answer.

No, I know the truth, and it's all due to Liam. I didn't want to leave. I liked staying with him. I liked waking up in his arms. Leaving feels wrong, almost like a betrayal. There's a connection between us I can't explain. He makes me happy, yes, but it's deeper than that.

"You're thinking awfully hard over a question that should be quick to answer."

I blink at my friend, forgetting what she had asked. She laughs.

"Okay, that expression tells me everything I need to know." She slams her hand down on the table. "Want to know what I think?"

"Do I have a choice?" I tease.

"What I think is, while you claim to love the city, what you seek is seclusion."

"What?" I ask, surprised, but her words hit close to home.

"Aside from work and school, you were a recluse." She holds up a finger when I go to protest. "Hear me out. It's not like you'd go clubbing with me. You'd rather stay in or stick to small gatherings."

"There's nothing wrong with intimate parties." I defend myself, but she's right. I never put myself out there for people to notice. My upbeat, too-friendly personality wasn't acceptable in my family's social circle. I've spent my entire life ashamed of who I am. It shouldn't come as a surprise I wanted to live in a big city. There, I could blend and disappear among a throng of people. Sugar Creek Falls is the complete opposite. Everyone knew who I was before I even blew into town. The longer I stayed, the more relaxed I became. I could be myself. I didn't have to put on airs. Everyone got to know the real me. And it turns out, people like me for who I am. The town filled a void I didn't realize needed restocking.

"There isn't anything wrong with that. All I'm saying is, smaller settings seem to agree with you." She dips a toasted pita into the sundried tomato hummus. "How's working with my brother?"

Thankful for the topic change, I ignore the twinkle in her eye and answer honestly, "It's been great. He gave me control of the office. I tackled the antiquated scheduling system and made strides with the bookkeeping and medical records. You should've seen the mess it was in. Poor Rachael could only do so much."

"The old bat needs to retire. She was old when I was little."

"I hope she doesn't go anywhere soon. Liam would be lost without her." I ignore the gnawing pain in my heart. The mere thought of saying goodbye to him causes palpitations.

"I'm not so sure she's the only one that would cause him to be lost if she left." She studies me thoughtfully.

"I have no idea what you mean." But I do. Because no matter how much I adore that town, I adore their town doctor even more. It's been a little over twenty-four hours, and I miss him. What does that say about me? What started as sex turned into more after the fourth. We turned into more. Surely, I'm not alone in this feeling.

It's just, we have so much working against us. He's coming off a recent heartbreak; although, the only mention of her was the phone messages. In fact, he hasn't been as grouchy lately either. Then, there's the fact he's Ansley's brother. Even so, I don't think she actually cares. He's older. Too old? Not entirely. There have been wider margins. Hell, there are tons of books written about older men and younger women. There is an entire trope dedicated to age gaps. Then, the debate about kids. He wants them. I don't—not right away anyway. I would be open to them once I work on myself. But I don't feel as lost as I did.

Yeah, there are many reasons not to be with him, but each one has a counterpart. There's one good reason for me to stay: love. Do I love him? I have my answer before even thinking about it.

Yes, I love his grumpy, domineering ass.

"When are you going to confess you're sleeping with my brother?" Humor laces the edges of her tone.

I could deny it, but she deserves answers. "You're not mad?"

"No. I expected it."

I shoot her a yeah-right look. She appears offended.

"It's true," she shrieks. "No one can resist the Seymour effect."

"I flippin' miss you."

"Me too. Is it serious between you guys?"

"I don't know. Probably not. I'm here at his encouragement."

"But does he know how deep you fell?"

"How did you know?" I shake my head. "Don't answer. I know you have some sort of sixth sense shit."

She laughs. "It didn't take much. It's written all over your face."

"Oh, God." I want to sink beneath the table and hide.

"Look, I know my brother. He'll push you to do the right thing, even if it goes against what he wants. That's just how he is. Have an open, honest discussion with him. See where you stand before you decide to take the job."

"I will. I promise."

"Anyway, I'll be back in town for the festival in a few weeks."

"You will?"

"Yeah, they're dedicating the park to my dad. I pretty much have to be there."

"Your mom will be glad to see you. Not to mention your brother."

"Mom guilted me into coming back. She wants me to convince Liam to give a speech."

"He's so adamant against doing it. Is he really that bad at speaking?" I ask.

"Yes, it's not an exaggeration. Liam froze before his valedictorian speech and told a fart joke to the entire school."

"What?" I laugh. "Was it at least funny?"

"'I have just released my own fragrance on the way here. Nobody in the car seemed to like it'," she deadpans.

I place my hand over my mouth and stifle a laugh. "It's kind of cute."

"Cute? Jesus, you must be in love." She rolls her eyes. "Anyway, you'll still be there regardless, right?"

"I'll be there. Even if it doesn't work out between us, I won't leave him high and dry." And my mind is made. If he still wants me to leave after I confess my feelings, I'll go, whether I accept the job or not. I dip the last carrot into the hummus, suddenly anxious to make the trip back. For once in my life, I feel good about going home.

CHAPTER THIRTY-FIVE

LIAM

"Here, sorry, I don't have anything else to offer besides almond milk." I hand Ciera a glass of water. Caramel lattes are the only sugary drink Evie allows herself, so a stocked refrigerator is useless.

"Water's fine. Sugar drinks make me heave. I'm surprised you gave up cow's milk, though."

"Mmhmm." I nestle into the porch swing and look across the field. I omit that the milk isn't exactly mine but Evie's. Ciera harped on me for months to switch to oat milk. Evie came along and turned me on to her milk in a matter of weeks.

"I still don't understand why you waited so long to tell me. You're near the end of your second trimester." I'm still in shock. I stayed up all night, pondering everything and wondering what the best scenario would be going forward, but I kept coming up blank. Worrying over Evie's reaction clouds my thoughts. She'll be here tomorrow, and I hope Ciera leaves town by then. Not that she won't be a factor going forward, but I want to break the news to Evie without my ex hanging around.

"I told you I wanted to get through the first trimester. Then, it was garnering courage. We didn't exactly end on good terms. Plus, you've avoided my calls this past month."

I puff out a breath. She's right on both counts. We didn't end on good terms, but it irritates me that I didn't know I was going to be a father. We should've discussed things last night, but I couldn't process anything. I was too shocked. I think I still am.

Am I happy to be a dad? Yes, of course, but the timing is wrong—not to mention it's with the wrong woman.

I scrub a hand over my face. Evie doesn't want kids. Will knowing that I'm going to be a dad change things? I was going to confess my feelings for her. But now? How can I when I'm a package deal? Is it better to let her go and save her from my chaotic life? I can guarantee one thing for sure. My life is bound to be messy with Ciera in it.

"Tell me what you're thinking. You've gone quiet on me."

I turn to the woman I had wanted to live the rest of my life with. Her hair falls in long, loose curls that are perfectly tailored. Her makeup is pristine. Ciera is exactly how Evie looked when she first arrived. The difference? Evie's style became more casual the longer she stayed here. She wore her hair in loose buns and lessened the amount of makeup. There isn't anything wrong with presenting your best self, but I want that casual girl who dresses up on special occasions, not the Instagram-ready socialite.

"I'm trying to figure out how to make this work logistically. You live in New York. I don't."

She licks her red-painted lips. "I was hoping we could give us another try."

I rear back. "What?"

She scoots closer to me. "I know it was wrong of me to leave the way I did, but Liam, I was scared. I didn't know what I wanted."

"What are you saying?"

"I want to move back. We're a family—the family you always

dreamed about. She rubs her belly affectionately, and my heart races. She can't possibly mean this. Yet, my mind entertains the idea. She's offering me what I always sought—a wife and child.

But that life is with the wrong woman.

"Ciera, we were flawed."

"How can you say that?" She has the audacity to appear hurt. She has to remember how bored and disgusted she was living here. She left for a reason. I didn't chase after her. There wasn't a grand gesture. A child can't bring people together. I have a stack of psychology textbooks to back my thesis.

"Because we were toxic together. You were never happy."

"I was happier in New York, that's true, but I can learn to adapt."

"That's just it. You shouldn't have to settle. It's okay to like city life. Many people do. I don't expect you to change."

Her eyes widen in surprise. "Since when? It was always your way, but I stood by you during everything."

That's true. She was there for my residency, crazy hours in the emergency department, the investigation, and our move here. We've been through a lot together. But she left and opened my eyes to our flaws. "I'm sorry my career took precedence over our relationship. That's on me. But it still doesn't change that we don't belong together."

"How can you say that? You had asked me to marry you."

"You left. And I had a lot of time to think and reflect. I realized we didn't love each other the way couples should. For that, I'm truly sorry."

"It's been five months since I left."

"Six, almost seven, and a lot can change in that time." It hits me like a ton of bricks. I was with Ciera for two years before moving back home and asking her to marry me. Marriage felt like the next step, something born out of obligation. I've known Evie for a little over two months, and I can't stop thinking about her.

Being apart from her for two days is maddening. Matthew was right. I wasn't grumpy because I missed Ciera. I missed the idea of us as a unit. With Evie, I fucking miss *her*. I love her.

And now, I have to tell her the very thing that may destroy us and ship her packing to Indy. God, why can't my life be uncomplicated?

"So, what am I supposed to do?"

"That's what we need to figure out. I promise you won't be raising the baby alone. I'll be there every step of the way."

"You'll be here. I'll be in New York." Her eyes glisten with unshed tears. I swallow past the lump forming in my throat.

"I haven't figured out the logistics, but I'll be supportive."

"Oh, that's rich. Do you think you deserve some type of badge?"

"What do you want me to say? We can't be together. My life is here. Your life is in New York. We'll figure it out."

She turns on the waterfall. Big, crocodile tears roll down both cheeks. There was a time when her teardrops affected me, but I have since learned she uses them as weapons. I'm so lost in how to correct this mess that I don't hear the car pull into the driveway.

"I don't want to do this alone."

"I'll think of something, but I need time to get it sorted," I say, trying to reassure myself. The situation isn't going to be solved overnight. It's too complex.

She pushes to her feet and steps toward the stairs. "I knew you wouldn't be there for me."

"I didn't say I wouldn't be there. I just need time to think." My feet chew the distance until I stand next to the mother of my child.

"Oh, I think the baby just kicked."

Startled, I place my hands on her stomach automatically.

Raising to meet her eyes, I smile. The first one to cross my mouth since Evie left. "Sorry, I hope this is okay."

"He's your baby, too." She grabs my hand and repositions it lower on her abdomen.

A small gasp cuts through the air, and I turn to startling gray eyes. I break apart from Ciera, as if I got caught with my hand in the cookie jar.

"Can we help you?" Ciera asks, placing her left hand on my biceps. And that's when I notice her engagement ring reflecting in the setting sun for the entire world to see.

Well, fuck.

CHAPTER THIRTY-SIX

EVIE

Can we help you?

We, as in they're a couple already.

My breath hitches as my gaze snaps to Liam, who looks as stunned as I feel, before shifting to a sizable diamond planted on a very important finger.

What. The. Fuck.

I was gone for one day. *One!*

And he is back with his ex in that span of time?

My stomach roils. I'm going to be sick.

"I, uh, was just going to my room." I grasp the handle of my carry-on tighter and side-step their perfectly aligned bodies. Her gasp slices through the air before I reach the front door.

"You're staying here?" Shifting movement sounds behind me, her tone ice cold. "What's going on?"

I spin around, prepared to answer, but the way she glares at Liam, the question wasn't intended for me. That's when I take her in. Long auburn curls framing a perfectly manicured face. She's beautiful. Of course she is. Those sharp, angular cheekbones belong on the cover of *Vogue*. She stands tall with the same haughtiness as my friends I left behind in Philadelphia. *The opposite of me.*

"Geneva, this is Ciera." *Geneva?* "Ciera, Geneva. She's my..." He pauses as our gazes connect. I raise an eyebrow, waiting for his answer. "Office manager."

And there we have it.

Wrong answer, asshole.

My back stiffens as I give Ciera the politest smile I can muster. "Nice to meet you. Sorry to shorten our meeting, but I had a long trip." My hands shake as I make my way into the house.

"She stays here?"

I don't wait for his reply as I beeline to my room. Tears prick my eyes, but I hold them in until I'm behind the safety of my bedroom door.

Geneva. Why, out of everything he said, does that hurt the most?

I sink to the floor as the world I created in my mind rips apart. Liam wasn't mine. He was never mine. I was a fool to think differently. But I never expected to drive up and see them hovered together with his hands wrapped around her. Several minutes pass before I push to my feet and pack my belongings. Forget the two weeks' notice. If Liam's getting back with his ex-fiancée, I'll leave tomorrow after work. I can't bear to see them parade in front of me. I wince at that thought.

"Evie!" Liam shouts as footsteps scamper up the stairs.

I wipe the spilled-over tears and shut the luggage. Liam barges through the door, wild-eyed and a little manic.

"I'm so sorry." He steps toward me, but I hold my hands up.

"Don't."

His face crumbles and plays with my heart. I stalk toward the window trying to create much-needed distance. I can't bear to look at him right now. I peer out the window and watch a red sedan drive away. Guess that answers who the car belongs to.

"Evie, let me explain."

"It's fine. I'm just your office manager." The chill in my voice makes me cringe. I sound as bitchy as his fiancée.

"That came out wrong."

I spin to face him. "If you want to get back with your ex, that's none of my concern. We weren't anything. It was only sex, remember?" The pang in my chest expands at those words. At least he has the decency to flinch.

"That's not true."

"Isn't it?"

"No, and you damn well know it." Each syllable slings at me as his anger rises.

"What I know is you looked pretty damn cozy on the porch."

His eyes close, tone softening. "It wasn't what it looked like."

"Seems to be the theme of the day."

"Ciera is pregnant. What you saw was me feeling the baby kick."

The hole in my chest opens wider, and I feel like I've been sucker punched. *Pregnant?* She represents everything he wants. A wife. Kids. The instant life he wants, whereas I can only offer time and a maybe.

I swallow past the ever-present ache in my throat, but I can't stop the crack in my voice. "I guess congratulations are in order."

"Yeah." His green eyes darken to a jade. He runs a hand through his hair and rests it on the back of his neck. Looking to the ceiling, he mutters, "Fuck. This wasn't what I..." He closes his eyes and shakes his head. "I'm sorry. I didn't mean to hurt you."

"I got the job. I told them I'd start Monday."

His eyes dart to the suitcase. I didn't mean to blurt out the news as if I have already accepted, but I can't stand here and listen to him tell me he wants to be with her. I should've seen this coming. I knew he was on the rebound. I knew better than to get involved with him. And I knew better than to open up to him and think my life could be normal. Normality isn't in Thornhill's blood. Our DNA code isn't wired that way. Far be it for me to want to break the mold. So, it's best to make him believe I'm leaving anyway. And from the way his face goes stoic, my plan worked.

"I guess congratulations are in order for the both of us."

The funny thing is, I don't feel like celebrating.

CHAPTER THIRTY-SEVEN

LIAM

"Thanks again for staying and helping me today. There's one more patient to check on—Aileen Dudley." I guide the truck across the narrow bridge and head farther east, hoping we make it back to the house before the impending storm.

I debated canceling today's rural check after Rachael called in sick, but these people depend on me. It's a rarity for her to call in, but the upcoming festival has pushed her stress limits. Considering how last night went down, I wasn't sure if Evie would stay and help.

Her leaving for Indy makes my stomach feel like it's inside a meat grinder. When I noticed her packed suitcase, I wanted to confess my love and demand she stays. That wouldn't be fair, though. She deserves so much more than I can offer. The honorable thing is to remain quiet and let her go. Let her hate me.

But it kills me.

"Really? I don't have anyone left on the list." Evie grabs the clipboard off the floorboard and scans through the names.

"You won't find Aileen on there. She wasn't scheduled. She

saw her obstetrician a couple of days ago and was diagnosed with Braxton Hicks. She's due next week. I just want to make sure she's doing okay." I worry about them not having access to a telephone or a reliable vehicle. Their house sits about fifteen miles off the main highway, hidden by overgrown trees. No one would ever know if they were distressed unless they used smoke signals. Evie's goal is to help underprivileged children. Well, she's about to get an education for other demographical needs.

Evie nods at my reasoning and pulls out the tote containing the patients' charts.

"You won't find her chart either. I didn't inform Rachael, so she wouldn't have known to pull it."

Evie places the tote back down and stares straight ahead, not uttering a word. The silence is stifling. The white elephant hovers over our heads like the looming black clouds in the distance. We can't move forward if we don't talk about the situation neither of us expected. It needs to be me addressing it, which is only fair. It's my issue at the root of the cause.

I turn onto a narrow gravel road one would miss if they didn't know it existed. Cornfields line both sides, separated by a ditch and further isolating us from distractions. Guilt burrows deeper. Evie deserves to know how much I care for her. Even with her moving to another town, she deserves to know this wasn't just sex for me. I don't think it ever was. My hands grip the steering wheel as the shaggy trees come into view. The timing could've been better, but I need to get this off my chest.

"Before Ciera showed up, I had planned on telling you how much I like you."

Evie's head snaps to me. "Why?"

Why? Why does she think? *Because I love you. I don't want you to go.* Although, that's highly inappropriate to say now that I fucked up everything between us. Confessing my love for her with these pressing issues doesn't seem right.

"Because I enjoy having you around. You make me smile and put me at ease. I can be myself around you. Plus, I really like you." So much that it hurt not having her here or in my bed last night. It was torturous with her so close and knowing I couldn't touch her.

"And now?"

"Now, I think it'd be selfish of me."

"Why do you think that?"

What is this? An interrogation? I feel as if the feelings police have me on trial and I'm tiptoeing around the truth.

Maybe you feel that way because that's what you're doing.

But how can I explain the way it makes me feel when I catch her sitting on the porch gazing at the horizon? I want to ask what she is thinking but am afraid to disturb the contentment settling in her expression. Or the way she sasses Mr. Cusack and the other cantankerous patients. She has a way of bringing out the best in people, but confessing that would reveal what I need to hide.

"Tell me how that makes you selfish," she spits out the words contemptuously.

My expression clouds with anger, suddenly tired of the odds stacked against us. Why can't she understand what I'm trying to say? I can push past the age difference. I can work the long-distance angle. But I don't know what to do about my ex-fiancée, and this vulnerability infuriates me to the point where I want to explode. "Because if I confess I fucking love you, I'd ask you to stay, and I can't do that. It's too selfish of me when I don't know what my future holds."

"Does anybody?"

I shoot her a glare. "You know what I mean."

Ciera hijacked my future in one night, which is a dick thing to think and isn't fair. It isn't her fault, considering I had a hand in making the child, but that vision of living on a farm with a wife and kids is what I always wanted. It's just I want that with Evie.

It wasn't that long ago you wanted that future with Ciera.

My hands grip the steering wheel. I'm the biggest asshole for wishing it was Evie carrying my baby.

My baby.

I'm going to be a father.

The more I think about it, the more it becomes real. And as much as I want to hate my circumstances, I can't.

I haven't a clue as to how this will work. With Ciera living in New York City, I'll travel a lot. How will I make time for Evie? How will that be fair to her? She deserves better than some older guy with a child living over seven hundred miles away.

"Look, I'm trying to do what's best for you. I think there's something between us. I can't deny our chemistry is off the charts, nor can I deny that I feel something more..."

"But," she prompts after my pause drags on.

"But I don't think it's fair to you. You deserve so much more than what I can offer."

She sits in silence for a beat as wheels crunch the gravel beneath us. I stare straight ahead, not daring to look at her. I'd cave if I did. That's how weak I am.

"When I went for my interview, all I could think about was getting back to Sugar Creek Falls. The constant noise grated at me. I had never experienced that before. I loved city life." She cocks her head toward me. "But as it turns out, I love country life a tad more. Or maybe it's the company."

I pull up to a debilitated, single-story house with a trail of dust following. The weathered siding is long overdue for paint. The broken shutters hang cockeyed and look as if a simple puff of breath would bring them down. I kill the engine and let out a defeated sigh.

"I can't be the reason you stay. You need to stay for yourself."

Her mouth opens, but a shrill scream pierces the air. Our heads whip toward the house, and my blood runs cold. I've recognized that sound before.

I grab the medical bag and dart from the truck.

You and that baby of yours are going to be okay.

CHAPTER THIRTY-EIGHT

EVIE

"Call nine-one-one," Liam shouts as we race to the house. He doesn't waste time knocking and barges inside. I hit the emergency button and give the details to the operator.

Another scream greets us as we step inside the house. A lanky-looking guy places his hands on his unruly red hair and gives Liam a bug-eyed plea.

"How many minutes apart?"

"She's screaming about every three to four minutes. But they're just Braxton Hicks. That's what the doctor said. She said we have nothing to worry about."

"Calm down, Cory. I'll take a look. Do you have any hand sanitizer?"

"No. That stuff is too expensive."

"Direct me to the bathroom so I can wash my hands. Meanwhile, I need you to grab some clean towels, about four or so, and a warm bucket of water."

"Yes, Doc. The bathroom is right through there." Cory points to the third door on the left.

"I can gather the water if you get the bucket," I say to Cory.

He nods and leads me to the kitchen, where I fill the bucket. As I wait, I take in my surroundings. Worn Formica countertops sit atop faded blue-green cabinets. The kitchen may be dated, but the area is clean. I glance back at the bucket and quickly shut off the water. At least the faucet is quick. I grab the bucket's handle and head to the hallway. Liam darts out of the bathroom and barks orders for me to follow.

"Thank God you're here, Doc," Aileen says right before she starts yelling. Her husband comes back in with some towels.

"Okay, Aileen, I'll check and see how far you're dilated."

"I just want to push," she says, gritting her teeth.

"No, don't do that."

Liam places a towel underneath her bottom and removes her underwear. When he spreads her legs apart, I almost toss up the sandwich I had for lunch.

What the hell is that?

"Okay, the baby is crowning. When the next contraction hits, I want you to push."

"You told me not to push."

"I thought these were Braxton Hicks. What about the Braxton Hicks?" Cory asks, pacing the floor.

"I'm going to kill you if you mention those aga—" She doesn't finish her sentence when another contraction hits. The baby's head pushes through, and I can't bear to watch. I keep my eye trained on Liam. To those worry lines between his brows. To the way his face sets in total concentration. But then, a flick of panic mars his expression. My gaze drops down, and there's no unseeing what unfolds next.

"Stop pushing," Liam demands.

"What? But you said—"

"Just stop. The cord is wrapped around the neck. I have to work it loose."

I swallow past the gasp lodged in my throat. The room goes

deathly silent aside from Aileen's pants. My gaze dips to Liam's hands. Is the baby's face supposed to be that color? Dread pins me in place, and I have never felt so helpless. Sweat forms on Liam's forehead, and I say a silent prayer. *Please, please, please be okay.* Liam hooks a finger under the loop and slowly loosens the cord over the baby's head. I let out a breath as Liam's shoulders relax ever so slightly.

"Okay, the cord is freed. Next contraction, I need you to push."

Cory finally leans next to his wife and grabs her hand. "You can do it, honey. You're doing good."

When another contraction hits, the baby's shoulders push through, followed by the lower half. A purplish-blue color tinges the skin as the baby lies silent in Liam's hands. Where are the cries? Shouldn't she be crying?

Liam wastes no time flopping the baby onto Aileen's belly and rubbing his hands up and down the baby's back. A beautiful cry belts out after what seems like the longest moment in time.

Liam releases a breath and smiles half-heartedly at the couple. "Congratulations on your new daughter."

Joyous sounds fill the room as tears stream down my face.

"Do we need to cut the cord?" Cory asks.

"No, we'll wait until the ambulance gets here. They'll have sterile supplies. Otherwise, we risk infecting the child." Liam turns to me. "What's the ambulance ETA?"

"They should be here any minute." As if on cue, sirens wail in the distance. "I'm going to wash my hands so I can help." Something I should've done by now, but I was too shocked.

When I exit the bathroom, Liam stands in the hallway, a lost expression on his face.

"How's momma and baby doing?"

"They're okay." There's a distance to his voice that makes my heart ache.

The sirens sound louder before cutting off. A moment later, the paramedics rush inside. While Liam explains the patient's condition, I step into the living room. It's a time capsule from the sixties. As I peer into the baby bassinet tucked in the corner, an unsettling feeling sinks in. I think we took a significant step backward. And I don't mean the décor.

Putting Liam and my impending situation aside, I see more pressing problems. There is a huge need for education on health care and well-being. This couple should've had an emergency birth kit ready, living so far away from a medical facility. They also should've been educated to tell the difference between false and actual labor. I can see where Liam's wellness center can be of good use. This community, among others, needs places like that. Maybe I should stay and help get this started. I could search for more grant applications and seek out donors. A text alert interrupts my thoughts. I glance at the screen and freeze.

> Jonathan: Time's up. Tell your doctor friend his career is over. You know I have the resources to finish him. You could stop it if you come home.

A moment ticks by, and another text pings through.

> Jonathan: I'm coming to you.

CHAPTER THIRTY-NINE

EVIE

The rain pours down by the time we end up at Liam's house. He hasn't spoken much since we left the Dudley's home. I fear him closing off and falling into the same descending spiral as before, where he can't get out of his head. I already sense him shutting me out. If I knew how to stop the comparisons surely floating through his mind, I would. But I know one thing; I can't leave until I make this right.

"That was the scariest thing I've ever witnessed." I grab a glass from the cupboard and fill it with water. Maybe I shouldn't mention what happened. Talking about it further cements those images of a lifeless baby in my mind. Those images won't go away regardless.

Liam grunts in response, clearly not wanting to discuss it. He shrugs out of his stained shirt and tosses it in the trash. He stands there staring at it. I take my time drinking the water, watching his back muscles flex. I want to ease his pain away. I'm struggling, and this tragedy was only a fraction of what he experienced in New York. I can't imagine the level of anguish he dealt with.

"If you hadn't checked on them, that little girl would've died. You saved her life. Possibly the mother's, too." I believe that and know he thinks it, too, even though he's spooked. It's too close of a reminder of his past.

I grab another glass and fill it, and then I step toward him. He turns when I approach, and those mossy green eyes rise to meet mine. My heart aches. There's so much hurt and longing in his gaze. I hand him the glass, pushing aside what I need to do in the corner of my brain to visit later. Before everything implodes, I want to release those haunting thoughts weighing him down if only momentarily. He takes the glass from my hand but doesn't drink. Instead, he stares at me. I run my hands along his chest, taking my time, committing every ridge and valley to memory. I make my way to the waistband of his pants. I continue to hold his gaze as I unbuckle the belt. His free hand slides over the top of mine, and he shakes his head. My phone buzzes inside my purse, drawing Liam's attention. I ignore it, not ready to address what that text symbolizes, and grip his belt tighter. I want this. I want to make him feel good one last time.

"Let me take care of you," I say, my voice raspy. Then I add, "sir."

He closes his eyes and sucks in a breath. Setting the glass down, he says, "I don't deserve you."

He releases his hold on my hand. I relish the small victory and drop to my knees, shoving his pants down. They fall to the floor. I grab hold of his cock and run my hand along his length, biting back a moan. *Damn*, I love this cock. I love every square inch of his body, but his dick is my favorite. Flashes of light spark through the windows, followed by a loud rumble. A shudder works through me, knowing what I have to do later. I fight through the feeling trying to overwhelm me and run my tongue along the shaft before wrapping my lips around the tip. I release with a pop and cup his balls, gently massaging them. He tips his head back, grabbing the back of my neck. I take that as a green light. I know what's coming. I know this will be our last night together before he shuts me out of his life for good. He doesn't realize I'm a step ahead of him.

He thrust forward, fucking my mouth, and I surrender. The tip of his dick hits the back of my throat, causing tears to form instantly. I swallow him down and take all I can. I know this isn't the time. We should pick up from the discussion in the truck earlier and explain how we feel toward each other. I should explain how my next move will protect him. But none of that matters right now. I want to satisfy him one last time. I want to have him for one more night. Our short-lived relationship will never be the same after tonight.

His breath quickens, and I know he's close. I look up at him, and our gazes lock. Whatever he sees is enough to tip him over the edge and have me swallowing every drop of cum.

Panting, he pulls me up and wraps his arms around me, squeezing so tightly I can barely breathe. His hands run through my hair, and it feels like he's on the cusp of crying. Or maybe that's me and my feelings spilling over.

I love you.

He pulls away far enough to land his lips on mine. The kiss starts slow and sensual before deepening. Can he sense this is our last night together? The way his tongue claims mine, it seems that way. Maybe we're both feeling vulnerable tonight.

I love you.

He picks me up and carries me to his room. He is usually vocal and demanding, but tonight, he hasn't said a word. Maybe he wants this to be our last night? I cling to him tighter, trying to keep my heart from breaking. I don't want this to end, but I have to protect him. If today taught me anything, it's that life is unpredictable. He's a good doctor. I won't let my burdens drag him down. He has a child that needs to be provided for.

I love you.

Tears prick my eyes as he lays me on the bed. Inch by inch, he peels my clothes off, kissing the revealed skin as he drags each article of clothing off. The rain beats against the window like tiny shards piercing my heart. I won't survive this night. My body is primed with anticipation by the time he has me naked and lying beneath him.

Thunder claps overhead as he enters me. The moment is so raw and intimate that I never want it to end. He moves inside me, and I let go, giving myself over to the moment.

The room becomes a symphony of thunder rolls and moans. Our bodies slap together in a harmonic cadence. Weaving his fingers through mine, he holds them above my head and drives into me with purpose. The pace continues until we're writhing in pleasure. A whispered, "I love you," escapes his mouth, and my heart breaks even more. Thrusting one last time, he holds the position before collapsing on top of me. I run my fingertips along the length of his back. He gives me one last longing kiss after catching his breath before he pulls away.

I lie there waiting for him to come back. As he cuddles next to me, I don't let him see the tears streaming down my face. When his breaths steady and his body falls limp, I slip from underneath him.

Staring at his angelic face, I itch to run my fingers along his strong jawline, to feel his scruffiness one last time, but I don't do anything while an incredible sense of loss swallows me whole. My voice is thick with emotion as I whisper, "Please forgive my betrayal, sir." I lean over and kiss his cheek. "I love you, too. More than you'll ever know."

I force myself to pull away and pad across the floor to my room, where my suitcases wait, knowing this regret will haunt me for the rest of my life. Women like me aren't born to be happy. We're born to fulfill needs and duties—the curse of a privileged life. I will make that sacrifice if it means saving the person who deserves more happiness than he realizes.

I make it out to my car and fire off a text.

> Me: I'm heading home.

CHAPTER FORTY

LIAM

The morning sunrays peer through the window, stirring me awake. I relish in the warmth for a moment hoping the nightmare of the last few days was just a bad dream. I reach across to pull Evie next to me but touch nothing but air. I lie still and listen for any signs of stirring. Dread settles in my bones. I palm the too-cold sheets and confirm what I already suspected.

She's gone.

Reluctantly, I plant my feet on the ground and push to stand. I race out to the empty hallway and throw open her bedroom door.

My heart sinks at the empty room and missing suitcases.

I don't even call her name because I know it's useless.

She's gone.

I skip down the stairs and beeline to the backdoor. A veil of blackness coats my heart as I stare between the shades. The faded Honda is gone along with my happiness.

She's made her choice, and it wasn't me.

CHAPTER FORTY-ONE

EVIE

"Hello, Jeffries." I drum up a smile, grateful to see the older gentleman, and shove my oversized sunglasses to the top of my head.

"It's good to see you, ma'am. Your parents are in the main office." Jeffries's no-nonsense voice makes me feel at ease. I know it's weird to admit, but the old geezer has been with the family ever since I can remember. He's the only one I can tolerate, aside from Miss Carmichael. Too bad she is no longer employed by us.

"Daddy's here and not at work?" Dad never works from home.

Jeffries hesitates. "He's following the doctor's orders."

"I see." I guess Mom wasn't lying about Dad's health scare. It makes coming home not that unbearable.

He gestures to the car. "I'll bring in your belongings and park the car."

"Thank you. No need to unpack. I can take care of my clothes." *I don't plan on staying too long.* As soon as I settle my score with Jonathan, I'm gone. I can't let any of them sink their claws into me. Otherwise, I'll never leave.

"Perhaps you want to change before meeting them?" He gives me a once over, the sparkle in his eyes twinkling brighter.

I glance down at my frayed jean shorts and puffy white halter top paired with red chucks. "What? You think this will push Mother over the edge?"

He clicks his tongue. "Never knew you for a rebel."

I punch his arm playfully. "Things are changin', Jeffery Boy." I wink at him and turn to walk down the sterile hallway, my sneakers squeaking against the snow-white marble floors. I've forgotten how cold and detached this house feels.

Sort of like my heart about now.

I hate leaving Liam that way, but I couldn't risk the fallout from Jonathan. Liam's demise won't be my collateral damage. He means too much to me, even though he was ending things with me. He wanted me gone. That much was obvious, proven by his lack of contact. He said he loved me, but that wasn't enough for him to ask me to stay.

But he was going to until he found out about his baby.

The voice of reason can go fuck herself. All she's doing is reminding me of things I can't have.

Three quick taps on Dad's door—one for the element of surprise, another for my protection, and the third for my sanity. I hear a commotion before pushing my way inside.

"Darling," my father's startled voice calls from behind the door. "I didn't expect you back so soon."

"Yes, funny how that works." I don't elaborate. Part of me isn't sure if he collaborated with Jonathan or not. "Mother said you've been having issues. Shouldn't you be resting?"

He tosses his hands in the air and looks around his office. "This is me resting."

I walk over to his desk. Mom lifts from her seat in front of Dad and turns to face me. She clutches her necklace and gasps. "What on earth are you wearing? Did you go out in public like that?" Her horrified eyes drop to my shoes. "Where are your heels?"

"I drove nine and half hours to get here. I wanted to be comfortable. Besides, I hawked them for rent." I flash her a dazzling smile because I speak the truth. My ex-landlord was more than happy to receive in-style Louboutins.

"Do you need money, darling?" Daddy asks, seemingly unaware of the financial strain they put me in.

I shake my head. "I have enough. What's this about you not feeling well?"

He bats his hand, as if dying is bothersome. "It was just a case of angina brought on by stress. I need to ease up on my workload."

"It would help if you'd be here. Then, your father wouldn't have to worry so much." Mom's head bobs in defiance.

Guilt settles into my bones. I hate that Daddy worries, but I can't live here. "Mother," I go to protest, but Dad cuts me off.

"Your mom brings up a good point."

I shoot a glare at Dad, as if he betrayed me.

He holds his hands up, making a stop motion. "Now, hear me out."

I clamp my mouth shut as my stomach sinks. There is never a good statement that starts with those words.

"I have a proposition for you."

"And what would that be?" I ask a little too sharply. Mom tsks. She can huff and puff all she wants; I won't succumb to their needs.

"It's no secret you want to help underprivileged people—kids in general. What if I set up a foundation where you can bring in donations while helping those kids you seem to care so much for."

I'm shocked Dad even knows about my plan. My dream. I've never told anyone besides Liam, and I know he wouldn't have talked to them.

"How do you even know that?"

"We know everything, dear," Mom claims before Dad can speak.

I narrow my eyes. "What do I have to do?"

Before my parents can answer, Jonathan walks into the room.

CHAPTER FORTY-TWO

EVIE

"What is going on?" I look at my dad and back to Jonathan.

"We have a business proposition I think you'll find rather lucrative."

My eyes narrow. "What?"

"You take the money to start the shelter. This will keep you busy and occupied and fulfill what you need," Dad says.

"Why do I anticipate a but?"

"You, in turn, marry Jonathan."

Wrong kind of but. This butt is an ass.

"There's no way I'm marrying this manipulative—"

"I wouldn't finish that if I were you." Jonathan steps closer to me. "Honey."

A sickening feeling washes over me. I glare at him.

"We'll leave you to discuss."

"Remember, darling, you're a Thornhill, not a vagabond." Mom's gaze sweeps over me. She curls her lips back in disgust. "Please change before dinner."

When my parents exit, I spin back to Jonathan. I want to

smack the smirk right from his devilishly handsome face. "What do you think you're doing?"

"Getting my way."

"It'll be a cold day in hell before I marry you. Are you that damn greedy that you would sacrifice a future wife and family?"

"We may not be in love, but we work together. It wasn't all bad." He erases the distance between us. My body recoils at his touch.

"It doesn't matter how it started. Only how it ended. And I remember it ending pretty badly."

"I seem to remember you wanting me on our last night together. I could see the lust swirling in those eyes." He steps closer, leaning next to my ear. "I could smell it."

Slap.

His chuckle is low and deep. He rubs his cheek, eyes narrowing. "Darling, I'd be careful if I were you. I don't think you want this type of life."

"I will not marry you," I say between gritted teeth.

"Oh, but you will. Or your little boyfriend's cozy practice will implode. I think he'll still need a license to practice, and rest assured, he won't have as much as a piece of toilet paper by the time I'm through. I would think his baby would need a good provider."

"How do you know about his child?"

His evil chuckle burrows deep inside me. God, I hate that sound. "You don't think I would let my greatest asset go off alone now, would you?"

"You had me followed?"

"I knew every step you took."

I think back to the stranger in town. How the man bumped into me and ended up in the office. How there was a familiarity about him, I couldn't place.

"You son of a bitch."

"Classy. You really shouldn't talk about your future mother-in-law like that. She wouldn't like it."

"You're crazy."

"Hmm, but sane enough to know your boyfriend won't be helping you out this time."

Jesus, he even knows about the car. What the hell?

"You don't know anything."

"Oh, but I do. He took the payout, by the way. And that's the real reason he wanted you gone from his life."

"No. He wouldn't."

Jonathan quirks an eyebrow. "I believe it came in the form of a grant last Thursday."

My chest tightens. Last Thursday, when he returned from the rural checks, he was so happy about the grant and federal approval. This happened right before my interview, right before he pushed me away.

But he whispered he loved me.

Yet made no promises to me.

I shake my head, refusing to believe the worst in Liam. "He wouldn't."

"Oh, but he did. It's funny what money does to people."

My eyes well up. He couldn't have.

"Didn't you wonder why he kept insisting you leave? He wanted you to choose the job so he wouldn't have to break your heart."

But he whispered he loved me.

"There were never any intentions of spending forever with you. He wants his second chance at a family. That's why he accepted the payout."

Tears stream down my cheeks, but I don't bother to wipe them away. "How many people did you pay off?"

"Enough."

"It doesn't make sense. Why waste the money?"

"That's pocket change. We'll have an empire together. You'll be by my side. You can even have your pet project helping people if you want." He leans over and tries to kiss me, but I push him away.

"No, it will never happen."

"We'll see." He licks his bottom lip. He steps back and pulls my phone from his pocket. "Jefferies wanted me to give this to you."

I snatch my phone from his hands.

"Unless you want his past plastered all over the local television stations, I suggest you think long and hard about my proposal. Oh, and he can kiss that government funding goodbye. Senator Glasnost's waiting on my call to pull the funding."

And then, he exits along with my hopes of a quick getaway.

CHAPTER FORTY-THREE

LIAM

"Hey, Grumpy-ass," my sister says as she invades my hiding space.

Tucked between two maple trees in Mom's backyard, I don't even bother to lift my head at Ansley's approach. I realize sitting hunched over with my elbows on my knees looks as pathetic as I feel, but I don't need any judgment. She hasn't stepped foot in this town since my father's funeral, and the first thing she wants to do is to hurl insults at me.

Fuck that.

I've gotten enough grief from friends. I don't need it from my family too. "I liked it better when you stayed away."

She ignores the "do not disturb" sign branded in my expression and sits beside me.

"You love me, and you know it." She bumps her knee into mine. "You also know I'm right."

I grunt because I do know she's right. She was also kind with the nickname, considering asshole would be more fitting. I'm barking at everyone, including my mom, but I feel handcuffed. I'm having a baby with a woman I don't love and let the one I do walk away. No, it was more like *run*. Evie ran so fast she didn't leave tracks.

God, it has been three weeks since she left, and I'm no closer to figuring out what to do about my situation. Ciera has blown up my phone daily—the concept of giving someone space lost on her —but we're no closer to an arrangement than when she first came. She acts as if the only way she wants this child is if I'm present. Even with all the drama, the question burning in my gut is how Evie is doing. I expected her to walk in after my sister. When that didn't happen, I spiraled deeper into darkness.

"What are you doing?" Ansley asks.

Slowly going insane.

"Contemplating life," I deadpan.

"You owe Mom an apology. She just wants you to say a few words about Dad tomorrow. That's not too much to ask."

"I know."

"Then, put on your big boy panties and give the damn speech. Quit sitting here, hiding like some little bitch boy, and give her what she wants."

"I'm not hiding." I wince, realizing I sound like a petulant child.

"Yeah?" She lets the question hang until I finally look at her. Her face softens, but she doesn't stop nagging. "It sure seems that way."

My nostrils flare. If she wants to go there, then fine. Game on. "I'm not the only one good at hiding, *sis*."

Ansley's eyes narrow. "Touché. But at least I can admit it."

"Good for you. You know I don't like speaking in front of crowds." My tone comes out harsher than intended, but I'm strung too tight. I'll snap with the least amount of annoyance.

"Wow, I thought Rachael was exaggerating when she told me how grouchy you've been." She places her hand on my knee and drops her voice. "What's really going on?"

"Nothing." I stretch my feet out and lean back onto the bench. A low hum of laughter and chatter from the neighbor's party filters toward us. It sours my mood further.

"Have you heard from Ciera?"

"Yeah."

"And?" she prompts.

"And it looks like I'm moving back to New York."

"What? You're getting back together with her?"

"No." That's the one definite in my life. "You can unscrew your face." It's twisted in disgust. Good to know what she really thinks of Ciera.

"Sorry," she says, bringing her hand to her forehead. "But move? You want to leave your practice and home?"

"I want to see my kid."

"I know the situation isn't ideal, but uprooting your practice and moving across the country isn't the best plan."

"What else am I supposed to do? Ciera won't move here without a commitment. I want to be part of my child's life, and Ciera blames me for messing up hers."

"But you'd be miserable. I mean"—she waves her hand along my body—"look at you. You're miserable just by the thought of it."

She's not wrong. "My well-being isn't important."

"You don't want to move."

"I don't have much choice."

"But you love Evie."

Also true, but how would she know? We barely talk. "You don't know what you're talking about. You just breezed into town. We haven't seen each other for over half a year. What on earth would make you believe I'm in love with Evie?"

"Because I know you. You're not as covert at hiding your emotions as you think." She cocks an eyebrow. "This grouchy bear thing you've perfected is nothing more than a reflection of your feelings. Face it, Liam, deep down, you're a nice guy. You're only grumpy when you're hurting. And you moved back here grouchy. I thought it was because of Dad at first, but then I remembered you weren't happy when I called while you lived in New York. You don't love Ciera. You love Evie."

"I can't be with Evie. She doesn't want an instant family."

"But did you give her a chance to choose? This entire scenario smells of misunderstanding, which is the absolute worst in breakups."

"It's *not* a misunderstanding." Evie made it pretty fucking clear what she wants. Or should I say what she doesn't want, which is me.

"She left my place early to tell you how she didn't want to leave. I get the unexpected pregnancy would derail the effort, but you dismissed her."

I flinch. "I didn't tell her to leave."

"And you didn't ask her to stay either."

"I did her a favor. She doesn't want kids. She sure as hell wouldn't want to raise someone else's."

"This isn't the nineteen-fifties. Stepchildren are as prevalent as the common cold."

"Did you just reference children as viruses?"

She scrunches her nose. "No. Maybe? I don't know. If you think about it, they kind of are. After the first set of friends has one, it spreads like wildfire, and before you know it, you're all attending little league games together."

Sadness creeps into my bones at that visual. "That won't happen with my son living in New York." I let out a sound that's a cross between a disgruntled moan and agonized groan. "The point is moot. Evie isn't interested in uprooting her life to become a part-time mom. She left in the middle of the night. It doesn't get any clearer than that."

"But did you tell her you wanted to be with her?"

"No, there's no point."

"Oh, big brother. You need to call her."

"She's better off in Indianapolis."

Ansley's gaze whips to mine, puzzlement clouding her features. "She's not there."

"What do you mean she's not there? Where is she?"

"She's back in Philadelphia, where she plans to stay."

Alarm grips my chest. It's one thing knowing she's pursuing what makes her happy, even if that happiness excludes me. It was the only thing keeping my sanity intact. But knowing she went home... well, it changes things. "She hates it there."

"Look, I don't know what happened. Evie won't talk to me about it, but she insists this is what she wants."

"Do you believe her?" There is no way she wants to be there.

"No. After the first month of rooming with her in the dorms, I knew she never wanted to go back." My sister lays an accusatory glance my way. "Why haven't you called her?"

My hands clench into fists. "I *have* called. I tried as soon as I got my ass out of my head." I spent the first day in a dark place. I dove into work, which was chaotic with Rachael still out sick. Evie had blocked my number by the time I finished the day. I was too angry to call my sister.

Fuck.

Why hadn't I called Ansley to check if Evie had arrived?

"Then, how do you not know?"

"She never answered. She blocked my number instead. I assumed that meant she was done with me."

"Supper's ready, you two," Mom hollers out the back door.

"We'll be right there." Ansley turns to me and says, "That's strange because she never mentioned blocking you. I'm going to get to the bottom of this."

"Don't."

"What do you mean don't?"

"Exactly that. Evie is my business. I don't want you to inter-fere. We'll figure it out after Dad's ceremony." I suck in a deep breath and let it out slowly. "For now, I'll apologize to Mom and make her happy."

"You're speaking?"

I shove down the sudden nausea and nod. "I'll speak."

BACK AT MY HOUSE, I dial Ciera's number. After what Ansley said about the timing of when I became a grump—which is the stupidest term ever, I'm not *that* grumpy—I got to thinking. I slipped into a dark time after the traumatic birth. I wasn't the best to be around.

"I'm surprised to hear from you already," Ciera says as she answers.

"I owe you an apology."

Silence greets me. A moment later, she says, "I know you do, but I'm curious as to what brought this on."

"It was something my sister said about my mood and the timing. The traumatic birth affected me more than I realized. I don't think I fully recovered. And because of that, our relation-ship was one-sided."

She lets out a sigh. "I'm glad you're recognizing it now. I just wish things would've been different between us."

I lay my head on the couch and stare up at the ceiling. How did we get to this point? I thought our future was set, only to find her in another state carrying the baby she never wanted and the girl I love living farther away and blocking my calls. What a tangled mess.

"Our expectations from the relationship were miles apart."

She laughs. "That's the truth. Well, you got your wish about a child."

"Yeah. I'm so sorry. I thought I was more careful than that."

"I was going to call you. Remember me telling you about the job I was trying to land."

"The one that would send you to Europe?"

"The very one."

My breath hitches. If she tells me she is taking my child out of the country, I don't know what I'll do. I'm struggling with the idea of being a semi-part-time dad. How would I handle being a once-in-a-while one?

"I found out today they chose me as their spokesperson. They're willing to wait until I deliver."

"What does that mean for the baby?" Sweat breaks across my forehead. I want to be involved in raising my child.

"I don't want to sound like an uncaring mother because I do love this child, but I can't raise him alone. I worked too hard to get where I'm at in my career. I don't want to miss this opportunity."

"What are you saying exactly?"

"Would you be willing to have full custody?"

Relief washes through me. This is the perfect solution. I could stay in Sugar Creek Falls. I could rely on my mom to help while I work. I could watch my child play with my friends' kids. I would be a unit.

"Of course, I'd be willing. I'll take full responsibility." Once I say the words aloud, I realize this may end my chance at reconciliation with Evie. I am a package deal now—one I'm not sure she'll want to unwrap.

"I feel like a horrible person." Her voice wavers as she sniffs. These tears are real for once.

"Listen to me. It isn't shameful to chase a career instead of motherhood. You're not any different than most men after divorces." I leave out the fact she never wanted to be a mom in the first place. Mentioning it won't give a positive spin to the conversation, and it would remind us of why we broke it off. I had blamed her, but it was really on me. Before asking her to marry, I should've been more mindful of her position. "And I'll, no, *we'll* always be here. You can still have a role in his life if you want."

"Look at us getting along."

"Maybe I should hang up before I say something stupid."

She laughs through a sob. "Thanks, Liam. I hope whatever girl invoked this change realizes how good of a guy you are."

She doesn't, and I don't know how to change that.

CHAPTER FORTY-FOUR

EVIE

"What are you doing?" I ask the staff person rifling through my suitcase.

"Sorry, ma'am. Your mother asked me to assist in getting you settled since it's been a few weeks."

My lips flatten to a thin line. It is not the woman's fault for invading my privacy. She's following orders.

"I'm perfectly capable of unpacking my clothes. I'm sorry my mom sent you in here, but I would appreciate my privacy."

"Yes, ma'am." She nods and ducks out of my room. I snatch the clothes she hung in the closet and toss them on the bed.

Maybe I'm being ridiculous. Or perhaps I'm fooling myself. If I empty my suitcase, I will never leave. I'll never see Liam again.

The ache in my heart burns at the thought of him. It has been three weeks since I left, and the pain of leaving is still as severe as the day I left him in his bed alone.

Is he back with Ciera? Is he excited about the family he wanted? Does he even miss me?

One phone call to Ansley would answer the first two questions, but I can't bring myself to ask. His lack of calling or texting speaks volumes for the last question. At the very least, I figured he would send a text to see if I made it to Indianapolis. As far as I know, he hadn't texted Ansley either. She would've told me otherwise—sisterhood over brotherhood and all that.

I fold the last pair of shorts, place them on top, and zip the suitcase shut. There has to be a way to get out of this mess without causing harm to Liam. I just have to figure it out.

"Miss Thornhill," Jeffries says.

"Yes?" I glance over my shoulder and eye his disapproval as he takes in the suitcase. I can't tell if he disapproves of my rebellion or my parents' entrapment.

"Your father wants to see you in his office."

"Thanks, Jeffries. I'll be right down."

"Yes, ma'am."

God, that's three ma'ams in less than twenty minutes. Give me laid back and country any day of the week.

I knock on my dad's office door three times before pushing my way inside.

"You wanted to see me?"

Dad looks up from his desk and frowns. I steel myself for the lecture of not looking the part—leggings and a sports bra aren't to be worn anywhere but the home gym—but he surprises me when he scrubs a hand over his face and sighs.

"Jeffries said you wanted to talk to me?" I prod, wanting to get this discussion over with.

"We need to review the funding for the center you wish to open."

I want to refute any proposal he offers on principle. The money comes with ties and obligations I don't want to fulfill. But if I refuse, that harms people who could otherwise benefit from it.

"What do you need to know?"

He sits back in his chair and folds his hands as he studies me.

"When you returned home, there was light in your eyes. They've dulled."

"I'm not following," I lie when I know exactly what he means. It took one day for their reminder of what it means to be a Thornhill to snuff the fire that drove me. To kill the spark that everyone outside this circle found endearing.

"You don't seem happy."

I scoff, which causes his eyebrow to rise. But come on. Happy? Is he for real? "How can I be happy when my will has been taken away?"

His jaw hardens, and I know I struck a nerve. But I'm done being nice. Dad doesn't need the added stress, but that doesn't mean lying to him. He put me in this situation. He knows Jonathan's vile and has no qualms about tying his only daughter to the guy.

"It's the best solution."

"Business before family, right?"

I swear his nostrils flare, and I'm pushing my luck, but he hasn't been the best parent. Liam gets a faraway look when he talks about his dad. What will my memories be? A Chanel bag and Louboutins? Very touching.

"I can see you're not in the mood to talk. Hopefully, your mood improves tonight."

I stand. Tonight is the environmental gala. I may put on a fancy gown, but I guarantee my mood won't improve. With a nod, I exit.

I need to find out if Jonathan's threat holds any clout. Does he have the senator in his pocket? Probably so. If I can get dirt on Jonathan, then I'll have leverage.

I step back into my bedroom and spy the suitcase.

Maybe tonight won't be so bad after all. I just need to play the part. Then, I can make my move and never come back.

CHAPTER FORTY-FIVE

LIAM

What did I agree to?

Standing on the podium, I wring my hands and clear my throat before stepping to the microphone. Why am I such a fucking coward when it comes to public speaking? I glance toward the noon sky and mutter under my breath, "I know you're watching us today, Pops. I sure could use your guidance."

I direct my attention back to the waiting crowd.

"I, uh, want to thank everyone for showing up today. This project was near to my dad's heart. Being a legacy, he always talked about giving something back to the community. I used to tease him and say that was what the prostate exams were for, but he failed to see the humor." My sister's eyes bulge as the entire crowd groans. I'm transported back to my senior year and my failed fart joke—tough crowd.

I grip the side of the pulpit and clear my throat again.

"Anyway, he had treated enough children for accidents that he saw a need for updated equipment in this park. Seeing his dream come to fruition would have made my dad smile."

Overcome with emotions, I hang my head and puff out a

breath. My gaze scans along the crowd, landing on Aileen holding her newborn. My chest tightens. Then, I look at my mom and sister, whose eyes glisten with tears.

"I miss my dad. He taught me the value of a community. He used to say many things could be accomplished when good people band together. That it's a choice to help your fellow neighbor, even when they are tough choices." I let out a small laugh. "He sat me down before I headed out for medical school and told me life is full of tough choices, but at the end of the day, you have to choose what makes you the happiest. You can never shine and give your all until you care for yourself."

I pause because, holy shit, my father came through. He did guide from above. And I know at that moment what I have to do. I glance down at my watch, catching the early time.

"I, uh, have to go."

A murmur breaks across the crowd as I exit off stage. My sister and Matthew race over to me with knowing smiles while the rest of the group looks confused.

Ansley hands me a slip of paper. "This is her parents' address. Ask for Jeffries. He'll help you."

Matthew pats my back. "Go get her, man."

CHAPTER FORTY-SIX

EVIE

Conversations surround me, but I've never felt so isolated. Sitting at the white linen covered table, I scan the ballroom. People in business rub elbows with senators and representatives. Deals once made behind closed doors are now whispered murmurs in the open. I've witnessed it all in my years of coming to these events. It strikes me that Jonathan is in the mix more than likely making some shady agreement. My frown deepens. I should garner intel instead of sitting here, sulking.

"This is a party. You could at least smile." Dad takes a drink of his whiskey and settles into the chair two seats away.

"I will as soon as there's something to celebrate." I don't bother to hide my disdain and bring my wine glass to my lips. Jonathan joining our table unbeknownst to me darkened my temper.

"Hmm," Dad grunts, and the pang in my chest tightens.

I've missed that sound. I miss my grumpy doctor. I can't help but wonder how the dedication ceremony went. Did Liam break down and speak? Is the festival going well? I hate that I'm not there with my best friend. I hate that I'm wondering what Liam and his friends are up to. I went from thinking the festival was lame to being sad for missing it. Or maybe I just want Liam.

"Sit up straighter, dear. Slouching is never a good look," Mom says, taking the seat between Dad and me. "It wouldn't hurt you to smile."

Why do people insist on others smiling? It's rude and annoying. "Once I have something to smile about, I'll do just that."

"You're with Philadelphia's most eligible bachelor. How can you not be thrilled?"

"Vivian, give it a rest," my dad says. My gaze snaps to him. Did he just put Mom in her place?

"But I—"

He holds his hand up to silence her. "Geneva is clearly not in the mood."

Why yes, he did. I mean, Dad isn't wrong, my mood could pucker the sourest lemon, but when did he get so observant?

Like a good little bird, Mom straightens her posture and settles back into her cage. Although I agree with Dad's messaging, I don't like the authoritarian way he handles Mom. This will be my life—my future—unless I make a change. Tears spring to my eyes. Liam showed a different side of love. One I deserve. I remind myself why I can't be with him. Not only will Jonathan use Liam's past to humiliate him, but he'll also find a way to void his medical license. Jonathan rubs elbows with powerful people. It is not beneath him to use that power to his advantage. He already threatened to pull the funding for his clinic. I need to get dirt on Jonathan.

I push to stand but sit back down when the band stops playing. The interruption draws everyone's attention to the stage.

"Oh, it's time." Mom's eyes gleam as she looks on with the other spectators. Dad's mouth flattens. *What is going on?*

I direct my attention to the stage, and my stomach dips when Jonathan makes his way to the lead singer. *This can't be good.*

"Act surprised, dear." Mom reaches across and pats my hand. "I want nothing but smiles. But not too big. You don't want to show off too many teeth. The pictures will turn out bad."

What is she talking about? Too shocked to even reply, I don't move as rage races through my veins. Surely she doesn't mean Jonathan is going to propose. How dare they ambush me like this? If they think they can railroad me into a marriage, they're more insane than I thought.

This isn't only about you. He has a child to provide for.

Jonathan grabs the microphone and gives the audience his million-dollar smile. I want to barf.

"I'm glad everyone is having a good time. Remember Black-well Incorporated is all about renewable energy. Open your pockets to sustain a viable environment. Speaking of opening pockets..." Jonathan reaches into his pants pocket, and I can barely breathe. Before he pulls out what could be the final nail in my coffin, a guy walks out of the shadows.

"Excuse me," the guy says, holding out his hand for the microphone. "May I?"

I suck in a breath when the spotlight moves to highlight the intruder and reveals *Liam*. He's here? How? Why? I sit trans-fixed, afraid that if I move, he will disappear.

Jonathan turns to the guy, his glare threatening. "I was about to speak. What are you doing?"

"I just need to make a quick announcement."

I do a quick sweep of the crowd. Everyone's attention is directed on the stage. Anger flashes through Jonathan's eyes, but he reels it in just as quick, as if he remembered the crowd. I know him well enough to know he wouldn't want to look like a fool in front of his associates. He'll play along until the narrative doesn't work in his favor anymore.

"That's what I'm trying to do, buddy." Jonathan gives a half-laugh to the crowd. A stagehand runs up to Liam and hands him a microphone. Jonathan starts to protest, but his words fall silent. A wave of murmurs descends around the audience. I stifle a laugh when he realizes someone silenced his microphone.

"What on earth is going on?" Mom asks. She goes to move, but Dad's voice comes out stern and direct.

"Sit still, Vivian."

"I, uh…" Liam shakes his head and laughs humorlessly. He clears his throat and begins again. "See, there's a dedication ceremony back in my hometown to honor my father. He was the town's physician. A good man. An honorable man who poured his life's work into a community. It wasn't until I was up there on the stage that I realized how off-course my life has gone."

I gasp. He actually fought his fear and spoke in front of the crowd. Pride sears through me. A sudden urge to rush to the stage and kiss his anxiety away overcomes me. It takes everything in me to stay seated, but I have to. I won't be the reason for his demise.

"Standing there, I remembered the day he sat me down and said, 'Son, life is full of tough choices, but at the end of the day, you have to choose what makes you the happiest. You can never shine and give your all until you care for yourself'. It made me ponder what I want people to remember me as. A doctor? A man who dedicated his entire life to his hometown, even if it meant sacrificing his happiness?" He searches the crowd, and his body relaxes when those beautiful eyes land on mine. "Or do I want to be someone who chases after their dream and doesn't let fear of the unknown get in the way? I don't know about you, but I want to belong to the latter category. No matter what challenges arise, I want to face them together."

Tears stream down my face, despite the smile stretching wide across my face. *Sorry, Mom, I couldn't care less about my teeth at this moment.*

Liam hands the microphone to the lead singer, jumps off the stage, and heads straight to me.

Mom's fist hits the table. "What is this?"

"I think this is our daughter branching out on her own."

My gaze cuts to Dad. He sits lazily in his chair, legs crossed. He's too relaxed for this to have been a surprise.

"You knew he was coming?" I accuse.

"We discussed things earlier."

"I won't stand for this. This is outrageous. He's a *doctor*," Mom says, as if being a doctor is equivalent to being homeless. She pushes to her feet.

"Vivian, sit down," Dad orders. Then, he turns to me and adds, "I think it's time for you to find that smile."

"Thanks, Daddy." The words choke in my throat. This is the first time he has considered my thoughts or feelings.

"Evie," the deep, baritone voice I've missed so much says as he approaches.

Our gazes connect and hold. The banquet room disappears as all my focus directs to the guy in front of me.

"I can't believe you came." I don't know when it happened, but I find myself standing before him.

"I had to. I had to make this right."

The spotlight shines on us. I shield my eyes from the bright beams as the band strikes into the chorus of Kiss the Girl by Samuel E. Wright from *The Little Mermaid*. The crowd cheers, egging us on.

Liam shrugs. "We better give them what they want."

I don't have time to respond when his lips find mine. We have so much to discuss. But for right now, we're good.

When we break apart, the room erupts into more clapping, and the spotlight disappears.

"You shouldn't have come. Jonathan is out to squash you. He knows certain senators who can bury the funding for your clinic."

"Then, we'll find another source. None of that matters if you're not in my life sharing it."

"But your reputation. He'll smear your name. Everyone back home will find out. What about your license?"

"Hey." He takes my face in his hands and leans down to kiss the tip of my nose. "I couldn't care less about my reputation. The people living there know me. That's the thing about small towns and what he fails to realize. A singular action doesn't define your reputation. It's a collective of choices made."

"But your license?"

"He has to prove I've done wrong. He can't."

"I'm so proud of you." And I am, not only for facing his fear and getting on the stage but also coming here for me. I don't know what this means for us, but it's a significant forward step.

"You're finished." Jonathan stalks to where we stand and grabs Liam's shoulder.

"Jonathan, I think you've manipulated my daughter enough." Dad's authoritative voice has a finality that makes Jonathan drop his hand. The great Jonathan Blackwall-Smith the Third wouldn't dare cause a scene, especially with my father.

"Sir, you can't possibly think this country boy is better. We have plans."

"It's not up to me." Dad gives me a warm smile. "All I want is for my daughter to be happy. That isn't with you." Dad leans in to kiss me on the cheek. "Family means more."

"Thanks, Daddy."

"Now, go before your mom unleashes the fury she's bottling inside her. I can only hold her off for so long. The driver's ready for you."

CHAPTER FORTY-SEVEN

EVIE

After telling the driver to take us to Liam's hotel, I lean back in the buttery-soft leather seat. Liam pulls his gaze from me and examines the limousine's interior. I can't imagine what this "Country Boy," as Jonathan dubbed him, thinks. I blush when laughter escapes.

"What's so funny?" He slides his hand over to mine and grasps my fingers. Contentment burrows into my bones. He feels like home.

"I find it ironic that you and your friends called me City Girl, and Jonathan called you Country Boy."

A slow, lazy smile tugs his lips. "What did you call me?"

I lick my lips, stalling. He quirks an eyebrow. "Dr. Grump."

He tips his head back in laughter. "I deserve that." His gaze darts around the limo again, giving a low whistle. "I can't believe this is your lifestyle."

"Was," I correct. "It *was* my lifestyle." A shiver skates down my spine. He'll never know how close I came to falling back into the same caged walls I worked to break free from.

"You don't think you'd miss this?"

I take in the vehicle's rich leather, the nameless driver always at the beckoning call, and my fancy dress that would've fetched me three months' rent in Chicago. The sheen from my feet draws my attention next. My exaggerated sigh lightens the mood.

"Not going to lie, I'd miss my heels." I tsk, drawing his laugh I wanted. As his laughter subsides, I grow serious. "When I was in Sugar Creek Falls, I never once missed this lavish lifestyle."

"Good thing because I could never compete." He scrubs a hand over his face, and my heart jumps at those promising words.

"Then, it's a good thing this isn't a competition."

Those jade green eyes bore into mine as a current of want jolts through me. I resist the urge to straddle his hips and give the greeting I so desperately want to share. There is much to discuss, and I won't derail this conversation. I also won't hold my feelings back this time. I need to take advantage of this second chance. They don't happen too often in life.

"Look, I know I messed up after Ciera came back, and you had every right that night to leave and block my number, but we really need to talk."

"Wait. What do you mean I blocked your number?"

He stills. "I called multiple times, and each one went straight to voicemail. It took me a few days to figure it out, but... why are you asking? You're the one who blocked me."

I snatch my phone from my purse. "No, I didn't. I thought you hadn't called or texted." I pull up my settings and look under blocked callers. My gasp pierces the air. "How did..." *Jonathan.* That bastard. "I had left my phone in my car when I first arrived, and our house manager gave it to Jonathan. He must've messed with it." I shouldn't be surprised, considering he invaded my privacy with my emails. The man holds zero scruples.

"Your dad's right. He is a manipulative prick."

The driver pulls in front of the Hilton, tabling our discussion until we're settled in the hotel room. The room is standard with a king-sized bed, desk, and combo dresser and television stand.

Liam removes his suit jacket and hangs it over the back of the desk chair as he loosens his tie. I lick my lips when he undoes his cuffs and rolls up his sleeves. The man is sexy.

Talk.

We are only here to talk.

Then, why do I want to toss him on the bed right now?

I shake my head, as if that will erase the X-rated thoughts swimming in my brain, and walk over to the bed.

"I don't know the best way to start, so I'm just going to be blunt." He sits beside me, hands on his knees. "I missed you. I know you want to accomplish all these things for yourself, but I missed everything about you. I missed seeing your mangled bunny slippers in the morning. I missed buying lattes after my run. I missed holding you at night and waking up beside you. I missed *you*. I love you, Geneva Thornhill. Right down to my very core. But I'm torn. I want to do right by you, but I don't want you to leave. Asking you to stay with me is the most selfish thing I could do, especially since it's more than me. You don't want kids right now, which I totally understand, and I was willing to concede, but that's no longer a possibility."

He was willing to concede.

"I've been doing a lot of reflecting on what I want and what makes me happy. I had this vision of how my life should look like, and I've molded my desires and dreams into this idea, but it all means nothing if I can't share it with you. If you're willing to share a life with my son and me, I'll move wherever you want: Philadelphia, Indianapolis, or Chicago. I don't care as long as we can be together."

My heart swells. "You're not moving to New York?"

"No. But you need to know it's not only me. My son will be living with me full time."

"Like permanently? What about Ciera?"

"Ciera had interviewed with this firm before moving to Sugar Creek Falls. They hadn't offered her the position at the time, but they contacted her yesterday. The only problem is the job's in Europe. She'll be moving to France, leaving me full custody of my son."

"That's great. I know you didn't want to miss any part of your kid's life." I want to jump in his arms and squeeze him. I can't explain how happy I am for him. His reluctance to tell me makes total sense now.

"I'm still missing out on the sonograms, but we FaceTimed during her last appointment. That's when I found out the little one is a boy."

Jealousy twists my stomach, confirming what I already figured out. I want that experience with Liam. I want an entire house filled with Little Liams.

He grabs my hand and weaves his fingers through mine. His woodsy scent wafts in the air, and I have to fight the urge to lean into him. But I missed him so much.

"That's why you need to think about what you really want and if you're capable of raising another person's child."

I soak in the sincerity pouring from every breath he takes. The way his gaze pleads for me to accept him and his son. I need to phrase my answer carefully, so he understands what I want. "When I said I didn't want kids, it was because I had to discover myself. How could I think about raising another little human without figuring out who I was first? But I spent these past three weeks thinking and came to a realization. This ideology of proving myself to people like my parents and old friends is pure bullshit. The only person I need to prove myself to is me. These past few months, I discovered who I was." A smile ghosts my lips. I was clueless about my self-discovery journey, but it became apparent after some serious reflection.

"I may not know everything about small-town living," I continue. "But for once, I found a place where I belong. I don't know if it's because I no longer hide who I am or because of a grumpy town doctor, but I found peace I never knew existed. That peacefulness shifted something inside me and made me realize I can accomplish good anywhere I go. That I am contributing. This entire time wasn't to prove myself. It was to be seen. You showed me that. You saw me."

"You touch more lives than you realize. You could never be invisible."

"Thank you." Tears sting my eyes, but I'm not through. "I can't think of anything more fulfilling than to fill that farmhouse with Little Liams. As for your son? You question if I could raise someone else's kid? The short answer is yes. He's a part of you—your creation. If he has a fraction of your personality, how could I not love him?"

"As much as I love hearing you say that, why do I sense reservations?"

I avert his gaze. This is the hardest part of the conversation. This is where I risk losing him. And damn it, I don't want to lose him, but I need reassurance. "That's because before I left—before we made love—you pulled away from me emotionally. I could feel it. I may have been saying goodbye, but you were, too."

"No," he rasps, but then he closes his eyes and shakes his head. "You're right. I was without realizing it. I was so confused, but I know what I want now. And that's you."

"How do I know you won't have another traumatic delivery and push me away?"

"You don't. And I can't guarantee I won't, but I recognize the trigger. I was serious before when I said the town would forgive my past, but the truth won't bury the guilt I still carry. The choices I made, regardless of whether they were correct, will haunt me for the rest of my life, but I refuse to let them define me."

"What are you saying?"

"I reached out to a colleague while waiting for my plane. She recommended a friend that specializes in birth traumas. I set up an appointment. Learning to cope with my guilt won't be a quick fix. Accepting my choices will take time and work, but I'm trying."

He looks so earnest and full of hope that my heart squeezes. This man, who was so closed off when I first met him I didn't think a tank could smash through his walls, is sitting beside me, pouring his heart out and trying. Whether it took losing me or gaining his son for him to recognize he needs help is irrelevant. He's doing this for himself and has taken the first steps. That's all the reassurance I need.

"I love you so much." Emotion chokes my words as threatening tears spill down my cheeks. His hands cup my face, and he swipes my tears away with his thumb. "Tell me I didn't mess this up between us. Tell me I'm not too late."

"You're not too late."

"I fucking love you." His lips crash onto mine. The kiss is frantic and urgent. It's future promises replacing past hopelessness. It's expectancy triumphing fear. It's intoxicating.

He pulls back, panting, the look in his eyes heady with want. "To hell with waiting or being too soon. I'll do this better later if you want, but marry me."

"What?"

"You heard me. Marry me. I knew I wanted you that first night when you waltzed over with a tray of champagne. I couldn't get you out of my head. You were on my mind before I ran into you in the hallway that first day. Why do you think I was so angry? I wanted to push you away because, somehow, I knew you were exactly the type of person I wanted. I can give you a better proposal later, but I want you to know I'm one hundred percent committed to you."

"I guess you'll have to start calling me Country Girl, then," I say, my smile matching his.

"I think I'll just call you mine."

"That's good because I only want your hands on me."

"That can be arranged." In one forward motion, I find myself lying on the bed underneath his massive frame. Heat darkens his eyes as he gently presses his palm on my calf and sweeps ever so slowly up the length of my leg. A quiver surges through my veins, which he doesn't miss.

The corner of his mouth lifts to a knowing smirk as his gaze holds mine. "Does my girl want more?"

His fingertips dip along the edges of my lace underwear, brushing teasingly along the area I want him most. "Yes, please."

That smirk flashes to a wicked grin. "Good. Now, get on all fours."

EPILOGUE
EVIE

Nine Months Later

I stand speechless, disbelief flashing through my mind as I stare at the double pink lines.

"I guess the opening ceremony isn't the cause behind your nausea after all," Ansley says.

We're in the bathroom of the new Vigo County Healthcare Clinic for Women. Ansley is the one who insisted I take a pregnancy test before the opening ceremony. She claimed I couldn't concentrate if I ignored my symptoms. I thought she was being impatient and nosy.

"Holy crap." I flash a broad smile at my best friend. "I don't know if I can wait until after the ceremony to tell him."

"Well, look at it this way. Liam's getting two dreams fulfilled today."

"Leave it to you to make a joke."

She shrugs. "Gotta save ya from the freakout."

I laugh and tuck the evidence into a plastic bag. The idea of placing a stick I urinated on in my purse is revolting, but these trash cans are empty. I can't dispose of it here. I blow out a breath. "Okay, I think I'm ready."

"Don't worry. I'll run interference, and you can tell him."

We step outside, where the small gathering of reporters stands along with our friends, family, and curious community members.

Liam stands looking proud as he holds his six-month son, Dallas. A reporter holds a microphone near Liam's face and nods to what he says.

I glance back at the building. This has been an actual labor of love. I've worked countless hours securing more grants and funding. The most shocking source was my father. He shifted the allotted funds for the facility he was going to give me to this one—a move that shocked not only Liam and me but Mom as well. I'm not sure she fully recovered.

Tensions have eased since I left home for good. I won't say she's happy, but she has come to terms with my choices. Dallas isn't allowed to call her grandma, but she can't deny how adorably sweet he is. That was, until he tossed his entire lunch on her silk blouse. I guess that's why I always had a nanny.

Jumping feet first into motherhood has been a breeze. Okay, that's a lie. I didn't know what the hell I was doing, but Liam bought me a ton of parenting books, which I devoured. It's a learning process, but what in life isn't?

"Hey," I say when the reporter leaves. The smile he greets me with melts my inside. I feel as if I'm the luckiest girl in the world. "Can we talk for a second?"

"I've got this little one." Ansley swoops in and takes Dallas from Liam.

Concern lines tighten his eyebrows, but he follows without saying a word until we're in a corner alone.

"Are you feeling okay?"

"Yes. Well, for the most part." I shake my head at his confusion. "Sorry, I'm not very good at this, so I'm just going to show you."

I pull out the plastic bag and display the results. His eyes grow large before snapping that gaze to me. "Is this real?"

"Yes!"

He picks me up and spins me around. Then, he plants his lips on mine and draws a slow, lingering kiss. When he pulls away, he asks, "Are you okay with this?"

"I've never been so happy."

"I need to make you an honest woman."

I punch his arm. "That's such an old man thing to say."

He chuckles. "I don't care. I can't wait to make you my wife."

"I'll get a date set now that the clinic will be up and running." I've spent so much time juggling this facility, a newborn, and his office. We haven't taken time for ourselves to plan a wedding. Plus, breaking it to Mom that I wanted a small countryside wedding wasn't a fight I was ready for.

"Sounds like the perfect plan. We have to prepare for that basketball team."

"I'm not having five kids."

"We're only three away." He pats my stomach.

"What if the baby is a girl?"

"That team isn't gender-specific."

"Oh?" I question, feigning surprise.

"Nope. Any team with our kids on it will dominate. That's the Seymour effect, City Girl."

I smile up at my cocky, not-so-grumpy doctor. "Well, it certainly worked on me." Then I add, "Sir."

His eyes darken with emotion as a low hungry growl escapes. "As much as I love the sight of you kneeling and waiting for me, I love the aftercare more." A wicked smile crosses his face. He isn't talking about life in general. He's talking about after sex. "You in my life is the best present I could have ever asked for. I was going to wait until after the ceremony, but..."

I gasp as he drops to his knee and pulls out a box from his lab coat. Tears prick my eyes when he opens the box and reveals a beautiful, contemporary engagement ring. Platinum intertwines and embraces the carat sized, round diamond like graceful ribbons. Two glittering accent diamonds nestle between the strands of metal. The ring isn't flashy or showy. It's perfect.

"You captured my attention from the first moment I laid eyes on you. I can't explain this draw. All I know is I want to be part of your life. I know you've already said yes, but will you accept this ring and make it official? Make us official? I want to be your equal in every step of the way."

"Yes," I choke out the word. "Yes, of course. I can't imagine spending my life with anyone else."

He slips the ring on my finger, and we both stare at it. I can barely see it through my tears, but my chest is full. I once questioned what was better, city lights or starry nights. I know unequivocally nothing compares to the glow he alights inside me.

And when he stands and plants a kiss I feel clear to my toes, I know I found my family. Sure, I could've survived on my own, but I belong here in Sugar Creek Falls with the man I love and a family I never knew could exist. I can't believe I'm living my dream.

EPILOGUE TWO
ANSLEY

One Year Later

"Are you sure you'll be okay? We could postpone the honeymoon?" Evie looks down at her three month old daughter and winces, guilt and longing etched into her expression. I hardly blame her. I'd struggle with leaving my newborn as well.

"I think Liam would kill me if I tried to talk you out of going." Standing by the barn away from the wedding party, I snuggle Britney closer to my chest and kiss the top of her baby-scented head. The soft pink bow tickles my nose as her eyelids flutter close. Nobody has a cuter niece than me.

"I know, but man, it's hard to leave the kids."

My eyes stray across the yard to find Dallas in Liam's arms, his little head nestled against the tuxedo's lapels. As if sensing an audience, Liam glances away from his groomsmen, Ethan and Matthew, and locks eyes with Evie. The look that passes between them tells me everything I need to know. They need to get away. Ever since she returned from Philly a little less than two years ago, they've hit go and never paused. Between getting the women's healthcare clinic up and running and being there for Dallas's prenatal appointments, followed by his birth and then Britney's, they haven't made time for themselves. Liam wanted to get married before Evie gave birth, but morning sickness hit her hard. She had insisted they wait until they got it under control. By the time that happened, it was late fall. She pushed their wedding off until springtime.

"You guys need this time. Mom and I will be just fine watching the little ones." My gut churns. While deciding what to do with my life, I agreed to come back to the town I vowed never to return and help Mom babysit my niece and nephew. What choice did I have? Mom can't handle a baby and toddler alone, and Liam and Evie deserve this break.

But that doesn't mean I like being here.

Dodging my past this entire week has been a challenge.

"Are you about ready?" Liam asks, eyeing his new bride while gently patting Dallas's back.

"Yes. Let's put the kids to bed and then grab the suitcases."

"They're loaded already in the truck. Matthew helped earlier with them." Liam turns to me. "Can you gather everyone and have them meet us out front?"

I smile stiffly and hand Britney to her mom. Evie's eyes shine with tears as she peers at her daughter.

"Stop it. You'll be fine," I say.

"I know, but these two are my life."

"Hey, what about me?" Liam feigns hurt, but the sparkle in his eyes tells me he's more proud than anything.

I love this for them, but I can't keep the green-eyed monster at bay. He claws at my insides like a bored billionaire starved for attention. I'm more like my brother than he thinks. My love for kids is why I pursued a teaching career, but I don't see a family in the near future. Not with my track record. The reason behind my failed relationships stands about twenty feet away, pretending to pay attention to Ethan.

If only I didn't compare every guy to him.

"You'll find out later," Evie says with a smirk, never taking her eyes off her new husband.

"Okay, you two. Save the eye-*fucking* for later." I mouth the curse word and shake my head. "I have people to round up before bleaching my eyes."

We part ways, and a few minutes later, everyone stands in the front yard, waving as the newlyweds take off toward their destination. I weave through the crowd, fully prepared to duck inside the house under the guise of babysitting. I've been able to escape unwanted company all week and don't want to push my luck.

When my feet hit the wooden porch, I stop short from a tug on my arm. I don't bother to turn. I know exactly whose hand is on my bare skin. I close my eyes, steeling my insides, but the attempt is futile. My breath still hitches when Matthew places his mouth next to my ear and speaks.

"You're done dodging me. It's time to talk."

ALSO BY KIMBERLY READNOUR

Cessna Wildcats Series:

Swinging Strike

Behind the Count

Full Count

On Deck (Prequel)

Caught Looking

Heartbreak Hitter (Cocky Hero Club)

Bad Boys Redemption Series

Second Chance Hero

Swing for the Fences

Bottom of the Ninth

Bad Ball Hitter

All American Boy Series

Celebrity Playboy

KB Everyday Heroes World

Sworn to Duty

An *Unforeseen Destiny* Series:

Impossible Love

Unexpected Love

The *Mystical Encounter* Series:

Visions

Deceptions

Vanished

ACKNOWLEDGMENTS

Thank you so much for reading *City Lights, Starry Nights*! I can't express enough my gratitude for your continued support. Starting a new series is always nerve wracking to me and I'm so grateful that you took the time to get lost in Sugar Creek Falls!

I can't begin my thank you's without starting with my daughter Logan. I knew she was talented, but she exceeded my expectations. I went totally off brand with an illustrated cover and didn't know how well it would be accepted. As I write this, I still don't know, but I absolutely love the artwork. I can't thank you enough for doing this for me.

To my trusty beta reader, Nichole. Thanks again for stepping up and reading my manuscript. Working on such a tight schedule didn't bother you at all and for that I am grateful!! I always love your insights and suggestions. They're invaluable!

To every single book blogger, bookstagrammer, and ARC team member. Words cannot express how valuable your shares, posts, reviews, and overall hype from the cover reveal to release day are to me. I greatly appreciate every single effort. Once again, thank you so much!

To my editor, Caitlin. Thank you so much for being there for me. Your insights and knowledge know no bounds! I love that you're a part of my team and put up with my last minute changes. Lol.

To my proofreader, Katie. You are the best! I thank my stars that you found me when I published my first sports romance. Our friendship means so much to me and the fact you want to read my words is a bonus!!

Linda and Alissa, thanks so much for everything you do! I wouldn't be able to continue my dream if it wasn't for your hard work at Foreword PR & Marketing. Thanks for everything.

Angela, you are still my rock! Thanks for being there for me and doing the things I don't want to do. Ha ha. But seriously, I appreciate the heck out you.

I hope you enjoyed book one in the Sugar Creek Falls series! I'm off to write ... to be continued.

ABOUT THE AUTHOR

Kimberly Readnour lives in the Midwest with her husband and a very snuggly cat.

Having a true passion for romance and HEA's, she took the leap from the young adult genre to romance and never looked back.

Kimberly worked as a Registered Nurse for fifteen years before hanging up her stethoscope. When she isn't running her own business, you can find her tucked away writing.

Contact me at:
kimberlyreadnour.com
kimberly@kimberlyreadnour.com

CPSIA information can be obtained
at www.ICGtesting.com
Printed in the USA
BVHW071018030123
655447BV00012B/85

9 781970 052015